A SEASON TO REMEMBER

BOOK 3

REBECCA HEFLIN

SEASONS OF
NORTHRIDGE

A SEASON TO REMEMBER

ACKNOWLEDGMENTS

To put my own spin on a song title,
this is dedicated to the ones I love.

This book was written during the pandemic in 2020. For many months I couldn't bring myself to write. The grief over so many lives lost was overwhelming. I could not have survived lockdown, and persevered and completed this book without the love and support of my husband, Ron. And even though I didn't get to physically see them, my sisters, my dearest friends, and my romance writers group made the insanity of the pandemic a little easier to bear. 2020, and now 2021, have taught me to cherish those close to me, even if I can't give them a hug.

QUOTE

You are not your mistakes:
they are what you did, not who you are.
~ Lisa Lieberman-Wang

1

Northridge, Mid-May

Oh, how the mighty have fallen, Georgia MacKinnon thought as she stepped into the musty, oppressive heat of the dilapidated old building. But beggars couldn't be choosers and all that.

She wrinkled her nose. The air smelled of rust, rotten wood, and something noxious like . . . poop. A sneeze tickled her nose and the back of her throat.

"Choo!"

A clatter erupted overhead, sending her heart racing to escape through her throat. "Jesus," she gasped, hand to the organ now pounding like a jackhammer in her chest. Closing her eyes, she muttered, "It's only a bird. It's only a bird."

The sound of scurrying in the near corner made her pause again and a shiver ran down her spine, from her highlighted hair to her Jimmy-Choo-clad feet. She didn't even want to *think* about what that could be.

"Hello?" Her voice echoed in the dim cavernous space before fading, leaving only silence in its wake. "Okay then." Glancing at her watch, she saw her prospective buyer still had two minutes until he was actually late for their appointment.

Clutching her tablet to her chest, she ventured further into what had once been a button mill, the sister building to the former cotton mill next door. That former cotton mill was now a thriving business with a dance studio, a retail store, and artist studios.

But this? This property was a far cry from the Hollywood mansions and Malibu beach houses she'd once sold as "Realtor to the Stars." She snorted and thought about the resemblance this dilapidated old building had to her life.

As her eyes adjusted to the gloom, she studied her surroundings. Unlike the building next door, this one didn't stand a second chance at life. The only thing in this building's future was a wrecking ball—if a stiff breeze didn't take it down first.

It hadn't taken a wrecking ball to destroy her life—just a thieving jerk—but the resulting damage was the same. She only hoped that, unlike this building, she'd have a second chance at the life and success she desired.

Leaves, sticks, rusted nails, broken glass, bird poop, and who knows what else littered the old wood floor. Some of the floor boards were loose and warped, their ends jutting upward, making it hazardous to the unwary. Though its brick-and-mortar walls were still standing, what was left of the roof provided little protection from the elements.

She had done her research though, and even without the decrepit building, the five-acre parcel was a prime commercial location. The town of Northridge was growing in this direction and with the land's commercial zoning, this could be the perfect spot for more boutiques, restaurants, and antique shops.

Across the street, the owner of the craft brewery Firehouse Brews had renovated the old nineteenth-century brick-and-mortar firehouse. On the opposite corner, The Secret Garden Nursery had a growing business where an old granary once stood. Yes, she could see this crossroads becoming Northridge's next commercial development.

She groaned as a trickle of sweat rolled down her back, making her twitch in discomfort and frustration. Despite the broken and missing windows, the May heat in the building was stifling. She plucked at her St. John Knits dress, wincing at the cost of her next dry-cleaning bill.

"Where *was* this guy, anyway?" Her time was just as valuable as his, she thought with annoyance. And as much as she needed the commission from this sale, she had a good mind to tell him so. And as both the listing agent and the selling agent, it would be a *nice* commission.

A noise made her turn toward the erstwhile doors. Silhouetted against the sunlight stood a tall, well-built man, hands casually stuffed into his pants pockets as if he'd been standing there watching her. *Finally!*

Swallowing her irritation, she painted a smile on her face, and in the Southern drawl that had sold more property than she could count, she said as she approached him, "Mr. Dunbar. I do hope you didn't have trouble finding the property."

The man stepped into a shaft of light pouring through one of the roof's many holes, and as she held out her hand to shake his, she blinked. *What the . . . ?*

Her knees went weak as she looked into the face of the last person she'd ever expected to see again.

LIAM DUNBAR STUDIED his wife's ashen face now just as he'd studied her from the door: with an eye to solving a problem. And if ever there was a problem to be solved, it was Georgia MacKinnon-Dunbar.

Mouth agape, she glanced from his face to her tablet and back again to his face. "But—" Looking back down at the tablet, she shook her head. "Why are *you* here?" She looked behind him. "You need to leave. I'm meeting someone."

"That someone would be me."

"But . . . I don't understand. I'm meeting a Mr. *William* Dunbar."

He shrugged. "Liam is short for William." Snorting, he shook his head, as it dawned on him. "You didn't remember my last name, did you?"

Her previously pale face grew red, and a trickle of sweat rolled down her temple. It was hotter than hell in the building, but he didn't think the heat was entirely to blame for her reaction.

She swallowed, licked her lips, and shook her head. "Of course I did."

"It didn't occur to you that *William* Dunbar might be me?"

Rubbing her temple, she stepped away and turned her back to him. "This isn't happening. This isn't happening," she muttered.

Despite the heat, Georgia looked as beautiful as she had the night he'd met her. Though she was a little more conservatively dressed now than she had been then, and her hair had been wavy and tousled that night.

He also remembered the way she'd looked when he'd last seen her—eyes dreamy and cheeks flushed with satisfaction, hair tousled from his hands, lips swollen from his kisses. He shook his head to clear the image.

Then she'd run out on him. Left without a word.

Now she stood before him with straight blond hair, pulled back into a sleek ponytail. But what he remembered most were blue-green eyes that shamed the Mediterranean Sea, full lips that lifted at the corner an instant before she smiled, and a Southern accent that dripped moonlight and magnolias.

The sleeveless sheath dress she wore, the color of a juicy tangerine, skimmed the subtle curves of her body, stopping just below the knee. And the flesh-colored stilettos that should have been ridiculous in the rough terrain of the property showed off her long legs.

Was it any wonder he'd been attracted to her?

He noted she wasn't wearing the gold band he'd given her. But then again, why would she? It wasn't as if they were in love or anything.

She spun on her heel to face him. "How'd you find me?"

He gave her a wry grin. "It's an interesting story really—one you might expect to see in a novel or movie. There I was looking at listings for old mills for sale in the South, and imagine my surprise when the listing agent for one of those mills turned out to be my runaway wife. Or at least someone with the same name as my wife. A quick Google search confirmed the former," he finished with a shrug.

Several emotions skittered across her face. Shock. Fear. Frustration. And something else . . . Disappointment?

"So you're not here to see the property then?"

He almost laughed. He'd just ambushed her, and this was what concerned her? "I am here to see the property. But this way I kill two birds with one stone."

"What—" The word came out breathy. She licked her lips and tried again. "What's the other bird? I mean, the property is one. What's the other?"

"I thought it would be obvious."

Her brows furrowed in confusion and she gave a subtle shake of her head.

"A divorce."

2

April twenty-first would have been his brother's thirtieth birthday. To mark the somber day, Liam had fully intended to take a punishing two-day trek on the treacherous Nankoweap Trail in the Grand Canyon before his friend's wedding the next day, but torrential rains and flooding had ended that plan. Instead, Liam found himself in a suite at the Aria in Las Vegas for a weekend of gambling, drinking, and any other potentially self-destructive behaviors he could think of.

He spotted her and her friend the minute he entered the club. She sparkled like the sun in the dimly lit club, with her shimmering blond hair and silver sequin dress. Her outfit was sexy by most standards, but in a Las Vegas club it was quite conservative by comparison. She laughed at something her friend said and reached across the pub table to smack her hand, making the knee-length dress rise to mid-thigh, revealing smooth, pale legs.

Her friend looked familiar. He tilted his head considering. A beautiful brunette, but a little too done up for his taste. A model or an actress maybe?

Ms. Sunshine turned to point toward the dance floor, presenting him with a wide (and deep) expanse of bare back playing peekaboo through her long waves. The back of the dress draped just above her ass. He swore if he stood behind her, he'd be able to see straight down it. Did she have on a lacy thong under there? he wondered. Or maybe nothing at all? The thought made him groan. Sexy, barely-there stilettos finished the outfit.

He stared a moment longer, debating with himself, but decided he was in no frame of mind to entertain a woman tonight.

Drinks and a high-stakes poker game suited his morose mood more. But for now, the heavy thump of bass from the dance floor provided a welcome distraction from the persecutory voices in his head.

He ordered a scotch neat then waited, scanning the crowd. Many would hit the casinos later. Some would go home with more money in their pockets than they'd come with. Others would go home broke. Some were high rollers, others wannabes. But they were all here for the same reason —to cut loose in the one city where just about anything goes.

His gaze landed on Ms. Sunshine again and found that, though her friend was gone, she wasn't alone. A tall hulk of guy stood next to her, skimming a finger down her bare arm. She stepped back, a look of revulsion on her face. Liam tensed.

The Hulk stepped further into her personal space until

she had nowhere else to go, with the wall at her back. Her hand pressed against his chest, but the guy didn't budge. "Holy hell," Liam muttered. He had no choice but to step in. Though Liam would relish an old-fashioned bar fight right about now, this was not the place for it, unless he wanted one of the many bouncers to toss him out on his ass.

He grabbed his scotch and another cocktail off the bar.

"Hey, that was my drink," a guy said. Over his shoulder, Liam told the bartender to give the guy another drink and put it on his tab.

When he arrived at the table with the drinks, The Hulk was still trying to make his case. Liam stepped up next to her. "Hey, babe. What's going on here?" He shouted to be heard over the thump of the music.

The Hulk stepped back and gave Liam a dirty look. Ms. Sunshine frowned at Liam before catching on. "Steve was just asking me to dance," she said, with a casual note, but Liam could hear a tremor in her voice.

"Well, maybe some other time, Steve. Right now, my girl's cocktail is getting warm." Liam gave him a friendly smile, but his eyes shot daggers at the man.

Steve gave it a thought or two then held up his hands as if to say "I don't want any trouble."

"See ya, Steve," Liam said as he handed the cocktail to Ms. Sunshine.

She took it with a grateful but confused look on her face. "Thank you, but why did you do that?"

Her words dripped with Southern charm. "Correct me if I'm wrong, but it looked like he'd outstayed his welcome."

The corners of her mouth lifted at that. "Yeah, you could say that."

"Where's your friend?" He lifted his highball glass to

gesture across the pub table where the other woman had been standing the first time he'd caught sight of them.

"Ladies' room. Wait, how'd you know I was here with someone?"

"I saw you when I came in."

She gave him a shy smile then looked at the glass in her hand. "What is this?"

Liam shrugged and grinned. "I don't know. I just grabbed the first drink I could get my hand on." Her reserved expression seemed out of place in a Vegas nightclub.

"Oh." She sniffed at it then wrinkled her nose.

"You don't have to drink it. It was just part of the ruse."

With a shake of her head, she set the glass down on the table. "Do you often come to a woman's rescue in a nightclub?"

"No. You're the first."

Even in the subtle lighting of the club, he saw the flush spread across her cheeks. "Thank you . . ." she said with a question in her voice.

"Liam." He nodded with the same question in his voice.

"Georgia."

Georgia? A Southern name to go with her Southern accent. "Nice to meet you, Georgia."

"Same here, Liam."

After a heartbeat, he said, "Hopefully the Hulk got the message and won't be back to bother you."

"The Hulk?" She laughed, a bright sound like the chime of crystal. "It fits."

"Well, enjoy your evening." He found himself hesitating, reluctant to walk away from this bright spot in what had otherwise been a shit day.

"Wait." Her hand landed on his forearm, light and

warm. "If you're not here with someone, stay." She lifted her eyes, the color of the turquoise waters off the coast of Greece, to his and all thoughts of high-stakes poker and other self-destructive behaviors evaporated.

GEORGIA DIDN'T KNOW why she'd asked the guy to stay but figured any guy who would come to the rescue of a woman he'd never met in a club must be a good guy. Then again, she'd learned she didn't have the best judgment when it came to men.

Even so, it didn't hurt that he was the nicest thing she'd laid eyes on since she'd arrived. Though he'd dwarfed the aptly named Hulk in height, he was far leaner. Even in her stilettos, he stood a foot or so taller than her.

Dark wavy hair, just the other side of needing a trim, swept across his brow and touched the collar of his blue dress shirt. His coal-dark eyes were fringed with lashes she'd kill for, and the cleft in his chin made her think of an olive-skinned Cary Grant. A hint of cologne—something earthy and expensive—teased her.

She'd been so thankful when she'd heard his voice and Steve stepped back. Clubbing was not her thing, and she had little experience with how to handle jerks who came on too strong. If her friend Audrey had been at the table, she would have known what to do. As a stunning Academy-Award-nominated actress, she probably had her fair share of aggressive come-ons.

Liam pointed to her drink. "What can I get you?"

"Oh, uh, just a glass of chardonnay." She'd learned over the years to nurse a glass of wine all night. It used to drive Erik crazy.

He signaled to a passing waitress. "Bring a glass of your best chardonnay."

Knowing she'd drink little of the wine, she winced at the expense. "Thank you, but I'm not a connoisseur or anything. The house wine would have been fine."

Liam just shrugged and took a sip of what she assumed was scotch. She'd often seen Erik drinking scotch when he was trying to impress someone. But she didn't get the feeling that this guy was trying to impress anyone.

Stop with Erik already. This was a weekend to blow off some steam, as Audrey put it. To do things Georgia MacKinnon would never do, just once—she glanced over at Liam's broad shoulders—like pick up a man at a club in Las Vegas.

"Would you like to get a table?" Liam asked, leaning in close so she could hear.

His warm breath on her cheek tickled in the best way possible. "Oh, we have one. Or we will in about ten minutes. We got here a little early. Please stay and join us."

"I wouldn't want to interfere with your girls' weekend." He studied her face and she felt as if she were the only person in the crowded club.

She waved off his protest. "Audrey won't mind."

As if saying her name had conjured her, her friend made her way through a crowd that stared and whispered as she passed. Though Georgia had many famous clients, she never understood how they handled constantly being the center of attention.

"Who's this?" Audrey asked, a perfectly waxed brow lifted. She set her crystal-encrusted Judith Leiber bag on the table and shook out her long deep-brown hair.

Georgia introduced Liam and told Audrey the story of her rescue.

"A real-life knight in shining armor." She eyed him from head to toe then looked back at Georgia. "I approve."

Heat flooded Georgia's cheeks. Leave it to Audrey to be direct.

"I thought I recognized you," Liam said as he nodded at her. "You were in *Home of the Brave*. Great performance. You should have won the Oscar."

"Thank you. It was a stellar group of actresses, so I was just thrilled to be included."

"Ms. Turner, your table is ready." A hostess lifted her hand to indicate the direction of the table.

Audrey glanced between Georgia and Liam. "You know, I'm getting a headache. Must be the music. I'm going to head up to our suite. But you two stay."

"Oh, but—"

Audrey pressed her lips to Georgia's cheek then whispered, "Have some fun. Remember, what happens in Vegas . . ."

Georgia nodded. Right. She followed the hostess to the table, full glass of wine in her hand.

"Should I recognize you?" Liam asked after they'd settled into the expansive booth tucked away in a relatively quiet corner of the club.

"What?"

"Are you an actress too?"

"Oh. No."

An awkward silence followed. Georgia had never picked up a man in her life. What were the rules? How did one play this game?

"What's the occasion?" he asked as he flagged down a server for another scotch, momentarily dispelling her panic.

"The occasion?"

"The reason you're in Vegas. A birthday? New job?

Divorce?"

"Maybe I just like to come to Vegas," she responded with a lift of her shoulder, twisting her wine glass in a circle on the table.

"No. That's not it."

She lifted her gaze to his. "How do you know?"

"Because you're displaying all the signs of a Vegas virgin."

Heat suffused her cheeks. "What do you mean?"

"Well, you're looking around as if overwhelmed by the sights and sounds. You didn't know how to handle The Hulk when he came on too strong. And you're nursing that chardonnay like it's the only glass of wine available and you want to make it last."

She looked away and sighed. She was beginning to regret not returning to the room with Audrey. "Fine. This is my first time in Vegas."

"Okay. So there must be a reason. Is it your birthday?"

"No. That's in June."

"A new job?"

"No."

"A divorce then?"

A sardonic laugh escaped her. "I'm here for my honeymoon."

He blinked. "You're m—? You mean you and Audrey?"

She shook her head. "Oh. No. Audrey's quite the catch and all, but we're each firmly ensconced in the hetero camp."

"Then where is your . . . husband?" He sat back, apparently attempting to put some distance between them in the event her groom appeared to claim his bride.

"I don't have one. That is, I'm not married."

He shook his head as if to clear it. "So you're on a honeymoon in Vegas because . . . ?"

"It was a non-refundable package," she said with a shrug. "Seemed a shame to let it go to waste."

"Ah. You're a runaway bride? Or was he a runaway groom?"

"Neither."

"What then?"

"Two months before our wedding I learned he wasn't the man I thought he was." *Quite literally.* Turned out Erik Lawson wasn't, well, Erik Lawson. It was just one of the many aliases he used. His real name was Jason Taggert, and as of two months ago, he was an indicted criminal being held without bond.

"Sounds like you dodged a bullet. Good thing you learned about that before the ceremony." He rotated the drink in his hand, enjoying the play of light on the amber liquid.

He didn't know what the asshole had done to her, but he meant what he'd said. Even though he didn't really know Georgia, it pained him to see her so hurt, but better now than later. "So you're not here to drink away your heartache," he nodded to her still half-full wine glass, "and you don't seem like the gambling type." He eyed her again. The clothing he manufactured wasn't haute couture, but he knew fine, expensive clothes when he saw them, and hers were. "Here for a one-night stand then?"

She jerked her head up. "No." She fiddled with her wine glass as if she were going to take a sip then changed her mind. "I'm just here to . . . have some fun. Do something daring. Impulsive even."

He lifted a brow at her. "Impulsive, huh?" He knew all about impulsive, only his impulses were usually dangerous. "And so far you've been cornered by a jerk, had a few sips of wine, and invited a strange man to your table. Sounds like a rip-roaring good time."

She drew herself up as if affronted then saw the smirk on his face. Her mouth lifted in a wry grin. "Right. Not exactly one for the books."

She was so damned beautiful. And so damned . . . sad. He couldn't say why, but he wanted to show this woman a grand time. Give her whatever she wanted. Keep that smile on her face and the shadows from her eyes, even if just for the night. "Well," he slapped his hands on the table, "let's change that."

"Change it how?"

"Whatever you want to do. Dance in this club," he indicated the dance floor with a jut of his chin, "or a different one. Watch a high-stakes poker game. Play the slots. See a show. You name it."

"A show? How would we do that now?"

"Oh, I have some connections. Is that what you want? Just tell me the show."

He could tell she was thinking as she bit her bottom lip. His gaze homed in on her mouth and he wondered if her lips were as soft as they looked.

"Cirque du Soleil's Zarkana?"

He pulled his phone out of his pocket, dialed the hotel's concierge desk, and told them he wanted two tickets to the ten o'clock show. "Done."

She looked at him, mouth agape. "How did you do that?"

"I told you. Connections." He didn't bother to tell her his suite came with show tickets every night. "The show is in the hotel, so we still have an hour to kill. Let's dance." He took her by the hand and led her through the growing crowd to the dance floor.

"W HAT THE FUCK?" Liam groaned, his hand over his face to block out the light pouring through the now-open curtains, the sound of the TV blaring in his ears.

"Who? What?" Beside him in bed, Georgia sat bolt upright, eyes wide with fright, breasts bared as the bed linens fell away.

"It's okay." He laid a hand on her arm, hoping to soothe her. "Someone apparently thought it would be funny to set the alarm to open the curtains and turn on all the lights and the TV for the ass crack of dawn."

The Aria was fully digital. Everything—from the locks and the lights to the curtains—was operated from either a phone or the tablet in the room. It was one of the reasons it was his preferred Vegas hotel. Until now.

The room's occupant could set a wake-up alarm to open or close the curtains or control the lights, TV, and music. This could be a nice feature, just not at—he peered over at the clock—six a.m., when said occupant had neither sched-uled nor expected it.

"Go back to sleep." He reached for the room's tablet and tapped to close the curtains and turn off the lights and TV.

She sighed, drew the covers up over her, and burrowed beneath them. He couldn't help smiling. She looked so innocent all curled up. Last night—and early this morning —she had been anything but.

He groaned as he lay back down. He didn't know what time they had finally fallen asleep, he only knew it had been in the wee hours of the morning. It hadn't been for long, but he'd slept deep and sound those few hours. Deeper than he could remember in a very long time, with no nightmares of his brother's death.

His heart rate returned to a normal rhythm, and he began to relax into sleep once more.

Georgia sat up again with a gasp, this time clutching the blankets to her, more's the pity.

"What?"

She looked around again, as if unsure where she was, then caught sight of him and gasped again, her hand over her mouth. Her eyes widened again, this time in surprise. She shook her head, horrified.

"Georgia. Lie back down. It's the ass crack of dawn."

"I . . . we . . . you . . ."

Propping himself on his elbows, he turned to face her. "Pick a pronoun and tell me what you're thinking."

Her eyes drifted shut, then she opened them and lifted the blanket to peer down at herself. "We did. We really did. It wasn't a dream."

"No, it wasn't a dream," he confirmed.

"I've never done this." She shook her head.

"Done what? Had sex? Because I'm fairly certain you weren't a virgin."

Ignoring his comment, she stared at him wide-eyed. "I've never had a one-night stand."

He chuckled. "Really?" Was she for real? "And who said it has to be one night?"

The horrified look returned to her face, and he chuckled again. He tugged her back down beside him and she complied.

Wrapping his arms around her, he pulled her to him. "We had a great time, right? I know *I* did."

She nodded against his chest, where he could feel the

heat of her blush.

He couldn't believe the next words that came out of his mouth. "Well, I'm free today until my friend's wedding this evening. Since you've never been to Vegas, we could explore the area around it."

One-night stands were totally fine with him, but for some reason, he didn't want this woman to think sex was the only reason she was here. He didn't want her to feel used. Especially not when her ex may have done just that.

"What do you mean?" She leaned back to look up into his face.

"We could see Hoover Dam and Lake Mead, or we could even drive to the West Rim of the Grand Canyon if we have time. Whatever you want. It's not daring, but it *is* impulsive. You game?"

She nodded again and he kissed her on the forehead. Another thought occurred to him. He'd been dreading the event, not only because he wasn't in the mood to celebrate but because he'd be flying solo. And he knew from past experience that single women would be vying for his attention. But if he had a date . . . "Would you like to be my plus-one for my friend's wedding?"

Georgia hesitated, gnawing on her lower lip. "I didn't bring anything wedding-appropriate with me."

"We could buy a dress. I hear they have a few shops around here," he said with a wink.

"Oh, um, no."

"Since you'd be doing me a favor by going, it's the least I can do." He waited, holding his breath. Her acceptance took on an unexpected importance.

"If you really want me to go . . ."

"It's all settled then. Now, how about we get a little more sleep? Then we can start the day."

"Okay." She snuggled against him once more, and though his body begged him to take her again, his heart was content to hold her close to him while he drifted off to sleep again.

GEORGIA RETURNED to the honeymoon suite she was sharing with Audrey to shower, change, and tell her friend her plans. She shouldn't have said yes to Liam. She had come to Vegas with Audrey, and now she was deserting her.

Just as she'd clicked the door shut, Audrey had come out of her bedroom wrapped in a silk robe, a broad grin on her face. "Just get in?"

Heat suffused Georgia's face. "Um, yes. Look, I'm sorry for bailing on you last night."

"Are you kidding me? I'm excited for you." She wrapped Georgia in a perfume-scented embrace then released her. "You look well satisfied."

Embarrassed, Georgia couldn't look Audrey in the face.

"Hey." Audrey lifted Georgia's chin. "You have nothing to be ashamed of. You're a young single woman who deserves to have a little fun."

The bedroom door opened again and a half-dressed guy with an impressive six-pack yawned and rubbed his eyes. "I was having a little myself." Mr. Six-Pack draped an arm across her shoulder.

Georgia narrowed her eyes. "Where did you go after you left the club?"

"To another club where I met Cooper. He's an aerialist with Cirque. Cooper, this is Georgia."

Cooper shot Georgia a grin.

"Are you going to see him again?" Audrey asked.

"Who?"

Audrey pursed her lips and sighed. "Your white knight."

"Well, he asked me to go to Hoover Dam and then to his friend's wedding, but . . ."

"Of course you're going to go!"

"What about you? I invited you here, I can't just leave you."

She patted the guy's bare abs. "Oh, I'm sure I'll think of something. Go. This weekend was meant for you. Enjoy yourself! It's *your* honeymoon, after all."

Georgia headed for her bedroom but stopped and glanced over her shoulder when Audrey called her name.

"Don't do anything I wouldn't do," Audrey said with a wink.

LIAM SPENT an enjoyable day with Georgia, driving to Hoover Dam then shopping for a dress for her to wear to the wedding.

By some tacit agreement, they didn't talk about anything consequential. No life stories, no career talk, no dreams and aspirations. But they'd found plenty of other things to talk about. And even the silences were comfortable.

Georgia picked out a dress in cool aqua that left her back bare to the waist. The dress stopped just above her knees, revealing those beautiful legs that had been wrapped around him most of the night, and she had smoothed out the waves of her hair so it was hanging down her back sleek and shiny.

Liam looked forward to removing the dress tonight and mussing up that hair.

Tomorrow they'd both have to return to reality—whatever that meant for her. For him, it meant making a stop at his New York apartment before heading back down South to check out his potential mill. But for tonight, they could keep the real world at bay a little longer.

The wedding reception was in full swing and inebriated guests were making the most of the D.J. He held Georgia close, swaying while Ed Sheeran sang about dancing in the dark, when she sniffled.

Aw, hell. This whole thing had been a bad idea. How insensitive could a guy be, inviting a heartbroken would-have-been bride to a wedding? What the hell had he been thinking?

He leaned back and lifted her chin. "Georgia. Don't cry. He isn't worth it." Her eyes glittered with tears and his heart ached for her. "Georgia," he entreated. He'd never been in love. Never would be. But he knew what it felt like to lose someone. And it hurt like hell, regardless of the reason.

She brushed a hand beneath her eyes. "I know. Of course, I know. But I'm supposed to be on my honeymoon. I'm supposed to be starting a new chapter in my life."

"And you are. It's just not the chapter you expected. And who knows? It could be even better." *Where the hell had that drivel come from?* He didn't know, but he would have said anything at that point to make her feel better.

She looked up at him, her lashes still damp with tears, lips parted, and he closed the distance between them, kissing her tenderly. He held himself in check, keeping the kiss tender rather than carnal, though he really wanted to take it up a notch. Or ten.

The song ended and he took her hand and led her back to their table.

At his prodding, Georgia joined the other unmarried women on the floor and succeeded in catching the bouquet. The look of astonishment and sadness on her face when she'd found the bouquet in her hands would stay with him.

Another unintentionally cruel invitation from him. What was *wrong* with him?

She plopped into her chair and turned up a glass of champagne she'd snagged from a passing waiter then set it on the table. This is the most he'd seen her drink since they'd met. She'd said she came to Vegas to get out of her comfort zone. To *do something daring. Impulsive even*, she'd said, which made him wonder . . . "What's the most impulsive thing you've ever done?"

Without hesitation, she looked him in the eye and said, "Sleeping with a guy I barely know."

He couldn't help but grin. "Happy to oblige with that bucket-list item."

She held up a finger. "Okay. Just so you know, sleeping with a stranger was not a bucket-list item."

"So, what is? Bungie jumping? Skydiving? Pole dancing?"

She snorted and gazed out at the dance floor where the groom danced around his bride to Bruno Mars' song "I Think I Want to Marry You," miming the words and pointing to her. He looked like a lovesick sap.

She picked up the bridal bouquet of roses the color of Georgia peaches and muttered, "Get married."

His stomach dropped.

She shook her head, and a blush crept up her neck and into her face. "You weren't supposed to hear that."

But he looked at her downcast face and thought, what the hell. "Let's do it."

"What? No. That's . . . crazy."

"And daring. Impulsive even. Why not? Nothing says

impulsive like a Vegas wedding. Besides, you're already here for your honeymoon."

She hesitated, gnawing on her lower lip.

"We can get it annulled in the morning. I promise. Agreed?"

"Really?" The tentative grin on her face could light up the Vegas strip. "That's definitely impulsive!"

He held out his hand to her and, with a nod, she took it. He led her out of the reception to the waiting limo and the first quickie wedding chapel they could find.

GROOMS WERE SUPPOSED to be nervous. Liam wasn't. Maybe it was because he knew this would be the shortest marriage in history. Maybe it was because he wanted to do something . . . crazy. Or maybe it was seeing Georgia walk down the aisle toward him to Ed Sheeran's "Perfect," a shy smile lighting her face.

The Lucky in Love Wedding Chapel's assistant had placed a snow-white veil on Georgia's head and tied additional ribbon around the bridal bouquet she'd caught earlier that just matched the aqua dress she was wearing. She looked radiant. And maybe a wee bit dazed.

Her asshat ex-groom didn't know what he was missing. His loss for sure.

When she reached him, he held out his hand to her, feeling for all the world like this was real. Well, it *was* real, it's just that it would be annulled in the morning.

Georgia glowed in the light from the chandeliers above. Her blond hair shone like spun gold, her cheeks like a ripe Georgia peach, and her eyes sparkled like the Mediterranean beneath a brilliant summer sun.

As he spoke his vows, he tried to remember he wasn't husband material. That he would never marry or have children. That he was destined to live his life alone, partly as penance for the things he had done and partly because he wasn't worthy of love.

But this beautiful woman in front of him deserved happiness and more. And if this impulsive ceremony in a tacky Las Vegas wedding chapel made her happy even for a short time, he wanted to give it to her.

"You may kiss your bride," the portly officiant intoned.

Liam stepped closer and, taking Georgia in his arms, pressed his lips to hers in a tender kiss. She tasted of the champagne she'd been drinking and a warm sweetness he couldn't name.

Yes, for tonight he'd give her whatever she wanted.

But it would end tomorrow, and while she might eventually get her happy ending, there would be no happy ending for him. He would do well to remember that.

GEORGIA WOKE UP, at first confused of her whereabouts. Then the bed shifted as the man next to her rolled onto his side, his broad muscular back facing her. Cheese and crackers!

Like Cinderella at the stroke of midnight, Georgia felt the need to flee. The weekend had been a fantasy. A whim. An isolated interlude to soothe the hurt over Erik's betrayal. No one needed to know. It *was* Las Vegas, after all . . .

But all good things must come to an end. She got dressed as quickly and quietly as possible in the darkened room. Carrying her sandals, she tiptoed to the door, sleep-dazed.

It wasn't until the elevator doors closed that she noticed the gold band on her left hand. She pressed a hand to her forehead. What had she done? Memories of the night returned. The wedding. The chapel. The marriage. And the promise.

But like someone leaving the scene of an accident, she panicked. There was no way in hell she was going back. Heart thundering, she removed the ring and tossed it into her handbag as the elevator door opened onto her floor.

Running from the mess she'd made had to be the most irresponsible thing she'd ever done. No. Marrying a man she'd just met had to be the most irresponsible thing she'd ever done. She blamed the entire thing on her unstable state of mind.

She'd fix it. She would. Just not now. Now she planned to pack her bags and drive to Northridge as planned, putting the neon lights of Las Vegas behind her.

BEFORE HE'D OPENED his eyes, Liam knew the bed beside him was empty. He sat up groaning, scrubbed his hands over his face, and blinked a few times, then shook himself. "Georgia?"

He glanced around the room then back to the upholstered chair beside the window where Georgia had tossed her dress the night before. It was gone. As were her shoes and purse. The only thing she'd left behind was the bridal bouquet, now wilted and looking the worse for wear.

He didn't know Georgia very well or, you know . . . at all. But for some reason, he never figured her for a runner.

Leaning back against the headboard, he gazed up at the ceiling. So much for an annulment. "Well, damn."

3

Northridge, Mid-May

"A divorce. Right. Of course." She wrapped her arms around her tablet and held it against her, trying to quell the nerves that sent a frisson down her spine. Not necessarily nerves of trepidation, but nerves of awareness that had been tingling since she'd first seen his face. Her traitorous body remembered him. Remembered his touch. The feel of his mouth on hers. Another frisson ran through her.

"If you hadn't run out on me the next morning, we could have handled this right away with an annulment as planned. Instead, I had to go search for you."

Georgia wanted to fidget under the annoyance of his dark stare but remained still. She wasn't proud of how she'd handled the whole thing, but she'd panicked. And it wasn't as if they'd exchanged their contact information.

Of course, she could have requested a copy of her marriage certificate from the Clark County Court in Las Vegas, and she would have . . . eventually. But she needed to get to Northridge, put the Las Vegas episode behind her, and get her business going first.

"I'm sorry. I—I've never been in that, um, situation. I didn't know what to do."

"Let's be clear, I've never been in that situation either, but I don't think running was the answer." At her uncomfortable silence, he continued, "Never mind. I found you, and we can agree that a quick divorce is the solution?"

She nodded, relieved. It was like she was a little girl again and had been caught misbehaving, only to find the punishment wasn't as bad as she'd expected.

"But first things first."

Her head shot up to his face in surprise. "What do you mean?"

He turned his back and walked away from her, inspecting the dilapidated structure. "Tell me about this place."

"Oh. Okay." Surely he didn't intend to keep the building, but she woke up her tablet and pulled up the specs anyway. "Well, it was built in eighteen ninety-two, brick-and-mortar construction. It has thirty thousand square feet of space. The property is a valuable five acres on an intersection that will likely be the next commercial development."

He waved her away. "No. I know all that. Tell me its history."

"Its history. Okay." Despite her confusion, she complied. "It's an old button mill that was owned by the Redmond family for generations. The business closed in the nineteen seventies. The oldest living descendant held onto the property, refusing to sell it. When he passed, his children decided it was time to cut the albatross from around their necks, and they put it up for sale."

It had originally been listed with Five Star Realty. As part of her purchase of the real estate business, Georgia kept the listings of those sellers who chose to work with her. "It's been on the market for almost ten years, but there've been no offers."

While she spoke, he walked around, patting the exposed brick walls, eyeing the crumbling roof and broken window panes, kicking at debris on the floor. He knelt down and brushed aside the detritus to reveal the floor beneath. Smacking it with the flat of his hand, he said, "There is nothing like heart pine."

He rose with the grace of an athlete, all one-hundred-eighty-some-odd pounds of him, dusted off his hands, and moved toward her. His inky hair was shorter than it had been in Vegas, and she decided she liked the slightly unruly length better, and her fingers remembered the silky feel of it beneath her fingers.

"I'll take it."

He'll take it? Just like that? How much money did he have? She thought about the lavish suite in Las Vegas, the limousine, and the VIP treatment he'd received. "But, don't you want to talk about price?"

"No. I want it. I'd give you a cashier's check for it tomorrow, but there is one wrinkle."

"What's that?" she asked as her heart sank. She didn't need a wrinkle. She needed an easy sale.

"It's zoned commercial."

"Yes?" she asked, confused.

"I need it for manufacturing."

"Manu—? But why?"

"Because, Georgia, I plan to manufacture clothes here."

"THAT COULD BE A TALL ORDER."

Liam crossed his arms over his chest and regarded his wife. "And why is that?"

"Well, because, other than Firehouse Brews, this whole area is zoned commercial."

"I am aware. But zoning can be changed."

"Look, you may think that if you come into a small town and throw around a bunch of money you'll get what you want, but it doesn't work that way in Northridge. Northridge is already a thriving town, with a solid middle- and upper-middle-class demographic. They don't want to see the idyllic environment destroyed by a noisy manufacturing operation."

"Who said anything about throwing around money? Or my operation being noisy?" He pointed across the street. "Besides, as you said, Firehouse Brews is not zoned commercial. It's zoned light industrial, and I'd bet my last dollar that my mill will be at least as clean, if not cleaner and more environmentally sound than Firehouse Brews."

She snorted. "Maybe as environmentally sound as Firehouse Brews but not much better. It's certified LEED Platinum."

He heaved a sigh of frustration. "My point is, my mill will not pollute the air, the water, or the peace, and while Northridge may not be in need of jobs, that can't be said of the area surrounding Northridge. And those people will only add to the Northridge economy."

She held up a hand in surrender. "Look, you don't have to convince me, but you will have to convince the Economic Development Council, who will then make a recommendation to the Town Council's zoning subcommittee."

"That's where you come in. I could have contacted any number of realtors to purchase this property. I didn't contact you just because I want to dissolve this marriage as planned, or because you're the listing agent, but because you're both a real estate broker and lawyer. You're the one who'll be responsible for convincing the powers that be. And since the sale is riding on that, I know you'll get the job done."

She studied him before nodding. "Fine. I'll provide you with the list of documents I'll need for the rezoning application before you leave," she waved her hand toward the outdoors, "to return to wherever you're from."

"Oh, I'm not leaving."

"I'm sorry?"

"I said I'm not leaving. I'm staying in Northridge to oversee the rezoning request, then the restoration and build-out of the mill, and the hiring of employees."

"But, don't you have people for that?"

"I'm a very hands-on person."

She knew from experience just how hands-on he was. Flashes of the backseat of a limo and roving hands sent a thrill down her spine.

"I'm not leaving until the mill is up and running."

Lovely. "And how long will that take?"

He shrugged. "Nine months, if all goes accordingly. A year, if it doesn't."

She nearly choked. "Nine months? A year? But—" Panic bubbled up, threatening to choke her. "Here? In Northridge? I mean, why not Atlanta?"

"Too far to drive seven days a week. I need to be here, on property, throughout the job. I can't be wasting hours every day in the car. I'm staying at the 1885 B&B."

Her biggest mistake living right here in Northridge for the next year? No, not her *biggest* mistake—Erik still held that dubious honor—but her most recent one. She groaned. Would her mistakes haunt her for the rest of her life?

And here, she'd thought moving back to Northridge she could start over with a clean slate.

GEORGIA PULLED into the winding driveway leading up to her grandfather's house. The sprawling white clapboard house stood on ten acres among Georgia pines and magnolias, boasting four chimneys, two sunrooms, two porches, and five bedrooms within its fifty-eight hundred square feet.

MacKinnon House had been in her family since it was built by her third great-grandfather Alistair Calder MacKinnon in the late 1870s. It had been renovated and remodeled over the years but had withstood the test of time, just like the MacKinnon family. The once five-hundred-acre parcel of land had been sold off over the generations by the family to expand the town of Northridge.

She'd lived here for five years, from the age of thirteen when her mother died to eighteen when she'd left for college. Now here she was back again at the age of thirty-two, feeling just as lost as she'd felt when she'd first arrived at thirteen.

With a heavy sigh, she parked her hybrid SUV in front of the open garage bay.

Another evening with her inquisitive grandfather. Another evening of sidestepping the additional circumstances surrounding her move back to Northridge. She loved her grandfather, which was one of the reasons she wanted to avoid the truth for as long as possible. She couldn't bear to see the disappointment in his eyes when he learned she'd lost almost everything.

No. Not *lost. Stolen.*

Unable to procrastinate any longer, she grabbed her tote from the front seat and stepped out into the late afternoon heat.

Dropping her tote bag onto the bench in the mudroom, she called out, "Grandad! I'm home."

"Georgia! In my study."

She found him seated at a walnut desk that had belonged to Alistair, the windows behind him lit by the lowering sun.

"Gimme some sugar."

Walking over, she bent and kissed him on the forehead then took up a guest chair and slipped the stilettos off her aching, swollen feet. "Ooh, that feels good."

"I've never understood how you ladies wear such shoes." He lifted a foot shod in a split-toe Oxford. "These are much more comfortable."

"And a lot less attractive—for women that is."

"Beauty over comfort, is that it?" he asked, his graying brows lifted.

"It is," she said with a nod.

He snorted. "How was your day?"

"Well. I think I sold the Redmond Mill today."

Her grandfather clapped his hands. "That's terrific news!

It's been on the market, what, ten years? We should celebrate!"

"There is one tiny problem though."

"Oh. What's that?"

"It's currently zoned commercial. It will need to be rezoned light industrial at a minimum."

"Industrial? The buyer isn't going to build a chemical plant or something?"

"No. Nothing like that. Believe it or not, he wants to restore the mill. He wants to manufacture clothing."

"Ah. I think I read about this young man in *The Atlanta Constitution*. He's the one who's going around the South buying up old mills, restoring them, and making everything from textiles to clothing. American Threads, or something like that."

Feigning knowledge she didn't have, she nodded and leaned back in her chair with a sigh. Her grandfather knew more about her husband than she did. In addition to not sharing their contact information, they hadn't shared much —well, nothing really—about their actual lives. She knew he was great in bed and could deliver on a fantasy-filled weekend in Las Vegas. Did that count?

"What do you think the odds are that he'll get the rezoning?" she asked, returning to the conversation at hand. "Firehouse Brews across the street is zoned light industrial."

Her grandfather tilted his desk chair back, folded his hands on his stomach, and considered. "First you'll have to convince the Economic Development Council. That shouldn't be too difficult, since it will bring more dollars to the community. And based on the photos I've seen of the other restored mills, they're not large bunker-looking buildings. They've kept the nineteenth- and early-twentieth-century charm of the original mills. And right now the

Redmond Mill is an eyesore. I think residents would be happy to see something, even a factory, in its place."

His fingers tapped. "It's doable. But it will all be in the presentation." He sat up and slapped a hand on his knee. "Let's schedule a meeting to discuss strategy. Right now, I'm famished."

4

The next afternoon, Liam entered the Firehouse Taproom, which he understood served as the tasting room for the local craft brewery, Firehouse Brews. The plaque outside the door said the building had once served as a livery stable and carriage house for the former Northridge Hotel. A chalkboard hanging on the opposite wall listed upcoming monthly tastings and featured food from local restaurants. Brilliant marketing.

Inside, the pub boasted exposed brick walls, a polished oak bar lined with taps ready to dispense the brewery's latest offerings, pub tables, and intimate booths. The glass shelves behind the bar held beer mugs, shaker pints, and pilsner and tulip glasses, as well as samplers for weekly flights of beer for those patrons who wanted to taste a little of everything.

He turned in the direction of the bar and a guy setting glasses on the shelf behind.

"What can I get you? The Engine Company Lager is selling well in this summer heat."

"Thanks, but I'm looking for Tyler."

"Hey, Tyler! There's someone here to see you."

"Be right there," a disembodied voice called out. Liam heard the scrape of a chair, followed by the sound of booted feet on the hardwood floor. A tall, blond guy came through the door.

"How can I help you?" he asked, with an amiable expression.

"Liam Dunbar." Liam stuck out his hand, and Tyler took it in a solid grip.

"Tyler Kincaide." Recognition appeared to dawn on the man's face. "You're the guy buying the old Redmond Mill." Tyler gave a slight shrug, "Small town. Word travels fast."

"Right. Well, assuming the property can be rezoned."

"So, what can I do for you?"

"I'd like to pick your brain when you have the time."

"I've got some time now. Have a seat at the bar." He turned to the bartender. "Pull us a pint of the Engine Company." He lifted a brow at Liam who nodded agreement.

After they had their pints, Liam settled in and took a sip. "Mmm." He lifted the glass. "Good. Really good." Who knew there would be a master brewer in such a small town?

"Thanks." Tyler lifted his own glass and sipped. "It is, isn't it?" he asked without a hint of arrogance, and Liam liked him instantly.

"I understand you had to have the brewery location rezoned."

"I did. And you'll have to have the mill property rezoned." Tyler hesitated. "I'm on the Economic Development Council."

"I know. I'm not asking for inside information or preferential treatment. I'd just like to take a look at your operation.

See if mine matches—or exceeds—yours," he said with a cheeky grin.

"You got it. Why don't you come to the brewery for a tour and I can show you."

Before they could actually schedule the tour, the door opened and a tall dark-haired man wearing a uniform walked in.

"Hi, Zach!" The bartender called.

"Hi, Nate!" Zach replied.

Nate lifted an empty glass, "Club soda with lime?"

"Yep."

Zach nodded at Liam as he clapped Tyler on the back.

"Liam, this is Zach Ryder, our local police chief. Zach, this is Liam Dunbar—"

Before Tyler could finish, Zach interjected, "The guy buying the mill."

It was a statement, not a question. Liam smiled. "Uh, yeah." He didn't bother with an explanation of the zoning caveat.

Zach accepted the glass of club soda from Nate and guzzled it down before continuing. "I read an article about you in *Newsweek*," he pointed at Liam with the now-empty glass. "Glad to see someone is going to do something with that eyesore. It should help cut down on petty crime. Kids going in smoking pot."

"Though my son may be a bit disappointed."

"How's that?" He couldn't imagine Tyler confessing to the police chief that his son smoked pot in the old mill.

"He's a violin prodigy, and when he's home, he likes to play in the old mill. Says it has great acoustics."

"Ah. You said, 'when he's home.' Where is he?"

"New York. Studying at Julliard."

Liam looked at Zach then back at Tyler, who was clearly the proud papa. "Wow! He must be good then."

Tyler rocked back on his heels, a wide grin on his face. "He'll be playing the great concert halls of the world someday, so I think he'll get over the loss of the mill as a venue."

"Zach's fiancée will be your neighbor—or rather her business will be your neighbor—she owns the sister building to the mill. It was a cotton mill."

"The dance studio?"

"The whole building. Her mom bought the building, built out the dance studio and dancewear shop, then leased out the artist galleries and retail space."

"Smart."

He felt Zach's eyes on him. "So how much noise will this mill of yours make?"

Right. Zach wanted to know if the noise from the mill would disrupt the dance studio. "Very little. We use the most energy-efficient, noise-reducing equipment available. I doubt she will hear anything more than the hum of the HVAC."

Zach nodded, seemingly satisfied.

"Did you need something?" Tyler asked Zach.

"Oh. Yeah. Can you add a couple more kegs of Tiny Dancer to our order?"

"You got it. Zach's wedding is the end of June," Tyler explained.

"Congratulations." His mind flashed to his "wedding" and he remembered how beautiful Georgia had looked that night. *Where the hell had that come from?*

"Tyler made a special beer for the occasion because that's the kind of guy he is. Named in honor of my fiancée, Olivia. It's a German pilsner, whatever that means." He laughed and set his glass down on the bar. "I just know it tastes good," he added, then shook his head at Nate's unspoken question of whether he wanted another club soda.

"Hey, why don't you come to the wedding?" Zach said, turning to Liam.

"Oh, no." He looked at Tyler then back at Zach, brows lifted. "I'm sure the guest list has long been set."

"Come on. I need to balance out the men-to-women ratio. Right now, it's about two-to- one, with all of Olivia's former dance company friends."

"Well, only if you think the bride won't mind." Liam thought it would be a good opportunity to meet more of the townspeople. If he could talk up his plan, show them he didn't intend to bring in a chemical plant, they might support the rezoning of the property.

"You're staying at the 1885 B&B?"

"Yeah."

"I'll add your name to the guest list and bring by an invitation and leave it for you. I gotta run." He tapped the bar, and with a nod to Nate, Tyler, and Liam, he left.

Tyler shook his head with a laugh. "Sorry about the interruption. Where were we?"

"You were inviting me to the brewery for a tour."

Tyler plucked his phone from his back pocket. "What works for you?"

As LIAM UNLOCKED the door to his room at the bed and breakfast, his phone buzzed in his pocket. Thinking it was the call he'd scheduled with his CFO, he swiped it open without looking. "Dan!"

"Um, no. It's not Dan."

Cole. His breath left in a rush. "Where have you been? I've been trying to reach you for the last *two* days."

"I, uh, had to take a break, ya know?"

Liam's chin dropped to his chest. "What's the drug of choice this time? Oxy? Coke? Or some new designer drug?" This was met by silence. "Cole?"

"I *needed* it, bro."

Liam pressed a thumb to his right eye where a headache was forming. His phone beeped with another incoming call —Dan, no doubt, but he'd call him back.

"Cole, you've been clean for six months. What the hell happened?"

"Man, don't give me that holier-than-thou shit."

"What the fuck, Cole? You were working, you were clean. What set you back?"

"I ran into a friend . . ."

That explained it. "You mean Jonah." Jonah wasn't Cole's *friend*, he was Cole's *dealer*.

A self-deprecating laugh came through the phone. "Yeah, man. Jonah. We were just going to catch up, ya know? Talk about old times, but he had this stash that he said was primo."

"Godammit, Cole." He knew getting angry wasn't going to help matters, but he couldn't help it. "Okay, okay." He tried to calm down. "And is there any left? Is it gone? Are you done?"

"Yeah, bro, it's gone. Don't get your panties in a wad. I'll be back at work tomorrow." Though Liam had offered him a job with American Threads, Cole had refused. He worked— when it pleased him—for a surf shop in Venice Beach.

Liam sighed and rubbed his forehead. "Okay. It was just a bump in the road, right?" He tried to convince himself.

"Yeah."

"Promise?"

Liam could almost feel Cole's huff of annoyance through the phone. "Promise."

"Call me tomorrow. And don't—don't ignore my calls anymore." He hit end before his brother could come back with a snarky remark. Then he called Dan back.

Try as he might to focus on the latest engineering schematics for the mill, Liam couldn't shake the worry nagging him since Cole's phone call. He lived in fear of getting a call from the police that Cole was dead of an overdose.

Or killed in a drug deal gone wrong like their mother.

Liam and his brothers were actually half-brothers, all born of different anonymous fathers, a mixed bag of mixed-race mutts. Liam carried the imprint of his father's Hispanic heritage with his dark hair, dark eyes, and olive skin, tempered with his mother's Irish heritage. Liam's younger half-brother Cole was African-American and had his mother's green eyes, which added a startlingly beautiful complexity to his features. Ben, Liam's youngest brother who he'd failed to save in an apartment fire, was fathered by an Indian man.

Liam's brother Cole had gone into the foster system when Liam went to prison for computer hacking, and it wasn't too long after that that Cole got sucked into drugs and addiction. Liam still struggled with the guilt of what had happened to Cole, not to mention Ben. He'd make a lousy parent, that's for sure.

His mother hadn't been the best role model either, though she tried to keep a roof over their heads and food on the table by working two jobs. And his anonymous father had long since left them to themselves.

Liam was eighteen when their mother died. Killed in the crossfire of a botched drug bust. Child services had had their hands full with cases, so it was just assumed Liam would take over the parenting of Cole, since legally he was an adult at the time, in age if not in maturity.

He knew Cole blamed him for landing him in foster care. And Liam readily took the blame. If Liam hadn't hacked the utility company computers, if he hadn't been caught, if he hadn't pled guilty to decrease his sentence, Cole would not have gone into the foster system. Wouldn't have been introduced to drugs by his older foster brother. Wouldn't have become addicted to drugs, wouldn't have dropped out of school, wouldn't be living his life picking up odd jobs, surfing off the California coast, and otherwise living the life of a drifter.

Liam absorbed that blame, letting it fester. He'd tried, but he would never be able to get his brother off drugs for good. To atone, he'd given Cole a job with American Threads. Cole had a gift with numbers, and Liam thought he'd take pride in having a job analyzing data from the mills' computers for efficiencies. That hadn't lasted more than a week before Cole called in sick and never came back to work.

With a dead half-brother and another drug-addicted half-brother, nothing Liam ever did could atone for his failures.

GEORGIA SMOOTHED the skirt she wore and took a deep breath before knocking on her grandfather's partially closed office door. She didn't know why she was so nervous. Maybe because this was where her grandfather had hoped she'd work. That she would join the firm after graduation, eventually become a partner and carry on the family business.

A distracted "Yes?" drifted from the far side of the spacious room.

"Morning, Grandad. Shelley wasn't at her desk, so I just came back."

"Oh, Georgia! Come in, come in. Shelley had a doctor's appointment this morning, so I'm flying solo until she returns."

She had to smile at that. If you could call it flying solo with the ten or so other lawyers in the office, not to mention the support staff. While Northridge alone wouldn't provide enough work for a firm that size, Fitzgerald and MacKinnon had a reputation that drew clients from the neighboring towns. Some as far away as Alpharetta.

Her grandfather was the epitome of the elder statesman and lawyer, seated behind a massive mahogany desk, horn-rimmed glasses perched on his nose, a document in his hands. He was Perry Mason, Atticus Finch, and Henry Drummond all rolled into one. His thick silver hair added to his distinguished appearance, reminding his opponents that with age comes wisdom.

Her grandfather removed his reading glasses and folded his hands on the massive antique mahogany desk. "Sit, and let's talk about the rezoning. What are your thoughts?"

Taking a seat, she licked her dry lips, recalling the time she'd argued her first case on Stanford's Moot Court Team. Her grandfather's approval had always been important to her. Not that he'd ever withheld it.

"Well, I thought the cover slide for the presentation should feature images of several of the restored and operational mills, so the council members could see up front that he isn't planning to tear down the existing structure and replace it with an unattractive prefab structure."

At her grandfather's nod of agreement, she continued. "Then present the architect's rendering of the building, complete with land and hardscaping, then into the LEED-certification plans before moving into the economics of the manufacturing operation." She looked to her grandfather before she continued.

"Solid strategy. Only once they're comfortable with the look and feel of the operation will they pay attention to the numbers." He rose from his desk and paced the confines of his office, in trial mode, as if presenting his opening argument. "Northridge itself doesn't need another manufacturing operation. It already has Northridge Plastics with its hundred-plus employees. And frankly, if the Larson family were trying to get that plant up and running today, rather than in nineteen seventy-four when they first built it, the Town Council likely wouldn't approve it."

He paused in front of his desk, facing her and jabbing his index finger into the desktop to make his point. "You have to convince them that the employees the mill hires will spend some of the money they earn in Northridge and that the retail operation Liam is also proposing will bring people into the town to shop and dine."

Her grandfather was something to see. She'd seen him in the courtroom a few times as a teenager and had been proud to be his granddaughter.

Perching on the corner of his desk, he folded his arms. "A field trip might also be in order. Take the Economic Development Council to one of the other locations. Maybe the one in Griffin. Let them see firsthand how the mill impacted the citizens and the economy."

"Good idea. I'll raise that with Li—uh, Mr. Dunbar." Heat rose in her face at the slip. "Solid plan. Thanks, Grandad." She made to rise, but her grandfather's hand on her arm stopped her.

"We haven't had much time to chat since you returned to Northridge. How are you doing?"

Her grandfather had been at an American Bar Association conference in D.C. when she'd pulled into Northridge exhausted from the cross-country trip. He'd followed that up with a week in Maryland visiting friends. And though he'd offered to postpone that, she'd refused. Not only did she not want her grandfather changing his plans for her, the time alone to organize her thoughts and her life were appreciated. She'd also been putting in a lot of hours at the office.

She felt his gaze on her. She'd seen that look before, but it was typically directed toward a less-than-forthcoming witness. *Here we go . . .*

"When are you going to tell me about your business and why you decided to come home to Northridge?"

Her mouth went dry again. "There's nothing to tell really. After Erik," she swallowed, "well, after he was arrested and the scandal broke I thought a change was in order." She smiled, but even she knew he wasn't convinced.

"Uh-huh." He smiled back at her, trying to make her feel at ease, but she knew his tricks. "I suppose a broken heart would make a girl long for the bosom of her family." He rose, returning to his desk chair as if he'd concluded his line of questioning. But she knew better.

"It must have been a Herculean effort to wind down a large successful business like yours, but I suppose the scandal would have made things difficult.

If he only knew. "It was, but then again, change is never easy, right?"

Before he could say anything else, his intercom buzzed, "Mr. Marshall, your ten o'clock is here."

She rose, taking advantage of the interruption.

"See you later," she said as she headed for the door.

"Georgia," her grandfather called after her.

Closing her eyes and taking a deep breath, she turned.

"You know I love you . . . no matter what."

There was a question there, but she just nodded and left.

5

Liam couldn't sit around waiting for the rezoning to be approved. He needed to be ready to jump if and when the Town Council approved the request.

He'd had to deal with rezoning in a few of the other towns, and once they saw the potential positive economic impact, their councils had salivated at the prospect. Often, they relished becoming models for future sites. With that in mind, he had a meeting with the architect from Atlanta to finalize the plans, then a meeting with the construction company from Macon.

In addition to buying the old mills to manufacture clothing and give the local communities a living wage, to the extent possible he tried to work with local architects, suppliers, and construction companies to handle the renovations.

This often meant building new relationships with each new mill project, but Liam was fine with that. With each new business came fresh ideas—better ways to do things, different approaches to not only the building itself but sometimes the setup of the manufacturing operation. It seemed each new mill was built on the improvements from the last project. They got better and better each time. Where he could, he took those fresh ideas back to the previous projects and implemented them there.

He pulled up in front of Firehouse Brews for his tour and meeting with Tyler and gazed through his windshield at the red-brick two-story building. Apparently, like him, Tyler appreciated the original late-nineteenth-century architecture, because he'd left much of it unchanged.

The glass and wood double doors that covered the bays where he assumed fire engines once awaited the call were painted a deep gray to match the stones that formed each arch. The same stones accented the three tall windows on the second floor. A brass plaque on the building, like those on the buildings downtown, declared it the "Old Northridge Firehouse, est. 1890."

Visible through the windows on the top half of the doors stood huge gleaming stainless-steel kettles and piping. An old-fashioned painted sign that read FIREHOUSE BREWS hung beneath the roof lintels. Two enormous tanks flanked the building's exterior, Firehouse Brews and its nineteenth-century horse-drawn fire engine logo adorning them. A restored version of the same fire engine stood to the left of the building.

When he entered the building, the scents of barley and hops enveloped him, and he inhaled the earthy aroma. Huge metal cauldrons lined one side of the exposed brick and masonry walls. Gleaming concrete floors, clean enough to eat off of, reflected the overhead lighting two stories up. Tyler had removed the second-story floor to make room for the massive tanks, pipes, and coils that filled the room.

"Liam," Tyler greeted him with a welcoming smile.

Liam turned to see Tyler striding toward him. "I know you're busy, so I really appreciate the time."

"Are you kidding me? I love showing off my baby. How about a tour?"

"I thought you'd never ask."

Twenty minutes later they reached Tyler's tidy office. Impressed, Liam said, "I like what you're doing with the water and the mash. Smart. And like your business, mine will eat up a lot of energy." Pulling up the guest chair as Tyler sat behind his desk, Liam continued, "The roof will be covered in photovoltaic tiles. Any excess energy generated will be stored for use on cloudy days. We should be able to generate eighty to ninety percent of the energy we need."

Tyler nodded in approval. "Northridge may look like we're stuck in the past, but we look to the future, and the Economic Development Council and Town Council support green energy."

"Good to know. Thanks for the tour. I know you're on the EDC, so I won't go into any other details with you until the meeting. I don't want to put you in a bad spot."

"I appreciate your understanding."

"But I assure you, I will sell this."

"I have no doubts," Tyler said. "Now, how 'bout a beer?"

GEORGIA LEFT her grandfather's law office and headed in the direction of what had once been a dusty old bookstore. According to her friend Alyssa, Kristen McKay had purchased the business and turned it into a popular coffee shop, café, and bookstore. It had quickly become part of Georgia's morning routine.

To say that Georgia was surprised to learn that Kristen had become a local businesswoman would be an understatement. Not that Georgia knew Kristen all that well in high school—she'd been three years ahead of Georgia—but from what Georgia remembered of the gossip, Kristen had been lucky to have food on the table back then.

In the fifteen years since she'd left, Northridge had changed quite a bit, yet so much remained the same. The same buildings stood, but many held different businesses. Many of the families had remained, but many new young families had made Northridge home. The town had a new laidback bustle to it. Busy, but relaxed. So unlike the energy of L.A., but she found it appealing.

She opened the door to the Beans 'n Books Café and was charmed once again by the tinkle of the bell, as the heavenly scent of baked goods and coffee invited her in. Patrons filled the tables, and a line of customers stood waiting to order at a counter along the left wall, which displayed the usual muffins and cookies, danishes and croissants. The warm pine floor glowed as if rubbed with beeswax, reminding her of Liam's comment about the Redmond Mill's heart pine floor.

Georgia scanned the tables for her friend. Alyssa Bailey had been Georgia's best friend growing up, and the only childhood friend with whom she'd maintained contact after leaving Northridge. Alyssa was married now with two kids and ran an after-school program at the community theater. They could go months without talking to one another, but when they finally reconnected, it was like they hadn't missed a beat. One of the many reasons she loved Alyssa.

"Georgia, over here!"

Alyssa's raised voice and waving hand caught Georgia's

attention over the hubbub of the busy café, and she made her way to a two-top in the far corner, near a rack of books on display. Georgia found herself in Alyssa's embrace, and some of the tension she'd been carrying since Liam showed up drained away.

Alyssa released her and stepped back. "God, you look amazing!"

"Thanks, so do you. New haircut?" Georgia had kept up with Alyssa and her growing family on Facebook, but nothing could replace seeing her in person.

"Yeah." She lifted a hand to her choppy dark waves. "With the kids, I don't have a lot of time in the morning, so this wash-and-go style suits."

Alyssa and her husband Dillon had a seven-year-old boy named Jameson and a three-year-old girl named Delilah.

"Very chic." Georgia pulled out the other chair and sank into it with relief.

This is the first chance she'd had to see Alyssa. She would have seen her at the wedding last month, but . . . And while Georgia had been back for two weeks, with the opening of her new real estate office, she'd been buried. That, and Alyssa had been on a family vacation in the Catskill Mountains in Upstate New York.

"You should order something," Alyssa nodded toward the counter, "then we can catch up."

After settling at the table with an iced americano, Georgia listened as Alyssa caught her up on the kids and Dillon. She was truly interested in Alyssa's life but, also wanting to postpone the inevitable conversation, Georgia beat Alyssa to the punch and asked for all her news.

"Okay, your turn. Tell me what's new," she prompted, taking a sip of her coffee. How are you? Anything on your asshat ex?"

She hadn't shared the full Erik story and probably never would for that matter. No way she would reveal just how gullible and naïve she'd been. It was all too humiliating, not to mention financially disastrous.

"Other than him being indicted for fraud and money laundering? No."

"I can't believe Erik Lawson wasn't even his real name. It's like an episode from a TV crime drama."

"Yeah. Isn't it?" Georgia asked with a sad smile. "I still think of him as Erik, even though his real name is Jason. But I can't call him Jason either."

Alyssa nodded and pointed a finger at Georgia. "Henceforth, he shall be called 'Not-Erik.'"

Georgia couldn't help the giggle that escaped. God, it felt good to be with Alyssa again.

After taking a bite of her morning glory muffin, Alyssa asked, "How was your, er, honeymoon? You said you went with a friend from L.A. What about it? Did you hit the jackpot?"

She wished! The money would've come in handy. "No." *Here goes nothing . . .* She licked her dry lips, leaned close over the table and whispered, "Turns out I got married on my honeymoon."

"Married?!" Alyssa clapped a hand over her mouth as heads pivoted in their direction.

Great. Heat flooded Georgia's face as she glanced around. "Yeah, hard to believe she married the guy, isn't?" Then she reached across the table and gave Alyssa's hand a squeeze. "Shhh."

"Sorry." Her voice dropped to a whisper, her warm brown eyes wide. "But what did you expect? Dropping a bomb like that? And why is it a secret? Is your new husband here in Northridge?"

"If you take a breath, I'll tell you." Where to start? "I invited Audrey Turner—"

"Wait—Audrey Turner? The *actress*?" Alyssa asked, her eyes wide.

"Yeah." Georgia waved her hand as if to say no big deal. "Anyway, she's the one who encouraged me to use my honeymoon to get away and cut loose, where, you know, what happens in Vegas—"

"Stays in Vegas," Alyssa finished with a smirk.

"Yeah. You know—shows, clubs, dancing, drinking . . . drinking."

"Not really your scene."

"No, but something in me snapped. After . . . well, after Not-Erik and calling off the wedding and the scandal, I just . . ." She shrugged.

"It's okay. I get it." She laid a hand over Georgia's and squeezed. "And? What happened?"

Georgia shrugged. "And our first night there I met a guy. In a club." She shook her head at the tropey-ness of it. "The connection was almost instant. I've never felt anything like it," she muttered almost to herself. "Anyway, we danced, saw a show. We danced some more. Slept together. We spent the whole next day together—Hoover Dam, Lake Mead, then more dancing and some drinking the second night at his friend's wedding—that's why he was in Vegas—"

"Okay. Wait. Back it up." Alyssa held up her hand. "You slept together the night you met?"

"Uh . . . yeah." Heat crept into Georgia's cheeks.

Alyssa reached out and gave her shoulder a shove. "You go, girl."

"Yeah, well, somewhere in there we got married. Well, to be specific, we got married the night of his friend's wedding."

"Oh. My. God." Alyssa sat back in her chair and eyed Georgia. "You got married in Vegas. How deliciously cliché."

"Apparently."

"You don't have an impulsive bone in your body. And you don't drink." She shook her head. "That must have been *some* guy."

Thinking about him coming to her rescue in the club, she could agree with that.

"Okay, so you slept together on the first night, but did you," she lifted her brows, "you know, consummate the marriage?"

"Yeah, and then some." She chewed her lower lip. When Georgia had woken up in the wee hours of the morning to the reality of what she'd done, there were three condom wrappers scattered on the floor. Three! Thank goodness one of them had had the presence of mind to play it safe.

"Must have been good the first night if you went back for more. So, what are you going to do?"

"Get a quickie divorce. Quietly."

"So there's no happy ending to this?" Alyssa asked, a note of disappointment in her voice.

Georgia drew back. "No! This isn't some rom-com. I hardly know the guy. There's no way we're staying married."

Alyssa nodded, took a sip of her coffee, thinking. "Where is he, by the way?"

Georgia sighed, then hesitated before answering. "You know the buyer I have for the Redmond button mill? It's him."

"Shut the front door! *That* was your appointment yesterday?"

"Yup. He found me—"

"Wait, what do you mean he *found* you?"

Georgia closed her eyes and confessed. "I woke up the

next morning, got dressed, and hauled butt before he woke up."

"You got married and bailed the next morning?"

She winced. "Yeah. Not my proudest moment. We were supposed to get the marriage annulled the next morning, but I panicked. I have no other excuse."

"Holy matrimony!"

"Frankly," Georgia continued, "I'd been a bit tipsy and didn't remember every detail of that night. I didn't remember the wedding until I was on the elevator and saw the wedding band. By that time, there was no way I was going back."

"So, what now?"

"Simple," Georgia said with a shrug. "We get a quickie divorce."

"We have a problem," Georgia blurted the moment Liam sat down for their lunch meeting at the Whistle Stop Pub.

"What kind of problem?" He laid the white linen napkin across his lap.

"A residency problem."

Liam shook his head. "I don't follow."

"States have residency requirements in order to file legal actions. Georgia requires six months residency in order to file for divorce."

"And you moved to Georgia when?"

"Three weeks ago."

Not long after their, *er*, encounter in Vegas. He rubbed his right eye with his thumb, as if it would ward off the headache building there.

"Where do you live?" Georgia asked.

"I moved to New York about two months ago, but I'm rarely there."

She woke up her tablet, did a quick search and groaned. "New York's requirement is two *years*!"

He lowered his head to his hands and groaned, then a thought struck him and he lifted his gaze to hers. "What about Nevada?"

"Six weeks. Already checked."

He stared at her a beat.

"No. I *can't* move to Nevada for six weeks. I just got here. I have a business to run."

"If you'd just stayed and faced the music like we'd agreed, we wouldn't be in this mess."

She at least looked chagrinned. "Fine. What about you? Can you move to Nevada?"

"No. I have a mill to get off the ground."

She threw up her hands in exasperation. "Okay. Where does that leave us?"

"We'll just have to wait," he said with a resigned shrug.

"Wait? But . . . *six* months?"

"No, five months and one week."

She rolled her eyes. "I can't stay married to you."

"Why? You have a boyfriend? A fiancé?" He didn't know why, but that thought sent a white-hot arrow of jealousy through his chest.

An affronted expression crossed her face. "Of course not! If I had a boyfriend, I wouldn't have been in Vegas. With you." She folded her arms over her chest and glared at him.

"I don't see what other choice we have. Six months is nothing in the scheme things."

"Six months of keeping this secret in a small town will seem like a lifetime, trust me."

"Six months is nothing. In the meantime, we rezone the

property and finalize this deal. I want this plant up and running by the end of next year's first quarter."

She stared at him, her teeth sunk in her lower lip. Releasing her lip, she heaved a sigh and nodded. "And you'll keep our marriage a secret?"

He nodded. "You have my word."

6

T he offices of MacKinnon Realty (formerly known as Five Star Realty) occupied a nineteen-seventies brick ranch-style house two blocks off Main Street in desperate need of an update. Or a wrecking ball. A far cry from the glass and steel two-story office she had previously occupied on Ventura Boulevard in Woodland Hills.

Some days she considered her personal no-alcohol policy. This was one of those days. Her Vegas mistake had not only followed her to Northridge, but now she and said mistake would have to remain married for another five months while keeping it a secret. Well, with the exception of Alyssa. Add to that needing to sell the Redmond Mill property ASAP so she'd have more than two nickels to rub together, to borrow a phrase from her grandfather, but it had to be rezoned first.

She jiggled her key in the ancient door lock. After a few choice words, the door finally surrendered, opening onto the dreadful office space. "I really have to get that fixed," she muttered, as she balanced her iced caramel macchiato in one hand and flipped on the lights with the other. The hum and glare of the bright fluorescent lights assaulted her senses.

Heaving a sigh of frustration, she grimaced in disgust. What she wouldn't give for the budget to gut this place and start over. Or better yet, to bulldoze it and build something with more charm than a bunker.

What she assumed had once been the dining room served as her office, the living room had become the reception area, and two of the three bedrooms had become two more offices, leaving the third-smallest bedroom for supplies, a copy machine, and an overall junk room.

The kitchen remained, which, though hideous, was convenient. She could bring food from home to save money on lunches, and she'd be able to offer refreshments to her clients. If the business was successful, and she was able to hire other agents, they'd have the breakfast area in the kitchen for lunches. The wood-paneled den, which served as an open office area with three small desks, would make a nice conference room (minus the paneling) to hold closings and other meetings.

When she could afford the renovations, that is . . . in a decade or so.

Not to mention the lack of curbside appeal. The exterior of the building, as well as the landscape, what there was of it, could really use an update.

But first things first. She needed a receptionist. She had two interviews today and hoped one would pan out so they could start ASAP.

If the sale of the button mill to her . . . um, husband, went through she could afford to slap some paint on the dull beige walls and replace the hideous rust-colored indoor-outdoor carpet that appeared to be older than she was.

Settling at her utilitarian metal desk that looked like

something from the Army surplus store, she sipped the excellent coffee and opened her laptop to pull up the digital file with the contract for the property.

Liam seemed to think the rezoning was a foregone conclusion. Unlike in the early days, any current manufacturing in the area was outside the charming nineteenth-century railroad town. Notwithstanding her strategy, she felt certain the townspeople would oppose its return.

The town's existence post-dated the Civil War by about five years, so it didn't boast any antebellum homes, but it had its share of notable historic homes dating to the early days, most in the American Craftsman style like MacKinnon House.

The town's economy was tourism, plain and simple. The old Georgia charm drew people who craved a day away from Atlanta where they could stroll the quaint historic downtown area, visit the trendy shops, and sample the excellent food and beverages Northridge's businesses were proud to offer.

Only about five square miles, the town proper was built on a ridge some twelve hundred feet above sea level and some two hundred feet above its neighbors, making Northridge's temperatures about ten degrees cooler than the surrounding area.

Even so, the summers could still be hot. And speaking of hot . . .

She rose to check the ancient thermostat. Eighty degrees. *Ugh.* "Please tell me the AC isn't on the fritz," she muttered. She adjusted the dial down a few degrees and crossed her fingers in the hopes that it would cool off. The last thing she needed right now was to replace the HVAC. That would surely bankrupt her.

Cursing Not-Erik, she turned her attention to the documents required for the rezoning and the notes for her next meeting with Liam.

LIAM WIPED the sweat from his brow with the bottom of his T-shirt as he, Tyler, and Zach slowed their pace a block from Main Street. "Good run," he panted. "Nice route."

Zach followed suit, using his forearm to wipe away the sweat. "Yeah. It lulls you into a false sense of ease with the beautiful historic neighborhoods. Then the hill into town kicks your ass."

Tyler rubbed his hands together, "Now we get to reap the rewards."

"If you haven't had Kristen's cinnamon rolls, you're in for a treat," Zach explained.

"Cinnamon rolls, huh? Kind of negates all that hard work I just put in," Liam said with a laugh.

"Nah. It all balances out." Tyler slapped him on the shoulder as Zach pushed open the door.

The bell tinkled overhead, and Liam nearly floated over to the coffee bar on the scents of cinnamon, sugar, and coffee. "I think I consumed five hundred calories just by breathing."

Tyler snorted.

Liam loved the warm welcoming feel of the café. The heart pine floors, exposed brick walls, and exposed wood beams added to the old-timey aesthetic. The tables were filled with patrons sipping coffee and tea, some working on laptops, others talking to their table companions.

"Looks like a popular spot."

"You know it," Tyler said with a proud grin.

Liam knew the owner, Kristen McKay, was Tyler's

fiancée and that they would be getting married later that year. The three men placed their orders with the barista, and Liam caught a hint of a Jamaican accent.

"Where's my woman?" Tyler asked.

The barista, whose nametag read "Calypso," rolled her eyes and gave a jerk of her head toward the back of the café. "She be in the office." Liam caught the pleasing lilt of a Jamaican accent.

"Grab a table. I'll be back," Tyler said as he headed in the direction Calypso had indicated where floor-to-ceiling shelves housed row upon row of books.

They had just plopped down in their chairs when the bell tinkled again and a well-dressed older gentleman came in, and something told Liam this was Georgia's grandfather, The Honorable Marshall MacKinnon.

Liam hadn't formally met him yet, but he fit the description. A tall, distinguished looking man, MacKinnon had a stellar reputation for fairness and was a keen judge of character if the words of Northridge citizens were to be believed, and he had no reason to doubt it.

The man stopped at their table, nodded a greeting to Zach, then thrust out a hand. "You must be the American Threads man."

Liam rose to shake the man's hand. "Liam Dunbar. And you're Marshall MacKinnon." The man's grip was firm but friendly. "Pleased to meet you, sir."

Marshall waved a hand at him. "Call me Marshall. Sir makes me feel my age. And please, sit," he said, gesturing to Liam's vacated seat. "My granddaughter tells me you're here to shake things up a bit," he continued.

Liam glanced at Zach then back at Mr. MacKinnon, wondering what exactly Georgia had told the man. "Yes, sir, if adding to Northridge's economic growth is shaking things up."

MacKinnon laughed, a jovial sound. "Nothing wrong with keeping things interesting," he said with a wink. Then he turned to Zach. "Give your lovely bride-to-be a kiss from me."

Zach nodded and Marshall MacKinnon made his way over to the coffee bar.

Tyler returned, pulled out his chair, and sank into it, a goofy grin on his face and his hair more mussed than when he'd left.

Zach cleared his throat, shot a look at Liam, then said with a cheeky smile, "And you thought he came in to get a cinnamon roll."

THE NEXT DAY, Liam entered Dominick's Pizza, and the scent of cured meats, aged cheese, and tangy yeast reminded him that he'd last eaten around six that morning.

For a small town, Northridge had some great eateries. From Beans 'n Books and the Whistle Stop Pub to Sweet Creams and Dominick's, he'd already had plenty of pleasant dining experiences in the short time he'd been around. A good crowd filled the booths and tables, so he waited to be seated. The door opened behind him, and he didn't need to turn to know it was Georgia. Above the cloud of pizza smells, the scent of jasmine drifted in, light but still discernible.

"Have you been waiting long?" she asked as she shoved her phone into the enormous tote bag she carried.

"No. Just got here. Busy today."

She blew a tendril of hair out of her face. "Lunch always draws a crowd."

Liam eyed her, noting that she appeared a little rough around the edges. She'd twisted her hair up in some sort of clip but some had escaped, and her usually polished nails were in need of attention. Not that any of this detracted from her beauty. He rather liked seeing her not so put together. But then he noticed the dark circles under her eyes, and the faint tinge of green beneath her peaches-and-cream complexion.

"Are you okay? You look a little pale."

She rubbed her forehead. "Yeah. Maybe I just need to eat something."

A server was clearing away a booth in the back. Perfect.

"Right this way," another server said as she showed them to the table.

Liam set the blueprints and other papers on the bench seat, but before they could slide into their seats, Georgia swayed on her feet. Alarmed, Liam grabbed her by the arm and pulled her against him. Her jasmine perfume and warm, lithe body sent his libido into overdrive and memories of their two nights together flooded his mind.

Get a grip, man. She's about to fall out.

"Here, sit." He guided her into the booth, took the tote bag from her—which felt as if it held bricks—and tossed it into the seat beside her.

"When was the last time you ate?"

She shook her head as if to clear it. "Um, I had a protein bar around eight."

As soon as he was sure she wasn't going to fall over, he took a seat across from her, handed her one of the paper menus on the table, and gestured for the server.

"I'll take a glass of iced tea. And she'll take a Coke."

"Oh, but—"

"The sugar will do you good. And do you have any bread or breadsticks?"

"We have our famous twisty breadsticks." Liam almost chuckled. *Famous?* "Bring us some of those. ASAP if you can."

The server nodded and left to do his bidding.

"High-handed much?"

"You nearly fainted. Clearly, you need sustenance."

She waved him away. "It's probably just the heat." He lifted a brow at her. "And, okay, hunger."

The server arrived with their drinks, and he was pleased to see Georgia take a big gulp of the icy Coke as she reached for a breadstick.

He looked over the menu and when he'd made up his mind and looked back at her, some color had returned to her cheeks. He breathed a sigh of relief.

After placing their order—a Greek salad for her, as well as another Coke, and a roasted veggie calzone for him—he sat back in the booth and eyed her, wondering what had caused that little episode.

She glanced up, a breadstick halfway to her mouth. "What?"

He shook his head and said, "You need to take better care of yourself."

She leaned forward as if she were about to share a secret. "Thank you for your concern, but just because you're my temporary *husband*," she'd whispered the last word, looking around to make sure no one heard, "doesn't mean you get to tell me what to do."

He folded his arms across his chest. "Fair enough. Shall we get to work?"

"Yes. Please." She pulled out the digital tablet she never

seemed to be without and swiped it awake. "Okay, so here's what we need to provide to the council with the request to rezone."

"'A plot plan of the lot showing the location of all present and proposed buildings, drives, parking lots, waste disposal fields, and other constructional features on the lot. And all buildings, streets, alleys, highways, streams, and other topographical features outside of the lot and within two hundred feet of any lot line.'"

"Got it." He held up a folder and she nodded.

She paused as the server placed their orders on the table before resuming. "'Architectural plans for any proposed or renovated buildings.'"

He lifted the rolled-up blueprint.

"'A description of the industrial operations proposed in sufficient detail to indicate the effects of those operations in producing traffic congestion, noise, glare, air pollution, water pollution, fire hazards, or safety hazards.'" A tendril of hair fell in front of her right eye, which she tucked away behind her ear. He recalled the silky feel of her hair when'd he'd fisted his hands in it, and his fingers itched to touch it again.

"Hello?"

He refocused to see Georgia waving a hand in front of his face. *Right.* "Check."

"'Engineering and architectural plans for the treatment and disposal of sewage and industrial waste.'" She lifted her fork to her mouth in an absentminded way, licking a drop of salad dressing off the corner of her mouth. His groin tightened.

Damn. Who knew talking about industrial waste could be so erotic? He shifted uncomfortably in his seat, but she didn't appear to notice. "Yep."

"'Engineering and architectural plans for the handling of any excess traffic congestion, noise, glare, air pollution, water pollution, fire hazard, or safety hazard.'"

"In with the blueprints."

"'A designation of the fuel proposed to be used and any necessary architectural and engineering plans for controlling smoke.'"

"N/A. The primary source of energy will be solar."

"Really?"

"Really."

"Cool." She nodded and continued, "'The proposed number of shifts to be worked and the maximum number of employees on each shift.'" She put the straw between her lips and sucked.

At his failure to respond again, she looked up with a questioning lift of her brows.

"Uh, got it." *Pay attention, man.* This is business.

"And the final catch-all, 'any other data or evidence that the Town Council may require.'" She set aside her fork, and dabbed at her mouth with her napkin. "Sounds like you've got everything covered."

"It's not my first rodeo."

She snorted, took another pull on the Coke, then sat back in obvious contentment, fully recovered from whatever had caused her to feel faint.

"When's the next meeting? What are the deadlines?" he asked.

"Well, we first have to present to the Economic Development Council, and their next meeting is June eighth. We'll need to have the aforementioned paperwork into them 'no later than fifteen calendar days before the next scheduled meeting,'" she said, apparently quoting the policy.

He checked the date on his watch. "Perfect. We can

submit the paperwork the end of this week, which gives us ten days to put together the presentation."

"Then we'd better get to work."

"TELL me something about yourself that isn't on your resume." Georgia set aside the tidy one-page document and sat back in her chair.

"Well, I'm gay."

She couldn't hold back the bark of laughter at this unexpected comment. "Okay then. Are you always this forthright?"

"Yes. My husband says it's both a blessing and a curse." The man sitting across from her shrugged, his brown eyes alight with mischief. She liked him immediately.

"What else?"

"My husband Jonathan and I just moved here from Charlotte. He's a plastic surgeon—lucky me," he patted his smooth swarthy face, "and is joining a practice in Atlanta. He told me to do whatever I wanted. Work. Don't work. But to enjoy whatever it was. I can't sit idle, so here I am," he finished with a lift of his hands.

"And you enjoy office work?"

"I enjoy keeping busy but don't want the pressure of a high-powered job in Atlanta."

"I can respect that. I don't think you have to worry about that here."

He looked around the dingy office then back at her. "I also have some design experience," he said with a lifted brow, leaving that statement to hang in the air, an unsubtle hint.

She ran a hand through her hair with a sigh. "Yeah. I just

bought this business and haven't had the chance," *or the money,* "to, um . . . renovate the place."

"I thought you were going to say detonate the place."

She laughed again. God, it felt good to let her guard down a bit. She liked this guy. "That either."

"I'm happy to help. Just say the word."

Georgia picked up the resume again. Fernando L. Lopez-England had a B.S. in Business from UNC, had lived in Charlotte for the past twelve years and worked in an art gallery, an interior design firm, and a law office. According to his resume, he was proficient in various computer software programs, had excellent communication skills, and was a self-starter. By all appearances, he was more than qualified for the receptionist job. But if he proved himself, he could grow into much more responsibility, and maybe get his real estate license, if he was so inclined.

"Well, Fernando—"

"Luis. Unless I've done something wrong and you're scolding me," he said with a lift of his mouth as he ran his fingers through his jet-black hair. "Luis is my middle name."

"Luis. If we can come to an agreement on salary, I'd like to offer you the job."

"And I'd like to take that job." He looked around again. "The first order of business . . . selecting some paint colors to liven up this place."

Liam's phone rang and his stomach plummeted when he saw the source of the call—LAC, or L.A. County, Hospital. This was the call Liam had been dreading. His legs went to jelly and he collapsed onto a chair in his room before he swiped to answer the call.

"This is Liam." His voice sounded breathy and . . . frightened. For good reason.

"Mr. William Dunbar?"

"Yes."

"This is Dr. Diaz. Your brother is Cole Dunbar?"

Liam closed his eyes and swallowed. The doctor had said *is*, not *was*. Maybe that was a good sign.

"Cole has been admitted to the hospital for further monitoring following a heroin overdose."

Liam didn't know whether to be relieved or upset. Relieved Cole was alive, but upset that his drug addiction had almost killed him.

"EMT's administered Narcan before transporting him here." The doctor continued, "He's stable and should be released tomorrow."

"Thank you, Doctor. Is he . . . is he awake? Can I speak to him?"

"He is awake." The doctor hesitated, "Mr. Dunbar, now is not the time to admonish him."

That was exactly what Liam wanted to do, but he knew the doctor was right. "I understand. I would just like to speak to him. To hear his voice."

There were mumbled voices on the other end then, "Hey, brother."

Cole's voice was raspy.

"Cole." Liam squeezed his eyes shut and drew in a deep breath. "How are you feeling?"

A drowsy chuckle came through the phone. "I've been better."

Liam practically had to bite his tongue before he said something he'd later regret. "I'm glad you're okay. I'm glad they found you." Tears burned his eyes, but he blinked them away.

"Are you?"

"What does that mean?" Anger tempered the fear and relief.

"Your life would be so much easier without a drug addict dragging you down."

Gathering his patience, Liam said, "Listen to me, Cole, you are my brother and I love you. I just wish—"

"That I weren't your problem?"

"No," Liam ground out. "I just wish I could help you."

"Did it ever occur to you that I'm beyond help?"

"No. And it never will." This was followed by silence. "Cole?"

"Yeah. I gotta go. They're taking me to a room."

"I'll call you tomorrow." But the line was already dead.

7

"This is what I love about small towns," he said, lifting his hand to indicate all the Memorial Day hoopla.

He needed this distraction. Cole was out of the hospital and had been admitted to an inpatient rehab facility at Liam's urging, but Liam still had a sick feeling in the pit of his stomach—Cole had been to rehab before and it hadn't kept him from landing himself back in a hospital emergency room from a drug overdose.

"You didn't have these kinds of celebrations in . . . ?"

"Chicago. No."

"Oh, come on. Chicago probably had a huge parade and fireworks."

"Oh sure, the *city* did. But I grew up in Riverdale, on the city's far southeast side. The only fireworks in Riverdale were those from gunfire." This resulted in silence from his frowning wife. "Let's not talk about the past. We're here on this Chamber of Commerce day," he gestured to the shimmering blue sky and white puffy clouds, "honoring our fallen heroes and celebrating hometown America. Let's just enjoy it. You must have been to hundreds of these celebrations growing up."

"Not really. I didn't live here until I was thirteen, but I have been to quite a few." She looked around. "I guess I didn't remember just how . . . American they were."

She looked adorable with her hair up in a sleek ponytail, wearing a red cotton sundress and flat sandals. Without her heels she barely reached his shoulders. As sexy as her usual heels were, he found he preferred her like this—breezy and easy going.

Local restaurants offered food, while locals manned craft tables and booths with everything from handmade quilts to stained glass. There was even a dunking machine where local celebrities volunteered to get wet on this warm afternoon, including Georgia's grandfather and Zach. Later there would be pie-eating contests and a cake walk. Proceeds from the activities would support the volunteer fire department. This was Americana at its best. He often wondered why he chose to live in big cities—first Chicago, now New York— and whether he could put down roots in any one of the small towns like this where he'd restored mills.

According to the town's newspaper—if the six-page document could be called that—students from the dance studio next to his future mill would be performing at the amphitheater, and various musical groups were scheduled to play. Then the community theater would be performing a scene from their upcoming production of *Brighton Beach Memoirs.*

He had a beautiful woman by his side, who just happened to be his wife—if only for five more months, he was confident the mill would be rezoned, and no one from the rehab facility had called him to say Cole had walked out.

At the moment, all was right with his world, and he'd learned from experience to savor those moments.

He saw Tyler had a booth set up and was serving his beer, while Kristen was serving up iced coffee, cookies, and cupcakes in a booth right next to his. A cold beer would be great later, but right now an iced coffee sounded good.

"Iced coffee?" he asked Georgia.

"I'm never one to turn down caffeine," she said with a shrug.

He snorted and shook his head.

Calypso made their orders, and resisting the strange urge to take Georgia's hand in his, they wandered the craft booths in companionable silence.

"If you get the rezoning, when do you plan to start on the building?" Georgia asked, taking a sip of her coffee.

"The construction company is ready as soon as we get the permits. I hope to have roofers there by the end of June."

"You work fast."

"Time is money." He studied Georgia a minute then asked, "Why did you leave L.A. for Small Town, USA?"

She tensed beside him, took another sip of her coffee, then lifted a nonchalant shoulder. "I told you in Vegas, after calling off the wedding, I needed a change. And home sounded . . . peaceful."

He was certain that wasn't the whole story, but intending to make the most of this beautiful day, he didn't push it. Besides, it wasn't his business. In less than six months, their impulsive marriage would be dissolved, and he'd likely never see Georgia again.

No point in getting wrapped up in her life.

GEORGIA RELAXED when Liam didn't ask any follow up questions. There was no way she was going to tell him her dirty little secret.

Two kids ran past them, ice cream cones in their hands. A couple walked their dog, holding hands and laughing. The atmosphere was one of happiness and . . . pride. These people were proud of their hometown. Neighbors greeted neighbors as if they hadn't just run into each other at Smith's, the local grocery store. You certainly didn't see that in L.A. It hadn't occurred to her how much she missed small-town activities this like one until Liam said something.

As a teenager, Georgia couldn't wait to get out of Northridge, away from her mother's troubled legacy. Away from those who pitied her orphan status, and those who watched her, waiting for her to make the same mistakes her mother had made before she left town in the dark of night, unwed and pregnant at eighteen.

Though it pained her to leave her grandparents, whom she had come to love, California, with its promise of thirty-nine million strangers, drew her. Strangers who knew nothing about her and her reckless mother. College had been the perfect excuse to leave. And law school was the perfect excuse to stay away. Her grandparents had been proud of her, though her grandfather not so subtly mentioned the possibility of her returning to Northridge and joining his law firm.

In theory, working with her grandfather was tempting. But in reality, California had taken hold of her and she wanted, no, *needed*, to prove she could make it on her own. The only time she'd been back to Northridge before now was to attend her grandmother's funeral.

"Why did you leave one big city for another one if you

like small towns so much?" she asked, shaking off the memories.

He took a minute to answer. "It doesn't really matter where I live. I'm rarely there. But maybe, like you, I needed a change."

"Then why not a small town? They seem to appeal to you. And as you said, you could live anywhere."

"I've considered it, but I've been so focused on buying and restoring mills that I just haven't taken the time to explore the possibility. The move to New York was a whim," he said, his tone suggesting that the thought had just occurred to him.

Liam grabbed her arm just as a group of kids came barreling through the crowd, narrowly missing her.

"Thanks." He'd let go as soon as they'd passed, but the heat of his hand on her bare arm lingered.

"I know you're not married—well, at least not to someone else—but do you have a family? Siblings? Kids?"

"I have a brother. No kids." His response was terse, and she wondered why that question seemed to strike a nerve, but she didn't press it.

"How about you? Any siblings?"

Turnabout was fair play, she supposed. "No." She kept her response short as well, hoping he would take the hint that she didn't want to talk about her past either.

"So it's just you and your grandfather then?"

"Yes." That wasn't a subject she wished to discuss either. She searched for a safe topic, but before she could find one, he'd moved away to toss his cup into a nearby recyclables receptacle, and when he returned, he said, "Let's go see who's on the dunking machine. I hear your grandfather and Zach are two of the dunkees."

"You've met my grandfather?" She shook her head. What

was she thinking? "Of course you have. You can't be in Northridge long without meeting The Honorable Marshall MacKinnon."

"He introduced himself at the café. He's like Northridge's ambassador."

"Indeed he is," she said with a smile.

"Maybe your grandfather or the police chief is in need of a cooling dip."

She laughed and shook her head. "I could never dunk Grandad!"

"Maybe not, but *I* could," he said with a grin.

"You wouldn't!" she said in mock horror.

"I would." He turned a cheeky grin on her. "After all, it's for a good cause."

Great balls of fire! Her knees went weak at the sight of his devastating grin. If he kept that up, she'd be hard pressed not to end up in his arms again.

And that couldn't happen.

"WHO IS THIS GUY I MARRIED?" Georgia muttered, closing the rezoning application she'd been working on. If she was going to help him with the rezoning request, she should familiarize herself with his business.

She'd spent a lovely day with Liam yesterday. After he'd successfully dunked her good-natured grandfather, they'd played ring toss then balloon pop and competed in corn hole. If she were honest with herself, it was the most fun she'd had in a very long time. Maybe . . . she shook her head at the idea that flitted through her brain. No. She'd already sworn to become the eccentric old spinster living in the family home, like Miss Havisham.

In the room of her adolescence, she sat at her childhood desk that looked out over the expansive lawn that swept down from the house to the woods beyond. Her late grandmother had redecorated the room since she'd left. It was no longer little-girl pink, and the four-poster bed no longer boasted a frilly canopy. It was an elegant guest room in cool blues, creamy whites, and rich browns.

Just below was the swimming pool her grandfather had built for her sixteenth birthday, and to the left, she could just see the roof corner of the old carriage house that had been converted into a guest cottage.

She didn't have much time because dinner would be ready soon. Margie Oldham, who cooked for the 1885 B&B, cooked two to three meals a week for her grandfather, often making enough for two or three meals at a time. Known for her traditional Southern cooking, Margie's meals weren't exactly health-conscious, but, boy, were they delicious! How her grandfather maintained his fitness level when he indulged in dishes like chicken pot pie, chicken and dumplings, and Margie's famous buttermilk fried chicken, she'd never know. She'd have to watch herself or she'd find a few extra pounds around her middle. Then her stomach growled, reminding her she hadn't eaten since the to-go salad she'd picked up for lunch.

Opening Google, Georgia typed "William Dunbar American Threads" into the search and hit enter. It yielded a slew of articles about him, including the recent one in *The Atlanta Constitution* her grandfather had mentioned. One headline from five years ago read IT SECURITY BILLION-AIRE SUMMITS EVEREST. "Wow," she breathed, at both his wealth and his exploits. No wonder he could write a cashier's check for the mill.

One thing she didn't find was a public social life. No

social media presence, no photos of him with beautiful women. You'd think someone with Liam's looks and money, he'd have women clamoring for his attention. If she didn't know better, she might think he was gay.

Scanning the rest of the results, she came across an exposé in *Newsweek* from two years earlier, and thinking it would be the most comprehensive resource, clicked on it.

The first line made her gasp:

For a convicted felon, William Dunbar—Liam to his friends—has led a storied life.

She *married* an ex-con? Boy! She could really pick 'em, couldn't she? Talk about frying pan to fire.

That's it! She threw her hands up in the air. No more men. She renewed her vow to follow in Miss Havisham's footsteps.

Shaking her head at the image, she scanned the article for the juicy bits, she read that he'd been convicted of computer hacking when he was nineteen and served three years in a minimum-security prison.

Sitting back in shock, she thought about Not-Erik and the crimes he'd committed. How could she have become "involved" with yet another felon? Is that how Liam got his money? Were the mills his way of laundering that money? Would she become an accessory by helping him get the rezoning he needed?

She shuddered. Her life was already in shambles, thanks to one felon. She wasn't about to aid and abet another. Tomorrow she'd tell him he needed to find someone else to represent him on the rezoning.

"Georgia?" her grandfather called from downstairs.

Phooey. She wanted to finish the article. "Yeah?"

"Dinner's ready. Come get it while it's hot. Margie outdid herself this time—chicken pot pie."

"Coming!" She bookmarked the article and closed her laptop.

She needed to get that divorce, and quick. November couldn't get her fast enough. And she needed to put some distance between herself and Liam. She snorted. Yeah, like *that* was possible living in Northridge.

THE NEXT MORNING, Georgia handed Liam the contract for the mill property. "Here's the contract. It includes a rezoning contingency."

Not wanting to have this conversation in public, she knocked on the door of his room at the 1885 B&B, and the moment he answered the door she stuck the contract in his face.

"All right," he said with some confusion, taking the documents from her. "I thought we were meeting at Beans 'n Books at ten. But since you're here," he held the door open for her, "come in."

She finally noticed he was standing there in a pair of jeans and no shirt, revealing the six-pack she remembered all too well. Every inch of it. His wet hair indicated he'd just gotten out of the shower. Her mouth went dry. Holy hamburger, he was hot.

"You coming in or not?" he asked, breaking through her daze.

She nodded, wordless, unable to speak. Words were beyond her ability at the moment. She entered the room, her gaze carefully avoiding the rumpled bed, the clothes draped over a chair, the pair of boxer briefs on the floor next to the armoire.

With her back to him, she blurted, "You're an ex-con and you didn't tell me."

Liam sighed behind her and she heard the scrape of beard stubble where he apparently scrubbed a hand over his face. "I don't keep it a secret, but I'm not in the habit of introducing myself like I'm at an AA meeting, 'Hi, I'm Liam, and I'm an ex-con.'"

She sniffed. "No, but you could have told me. You had a day and half to tell me this in Las Vegas. And you didn't."

"You were the one who said we should keep things light. No talk about our real lives."

Well, shoot. He was right. "Fine. But now I know, and I can't represent you for the rezoning. I can't be an accessory to a crime."

"A . . . what?"

"If you're using the mills to launder money, I won't be an accessory."

He laughed. He actually laughed.

She spun to face him and groaned. "Could you please put on a shirt?" Seeing one lying on the foot of the bed, she grabbed it and held it out to him.

He took it with a smirk and pulled it on. When his head popped through the neck, he continued. "My mills are a legitimate business. *All* my enterprises are legitimate."

She folded her arms, determined to get to the bottom of this. And now that he'd clothed that six pack, she could concentrate. "Did you hack the Chinese government or something?" She asked, her voice quiet as if someone was listening in.

He snorted. "No. Nothing so glamorous or clandestine."

"Then who?"

He sat down on the chair as if the weight of his past were too heavy a burden to bear. "I hacked ComEd, and trust me,

I, and more importantly, someone I love, paid the price for my stupidity."

"ComEd?" Her brow furrowed in confusion.

"The electric and gas utility company that provides power to most of Northern Illinois, including Chicago."

"Why would you do that?" She dropped her arms by her side.

"So our electricity wouldn't be cut off."

"Our?"

"Me, my brother, and my mother. The power was about to be cut off for non-payment, and it was January. Do you know what January is like in Chicago?"

"Cold, I would imagine."

He barked out a laugh. "*Colder* than you could possibly imagine."

"That doesn't sound so horrible. A first-degree misdemeanor at worst. But you served three years in prison."

"Yeah, well, while I was in their system tweaking our account to make it look like the past-due amount had been paid, I 'paid off,'" he made air quotes with his fingers, "dozens of other past-due bills for people. Enough for a third-degree felony charge. If I had just 'paid off' ours, my intrusion might have gone unnoticed," he added with a rueful smile.

"Oh." She thought about that a moment. He'd "paid" bills of people he didn't even know? "You paid off the past-due bills of people you didn't even know?" she asked, stating her thoughts out loud.

"Yes. Why?"

"The purpose seems somewhat noble, even if illegal. Like Robin Hood."

He rose to his feet. "Georgia, I'm no Robin Hood. I

ripped off ComEd for over thirty-five hundred dollars. That's hardly noble."

"No, but the reason you did it is." She leaned against the foot of the sleigh bed, somewhat in awe of what he'd done. He was no Not-Erik. "You prevented people who couldn't pay their utility bills from freezing. You didn't hack ComEd to steal money or information. You didn't gain access to people's credit cards or bank information and try to sell it to the Russian mob. You were only trying to keep your family and other families warm."

"It did help in my sentencing hearing, but the fact remains, I'm a convicted felon."

A brief moment passed and then she asked, "What did you mean someone you love paid the price?"

He looked away, his gaze toward the window overlooking the B&B's backyard. "That's a story for another time."

He sounded so . . . tired that she didn't push it. "Okay."

Picking up the contract where he'd tossed it onto the side table, he said, "I'll review this and get back to you."

"Sure."

She turned to go, but when she had her hand on the doorknob, he asked, "Do you want me to find someone else to represent American Threads for the rezoning?"

"No," she tossed over her shoulder. "I'll do it."

8

———————

A week later, Georgia rubbed sweaty palms on her skirt, and glanced around the table at the members of Northridge's Economic Development Council. There were a few friendly faces—Kristen and Tyler —but most were strangers or only recent acquaintances.

About half of Northridge's population had turned over since she'd last lived there.

Liam sat next to her looking cool as a cucumber in his navy suit, white dress shirt, and burgundy-striped tie. He looked good in a suit. He looked good in everything she'd seen him in, from blue jeans to open-necked dress shirt and slacks. He looked even better in nothing at all.

He smelled good too.

Focus, MacKinnon. A lot was riding on the sale of this property. And the sale of this property was riding on the rezoning, which in turn was riding on their presentation.

Carter Watson, the council's chair called the meeting to order.

Liam leaned over and whispered, "Chill. We've got this."

She shivered as his warm breath tickled her ear and flashes of a dimly lit hotel room and skin on skin filled her head.

Snickers! She clenched her thighs together and nearly groaned. He sat back, the corner of his mouth lifted, and she wanted to kick him in the shin with her pointed-toe stiletto.

While Carter went through a discussion of the last meeting's minutes, Georgia walked through their plan in her head. She'd begin with her part of the presentation, which, in addition to photos of a few of the other restored mills, included the history of the Redmond Mill, the historical impact of mills in the South, and Northridge in particular, then the plans for the structure.

Liam would follow up with a brief history of his company, the environmental and economic impacts of the other mills he'd purchased, restored, and re-opened in their respective communities, then on to the economic numbers, and finally the environmental impacts on Northridge specifically, leaving time in their allotted twenty minutes for questions.

Overall, she felt confident about their approach, but when it comes to small-town politics, you never know what obstacles you're going to face. They were first up on the agenda, which she was happy about. Get it over with rather than wait and worry during the meeting. She nodded to Kristen, who gave her an encouraging smile and a nod.

Before the meeting, Liam and Tyler had exchanged a few words. She knew that Liam and Tyler had met last week.

Liam nudged her in the ribs. "You're up," he whispered.
"Right."

Damn, I married well, Liam thought with a rueful grin as he watched Georgia give her part of the presentation. In a navy pencil skirt and white silk blouse, she presented a polished business look, but her Southern accent had the council members eating from her hand. She was one of them—at least many of them—and her charm and warmth drew them in. If she took after lawyer-grandfather, he likely had juries enthralled the moment he presented his opening arguments.

She might be nervous, but you'd never know from watching her. Clicking through the slides, highlighting important information, smiling and looking every individual in the eye, she gave a smooth argument on behalf of the rezoning. He'd always been turned on by smart professional women, and Georgia was no exception.

He wondered, not for the first time, if she'd be interested in carrying on a relationship while he was in Northridge. Though they were married, there would be no strings attached. His mind had just begun to wander further down that path when the gentleman sitting next to him said, "Mr. Dunbar, I believe you're up to bat."

Heat flooded his face. *What the hell?* There was a time and a place for sexual fantasies, and this was not it.

"Right." He rose, buttoned his jacket and took the laser pointer from Georgia, who wore a quizzical look on her face. He shook his head and, like a man stepping up to home plate, focused his attention on the matter at hand.

Cleary, Georgia MacKinnon was a distraction he might be better off without.

THAT AFTERNOON, Georgia walked into the office and the overwhelming scent of paint assaulted her. Bile rose in her throat, but she covered her mouth with her hand and swallowed hard, suppressing the urge to vomit.

Luis stood on a ladder in the reception area, paint roller in hand, covering the once-white walls with a muted gray-green.

"What are you doing?" she asked after dropping her tote bag on the army-green armchair.

He paused, roller in mid-air, "Sugar, I thought it was obvious. Painting."

"I see that. I mean, I didn't even ask you to."

"Pfft. It's no bother."

She shook her head. "That's not what I mean. I might have had a say in the matter." She folded her arms beneath her breasts in annoyance.

"You don't like it?" He eyed the walls critically, not at all put off by her tone. He only had one wall left, and she had to admit the color already created a sense of comfort and calm.

"Well, no. I do like it. It's just . . . you might have cleared it with me first."

"Surprise!" He winked at her with a cheeky grin.

She sighed. An unexpected expense. "Leave the receipt and I'll reimburse you."

"No need. It's my treat. Trust me, after two weeks in this dreadful cave, it's as much for me as it is for you. Besides, I really enjoy the work. Enjoy seeing the fruits of my labor."

Hands on hips, she studied him, unsure how to respond. She didn't want to take advantage of him. Then again, if he truly liked painting, why deny him the pleasure? And, truth be told, coming into the bunker every day *was* depressing. "Okay. But maybe next time, ask me first."

"Deal. There's a couple of messages on the desk, and

your friend Alyssa dropped by. Said she'd catch up with you later."

"Thanks."

She looked around the room again. Right now, she avoided clients coming by the office, preferring to meet at the Beans 'n Books or the Whistle Stop Pub, too embarrassed by the office. Paint did wonders for it, but it still had a long way to go. New window coverings, light fixtures, office furniture, a new couch—not to mention new flooring to replace the decades-old carpeting. The kitchen could use some amenities too, like coffee, water, some snacks . . . new appliances that weren't harvest gold.

As if reading her mind, Luis descended the ladder, and joined her in studying the space. "We need a sofa, chairs, a coffee table, and maybe a console table over there," he said, pointing to a wall between two windows.

The thought of spending money on those items made her wince.

"You know, I'm also a wiz at reupholstery and furniture restoration. I bet I could find some secondhand furniture and repurpose it."

She turned to look at him and he met her gaze in a moment of perfect understanding. He'd guessed she didn't have the money to redecorate the office, but instead of asking the question, he'd found another way of solving the problem.

"Thank you. Just . . . go easy on the cost, okay?"

"Pfft." He waved a hand. "I once furnished my entire two-bedroom apartment in Charlotte for less than five thousand dollars. Even had a writeup on it in a local magazine." He went hands on hips as he eyed the space again. "This will be a piece of cake."

"I like cake."

"Me too." He gave her a shoulder nudge. "Chocolate, of course."

"Of course. Is there any other flavor?"

"MR. DUNBAR, THIS IS MS. GIBSON."

Liam's stomach dropped in recognition of the name of the director of the drug rehab facility where Cole had agreed to be admitted.

"What can I do for you?" he asked, trying for a casual tone.

She hesitated, "I'm sorry to report that your brother is in violation of a number of the facility rules."

"I'm sorry to hear that." He bit down on the anger and frustration as if he were biting his own tongue. He'd only been in a week!

"He's been counseled several times on his failure to comply with the schedule, staying up well past the eleven p.m. bedtime and not getting up at the required seven a.m. wakeup call. Facility personnel have had to enter his room every morning since he's been here to wake him up."

Before Liam could comment, she continued. "He's also not abiding by mealtime schedules and has often been found wandering the facility in places where he is not permitted."

"I'm sorry." He rubbed the tension in the back of his neck, pacing the confines of his room.

"But what is most concerning is his failure to attend the mandatory therapy sessions. Mr. Dunbar, your brother cannot get well without these therapy sessions."

"I understand. I know it is frowned upon this early in the

program, but if you think it would help, I'd be happy to speak with him."

"Thank you, but I don't believe that would be helpful. We have reviewed the rules with him once again and reminded him that he signed a contract when he was admitted that he would follow them. I'm afraid that if your brother does not abide by the facility's rules, we will have to discharge him."

"Please, Ms. Gibson, give him another chance." Liam hated begging, but when it came to his brother, he would get down on his knees. "Perhaps now that you've repri-manded him, he will try to do better." Liam didn't believe it for one minute, but he had to try.

There was a heavy sigh on the other end of the phone. "We will give him one more week. If there is no improve-ment in compliance, he's out. I'm sorry. We have our other residents to consider."

"I understand," Liam said in resignation, scrubbing a hand over his face. *And then what?*

TUESDAY MORNING GEORGIA entered the office to find the hideous carpeting gone and in its place just the bare concrete floor. "What the—?"

"Morning, sunshine. Isn't it wonderful? No more moldy carpet!" Luis lifted his hands as if he'd just performed a miracle.

"But concrete? What's going on the floor?"

"Nothing. Well, nothing but some concrete stain, anyway. Then an area rug."

"Concrete stain?"

"Navy stain to be exact. The navy will make the gray-green walls pop, and add an elegance to the feel of the space."

"If you say so." She set her tote bag on Luis's desk.

"Trust me on this."

"I suppose I must." She looked around for any other new surprises.

Gone, too, were the awful utilitarian fluorescent lights. In their stead, he'd installed discreet recessed can lighting. She examined the crows-foot pattern on the ceiling and the near-undetectable patch job.

"How'd you learn to do all this?"

"YouTube. For a while, I flipped houses in Charlotte."

"Really?" That intrigued her. If she had the money, she'd love to buy something, fix it up, then sell it.

Before she could explore that further, the door opened, and Georgia turned to see Liam standing there.

"Well hello, tall, dark, and handsome," Luis muttered.

"I thought you were married," Georgia whispered.

"Married. Not dead," Luis replied, his gaze never leaving Liam's form.

Liam looked around, brows lifted. "Looks like some redecorating is underway. Should I come back later?"

"Oh. No. It's a work in progress." She eyed Luis then turned back to Liam.

Liam stuck out his hand to Luis. "Liam Dunbar."

Luis took it, eyebrow lifted, and shook it. "Nice to meet you. Luis."

"Luis is my receptionist and . . . decorator."

"Interesting job title." Liam took in the freshly painted walls, the bare concrete floor, and the ugly couch and chairs before meeting her gaze with a questioning look.

"Let's meet in my office."

Luis groaned. He had yet to ply his magic on that dungeon-esque room. Oh well. No help for it.

Liam halted just inside her office, obviously taking in the bare, nail-pocked walls, the military-grade desk, and the curtainless windows. She bit her lip.

"Love the look. Are you going for nineteen-forties army retro?"

"Yeah."

"I think you've nailed it."

She couldn't hide her smile. "The reception area was the priority. What can I do for you?"

"Any word about the rezoning?"

"No. But I don't expect anything for at least another week."

He nodded then paced her office.

"That's why you dropped by?" She tilted her head, noticing his tense shoulders.

Turning back to her, he reached into his jacket pocket and pulled out an envelope. "My attorneys would like you to sign this post-nuptial agreement." He frowned at the envelope before handing it to her. "If we'd been able to get a quickie divorce, this wouldn't be an issue, but with five months to go . . ."

She took the document from him then closed her office door. "You told your attorneys about the marriage?"

"They're my attorneys, Georgia. I hired them for a reason."

"Right. Of course." A man of Liam's wealth would have a bevy of attorneys at his beck and call. Which raised a question. "Liam, why did you ask me to handle the rezoning when you have lawyers on speed dial?"

"One, you were the listing agent and have a vested

interest in the outcome of the rezoning decision, and two, you're local."

"Ah." She folded her arms, the agreement crinkling in the process. "You thought me being a hometown girl would sway the opinion of the EDC."

"Couldn't hurt."

She didn't know why, but she felt used. Silly, considering she would earn a nice commission on the sale of the mill. Had he said anything that wasn't true?

Walking over to her desk, she pulled the agreement out of the envelope and opened it. And although she had no intention of asking for anything from him in the divorce, why did the thought of him asking her to sign the document leave an empty feeling in the pit of her stomach? She flipped through the six-page agreement and, seeing nothing out of the ordinary, picked up a pen.

"You don't mind?" Liam asked, his tone sounding . . . embarrassed.

Holding his gaze, she said, "I never expected anything from you, Liam." She signed her name, hesitating for a moment over the signature *Georgia Elizabeth MacKinnon-Dunbar.*

She held the signed document out to him. "Need a pen?"

He took one from his pocket and bent to sign in a scrawling hand *William Nathanial Dunbar.*

"I appreciate your understanding. You'll receive a copy of the fully executed document from my lawyers." He stood a moment then, at her silence, took his leave.

So much for the warm and fuzzies she took away from their recent encounters. She and Liam would get a divorce in November and they would move on with their separate lives.

"Don't get involved, MacKinnon."

Luis stuck his head in the door. "Did you say something?"

"No. Just talking to myself."

LIAM CURSED HIS LAWYERS, even though he knew they were only recommending what was best for him. If he and Georgia had gotten the annulment the next morning as planned, no harm no foul. But staying married for another five months before they could get a divorce changed everything in his lawyers' eyes. And while he didn't think Georgia married him to get his money, it was best to head-off a potentially messy situation.

Still, the look in her face when he'd handed her the enveloped haunted him. She gone from warm to leery in the blink of an eye. And after the day they'd spent together on Memorial Day and her reaction to his criminal record, it was doubly difficult to treat her as if she were a gold digger.

Shoving the envelope back in his jacket pocket, he headed in the direction of Main Street, determined to shake off the pall that now surrounded him. Turning the corner, he surveyed the town with a critical eye. Northridge intrigued him. He had a soft spot for quaint small towns, but he admired Northridge's philosophy—a mix of appreciation for its history coupled with a desire to remain relevant in the twenty-first century.

The upcoming film production for the feature film *Battle of the Heart*, the marketing savvy of its Economic Development Council, and the Town Council's leadership were all indicators of forward-thinking.

Shops, restaurants, and galleries lined both sides of the street. Charming baskets hung from the old-fashioned light posts, their contents spilling out in yellows, purples, and bright greens. Café tables sat in front of Beans 'n Books alongside a cart displaying books by Georgia authors. Awnings announced businesses like Pints and Paints, Sweet Creams, and Forget Me Not's Florist.

The town was affluent, but warm and welcoming. Maybe it wasn't strange that Georgia had returned home.

Even so, he reminded himself not to get attached to Georgia or Northridge. By the end of the year, he'd be moving on to his next project and Northridge would just be the location of another mill. And Georgia would be his ex-wife.

9

S eated at the breakfast table, Georgia took one look at the lumpy oatmeal her grandfather preferred for breakfast and bile rose in her throat. "Crap." She clamped a hand over her mouth and bolted from the room.

"Georgia? Georgia?"

She heard her grandfather's footsteps over her retching. She hadn't had time to even close the door to the powder bath. He knelt beside her and held her hair back while she lost the limited contents of her stomach. Utterly humiliating. When she finally finished, he rose and ran a cloth under the faucet before handing it to her. She wiped her mouth and collapsed into a heap on the floor.

"Better?"

She was afraid to nod for fear the nausea would return. If there was anything she hated more than nausea, she couldn't think of it. Oh wait. Not-Erik. She hated Not-Erik more than nausea. And that was saying something. She gave her grandfather a wan smile. "I think so." Closing her eyes, she leaned her head against the wall behind her. "Wow. I haven't been sick like that since I was a little girl."

"The time you ate too many tangerines?"

"Yeah. That." To this day, she couldn't stomach tangerines, and with their mention, her stomach pitched again. *Breathe.* In through the nose, out through the mouth. A few breaths later, the nausea eased.

"What did you have for supper last night?" her grandfather asked as he offered a hand to help her up.

"Oh. Uh," she frowned, "I had takeout from the Chinese restaurant in Doraville." She'd picked it up on the way back from a showing. While it hadn't stacked up to the Chinese food in L.A., it hadn't been bad, but had it made her sick?

"Maybe steer clear of the lo mein for a while."

"Yeah."

"Come. I'll make you some dry toast and tea." He kept a hand on her. "You got your sea legs?" he asked with a smile.

She nodded but clamped her lips shut to ward off another round of nausea.

A FEW DAYS LATER, Georgia pulled out a chair on the Whistle Stop Pub's covered patio and dropped into it, utterly exhausted. She'd rather be taking a nap than meeting Alyssa for lunch, but she pasted a smile on her face when the server greeted her to take her drink order.

"Do you have ginger ale?"

"Yes. Would you like an appetizer while you wait?"

Georgia's stomach roiled. "Uh. No. But could you bring me some crackers?"

The server gave her a funny look but nodded.

When Alyssa arrived, she took in the packs of saltines and ginger ale. Pulling out her chair, Alyssa sat down, studying Georgia, and the look on Alyssa's face gave Georgia pause.

"What?"

Alyssa shook her head. "Nothing."

"That's not a 'nothing' look."

Alyssa waved a hand in Georgia's direction. "It's just that . . ." She eyed Georgia again critically. "I know that look. That feeling. Because . . . because that's how I felt with my first pregnancy," she finished with a shrug.

Pregnant? As if her stomach weren't bad enough, it dropped at the thought. *No. I can't be.* She shook her head as if that would make it so. Of course she wasn't pregnant. How could she be? It was just a touch of food poisoning, that's all.

Food poisoning that came and went over the last few days, a voice in her head said.

When she didn't respond, Alyssa continued. "Answer me this . . . have you been dizzy? Nauseous? Exhausted? Are your girls sore?"

Georgia felt herself pale even more. She'd had that dizzy spell in Dominick's last month. But no, she'd just needed food. She'd felt much better after she'd eaten. Then again, she had thrown up a few days ago, but thankfully, not since. As for exhausted, yes, of course. After all, she'd been burning the candle at both ends to get her new real estate business off the ground.

As for her breasts—she resisted the urge to cup them and test their sensitivity—they'd been a little tender, but nothing out of the ordinary . . . Too much caffeine did that sometimes, and heaven knew she'd been consuming a lot of caffeine lately to counter the exhaustion.

"When was your last period?" Alyssa prodded.

"I don't have periods. I am—*was*—on the shot." Her mouth suddenly dry, she reached for her glass of water. "I was getting the shot every three months, but I didn't see any reason to go for my appointment right after Not-Erik and, well, you know." Georgia stared across the patio, not seeing the café tables and patrons. She was on a cruise down Denial River.

"Is it possible it's Not-Erik's?

"God, no! The Great Debacle happened two months before . . . before Vegas." *Vegas.* Georgia shook her head again. "But we used protection," she said to herself. At least she was pretty sure they'd used protection *every* time. There were lots of "times."

"The only birth control that's one hundred percent effective is abstinence. Take it from me. Delilah was a bit of a surprise."

At Georgia's pained expression, Alyssa reached across the table and laid her hand on Georgia's. "Honey, you need to pee on a stick, ASAP."

LIAM SCROLLED through the photos on his phone, looking for the ones of the mill he'd taken the day after he'd first inspected it.

Scrolling too far, he swiped up to the more recent photos, stopping abruptly at a photo of him and Georgia at their wedding, no less. He sucked in a breath. Funny, he'd forgotten the officiant's wife had commandeered his phone and taken pictures during the ceremony. He doubted Georgia even knew the photos existed.

He enlarged a photo of the two of them standing face to face before the officiant, apparently saying their vows. Vows! He shook his head. He'd actually sworn to love, honor, and protect Georgia until death with no intention of ever upholding those vows. Then again, neither did she.

What the hell had he been thinking?

He hadn't been, that was the problem. She'd come along on one of the somber anniversaries he marked and pulled him outside the bitter thoughts in his head. And he'd wanted to make her happy. To give her whatever she wanted. To fulfill her every fantasy. Including an impulsive Las Vegas wedding.

Unable to resist, he scrolled through a few more pictures. There was one of her laughing at something he'd said, right before the ceremony. He didn't consider himself a funny person, and he wished he could remember what he'd said that had tickled her so.

He stopped again on a photo of their ceremonial kiss, only from the photo, there had been nothing ceremonial about it. He held her snug up against him, one arm at the small of her back, the other gripping the back of her neck. For her part, she had one hand embedded in his hair, the other holding the bouquet she'd caught at his friend's wedding.

He could still remember the feel of her against him, the taste of her lips beneath his. Her warm, supple body pressed to his as if she couldn't get close enough. He also remembered he'd been . . . happy. Joyous almost. Feelings that were otherwise alien to him.

His finger hovered over the little trashcan icon, but he couldn't bring himself to delete the photos. *Damn.* He'd delete them when their divorce was final.

Locking his phone, he shoved it into his back pocket without bothering to find the photos of the mill he'd been looking for in the first place.

A HALF HOUR LATER, Georgia and Alyssa sat on the floor of Alyssa's master bathroom waiting. It was currently the only bathroom that offered total privacy. The office wasn't an option with Luis there, and her grandfather's house wasn't an option, since he was working from home this afternoon.

Three sticks lined up on the countertop like judges on an appeals court bench waiting to rule on her oral argument.

Georgia drew her knees up, wrapped her arms around them, and laid her head down. *How long could five minutes be anyway?* "I'm not pregnant. I'm not pregnant," she said as if it were an incantation.

"You still do that."

"Do what?" Georgia looked up in surprise.

"Repeat a sentence when you want to reassure yourself or want something to be true."

Georgia shrugged. "If I say something enough times, maybe The Fates will listen."

The timer on Alyssa's watch buzzed.

"Oh, God." Georgia groaned. "You look…" she told Alyssa, her hands clenched around her knees, her eyes squeezed shut. "I can't." She laid her head back down on her knees, muttering to herself, "I'm not pregnant, I'm not pregnant."

Alyssa rose and, moments later, sat back down on the floor beside Georgia. "Congratulations? You're pregnant."

So much for The Fates listening to her mantra.

"I guess that advertising campaign was wrong," Alyssa said, staring at the sticks in her hands.

Georgia gave her a quizzical look, not following.

"You know—what happens in Vegas stays in Vegas,"

Alyssa explained, as she wrapped her arm around Georgia's shoulders.

Yeah. Sometimes it shows up again when you least expect it.

PLEADING A HEADACHE, Georgia went straight to her room after she got home from Alyssa's.

She collapsed onto the bed and pulled a pillow over her face.

How had her life gotten so off track? It seemed one minute she had an enormously successful business, a man who loved her, a beautiful beachfront home, and a promising future, and the next she'd lost said business, her home, her reputation, and her money, thanks to her felonious ex-fiancé. And now, for all intents and purposes, she was married to a total stranger, planning a quickie divorce as soon as legally possible, and was pregnant with said stranger's child.

What on earth was she to do?

Unlike her mother, she couldn't run away from this.

It's not as if she never wanted children, but she'd imagined something very different. A husband who loved her, a home, financial security. Groaning, she threw the pillow off the bed and rolled onto her side.

Go to Vegas, they'd said. *It'll be fun*, they'd said.

Here she was, just like her mother. One irresponsible night (or two) and she was pregnant. Pregnant! Not out of wedlock, at least not in the legal sense, but to everyone else in town, she'd be the apple that didn't fall far from the tree. And what would she tell her grandfather? *I'm pregnant. Pass the potatoes, please.* How can she shame him all over again? And how can she face his disappointment?

She'd tried so hard to be the good girl. To follow the rules, to work hard, and to what purpose? Broke, soon-to-be-divorced, and pregnant.

Oh yeah. She'd make her grandfather right proud.

A FEW DAYS LATER, Georgia sat on the medical table, the exam gown open down the back, the paper "blanket" crinkling in her hands as she pleated and unpleated it.

"Chill," Alyssa said, reaching over to squeeze her hand. "Everything will be fine."

"I'm pregnant," she said. "How can everything be okay?"

Before Alyssa could answer, the doctor came in.

She stopped short when she saw Alyssa. "Hi, Alyssa! What are you doing here?"

"This is my friend, Georgia. I'm here to offer moral support."

"Ah." Dr. Grimshaw stuck out her hand to Georgia. "Hi, Georgia."

"Hello." The greeting came out breathy and nervous, and Dr. Grimshaw patted her on the leg. "Everything will be fine."

Georgia shot Alyssa a look and Alyssa shrugged.

Dr. Grimshaw opened up her laptop and reviewed Georgia's information. "So tell me, do you know when you may have conceived?"

"April twenty-third or twenty-fourth," Georgia and Alyssa said in unison. Georgia shot a glance at Alyssa and grimaced at the look of surprise on Dr. Grimshaw's face at their dual response.

"Okay. That's pretty certain."

"That makes you about eight weeks pregnant, but let's do the exam."

"Do you want me to leave?" Alyssa asked.

Georgia held out her hand and Alyssa took it. "No. Stay."

GEORGIA CRAVED caffeine like an addict craved heroine. At least she could still have one coffee a day, according to Dr. Grimshaw, even if it was decaf.

The doctor confirmed what the three pregnancy tests had already revealed, and the results of the ultrasound indicated a due date of January twenty-fourth.

It was really happening.

Leaving the heat of the summer day outside, she entered the cool, heavenly scented café. A iced mocha (decaf) would hit the spot.

She spotted Kristen behind the coffee bar talking with Olivia James. Like Kristen, Olivia had been three years ahead of Georgia in school. Funny, she seemed to recall they'd hated one another in high school. Georgia never knew the backstory, but she guessed time really does heal all wounds because now they seemed thick as thieves huddled over what looked to be a bridal magazine.

Georgia had read in *People Magazine* that Olivia, previously an internationally famous ballet dancer with The Joffrey Ballet, had ruptured her Achilles tendon, abruptly ending her career. She'd come home to handle her mother's estate and never left. Now she and Zach, her high school sweetheart, were getting married later this month.

"Hey, Georgia," Kristen called to her. "You remember Olivia?"

"Yes, though I doubt Olivia would remember me." She smiled at the tall beautiful brunette.

"Of course I do! You used to come to my mother's house when your grandfather visited. Good to see you again."

"Thanks. Good to see you."

"What can I get you?" Kristen asked.

"Iced mocha, please."

As Kristen moved to make her order, Georgia remembered, "Oh. Make it decaf."

Georgia braced a hip onto the barstool next to Olivia while she waited, and glanced at the photo of a wedding cake in the open magazine. "Wedding plans?"

"Oh. Just the last-minute details at this point. What do you think of this cake top?"

Georgia leaned over, studying the photo of a simple three-tier cake topped with fresh flowers. "Beautiful. Simple. Elegant." Then she scrutinized Olivia in a sundress the color of an Irish spring and nude ballet flats, her dark hair twisted into a bun with wisps framing her face. "It suits you."

"Thanks!"

Kristen set Georgia's coffee in front of her, and she snatched it up like a woman parched from a week in the desert. Georgia took a long pull of the cool, sweet beverage and closed her eyes in pleasure. It might not be caffeine, but at least it was coffee. She opened her eyes to find Olivia and Kristen staring at her. "Sorry. I'm, uh, limiting my coffee intake, so this is like manna from Heaven."

Kristen's eyes narrowed, but she didn't say anything.

"You should come." Olivia said.

"Come where?" Did she miss something in the midst of her coffee-induced orgasm?

"To the wedding."

"Oh. No. I couldn't. I mean, I'm sure you have the seating chart done and everything."

"Your grandfather is coming. If I'd known you were moving back I would have invited you. It's Saturday, June twenty-sixth, but I'll drop an invitation off at your office so you have all the details. And feel free to bring a plus-one."

Georgia felt the heat rise in her face at the mention of a plus-one. *How about a secret husband?* she thought. *Does that count? Or maybe the bun she had in the oven?*

"Gotta run. I promised Jennie I would help her pick out a nail polish for the wedding." She grinned at Kristen, and continued for Georgia's benefit. "Jennie's my stepmom. Since my mom is . . . gone," a pained expression crossed her face, "Jennie's giving me away at the wedding," she explained to Georgia.

"Grandad told me about your mom. I'm so sorry. She was always kind to me."

"Thank you." As Olivia gathered her things and left, Georgia, utterly exhausted, climbed onto the barstool she'd been leaning against and sighed.

"Tired?"

"Very."

"Probably caffeine withdrawal."

"Probably."

"Or getting your new business off the ground."

"Likely."

"Or pregnancy."

Georgia covered her mouth in an attempt to keep the mouthful of coffee from spewing all over the bar. She swallowed. Then swallowed again. "How—"

"Been there. Know that look." Kristen circled a finger around Georgia's face. "A mix of green around the gills, pink in the cheeks, and blue under the eyes."

Georgia looked around the café, quiet in the late afternoon. No one paid them any attention, and she slumped in relief.

"Don't worry. Your secret's safe with me. If that's what it is, I mean," Kristen said with a shrug.

Georgia nodded. "It is. For now anyway. Thank you."

"Just a piece of advice. If you haven't told the father, you should. Trust me on this." Kristen wore a pained look, but her gaze was steady.

Georgia's grandfather had filled her in on all the drama. Turned out that Kristen's seventeen-year-old son Seth was Tyler's, only father and son hadn't found out until last year. According to her grandfather, it really blew the lid off Kristen's developing relationship with Tyler. But they'd found their way back to one another, and now Kristen and Tyler were engaged.

"I will." She swallowed again, dreading the conversation with Liam, especially after the post-nuptial agreement. She'd make it crystal clear that she didn't want or expect anything from him. The last thing she wanted was to be tied to someone who was practically a stranger.

10

"How do you know it's mine?" Liam glared at Georgia, outraged.

"You're the first—and last—person I've slept with in the past five months! Unless there is some kind of delayed reaction, it's yours. If you don't believe me, feel free to take a paternity test." She handed him a brochure. "I checked. You can get a DNA test before the baby is born. It can be performed now, after the seventh week of pregnancy."

He glowered at the colorful paper in his hand without seeing it. "How the hell?"

When there had been a knock on the door of his room in the B&B, he'd assumed it was housekeeping with the extra towels he'd requested. He'd been surprised to see Georgia standing there looking nervous and uncertain. And now he was even more surprised by the bombshell she'd just dropped.

"Are you sure we used protection *every* time?" She crossed her arms beneath her breasts.

"I—" he thought a minute, a sinking feeling in his gut. "Yes. I wasn't that drunk. I repeat—how the hell?"

"If you'll recall your sex-ed class, the only surefire method is abstinence. And we definitely were not abstinent."

No, we sure as hell weren't. But still . . .

"Look, I'm not expecting anything from you, if that's what you're worried about, and given the post-nuptial agreement, I'd say you probably are worried." She opened her tote bag and pulled out a folded document. "I have a Voluntary Relinquishment of Parental Rights form here if you'd like to sign it." She held out the completed form.

Unexplained anger flared. Why should he be angry that she's offering him an out? He'd be free and clear. But no. He was a man who didn't run from his responsibilities. "That's the least of my worries. And if you think I'm just going to walk away and leave you with the cost of raising a child alone, you have another think coming."

"Okay. I don't know what you're thinking. I just wanted you to know I'm prepared to handle this on my own."

"*Handle* it? You're not thinking—"

"No." She set the forms on the table next to the loveseat. "Though I can't say the thought didn't cross my mind, given the circumstances. But no. I'm keeping the baby." She laid her hands over her flat stomach as if cradling the child that grew there.

He nodded in relief. He didn't know why the thought of losing a child he never expected to have bothered him, but it did, especially since he wasn't cut out to be a father. Look at what had happened to his two brothers under his watch. No. He wouldn't raise this child, but he would see to it that he— or she—would want for nothing.

"And the divorce?" he asked.

"I see no reason why this should change things."

"Okay. It's more complicated with the child, but I give you my word, I will pay a generous child support."

"I don't want—"

He held up a hand cutting her off. "This isn't up for discussion. The money will be set aside in a trust. Use it. Don't use it. But it's there."

"One more thing."

He tensed.

"This is our secret."

ANOTHER SECRET TO KEEP.

Liam stared at the glass of scotch in his hand. The refrain *How the hell?* echoing in his head. How did a Las Vegas fling turn into marriage and a baby? Tilting the glass, he swallowed the remaining contents, enjoying the heat as it spread down his throat and into his chest.

Liam Dunbar a father. Karma clearly had a sick sense of humor. He'd laugh at the irony of the situation, if it wasn't so serious. The last thing the world needed was a child from Liam Dunbar. And the last thing a child needed was Liam Dunbar for a father.

His promise of financial support had been in earnest. He might not be able to be the parent a child deserved, but he'd be damned if his child would grow up financially insecure like he and his brothers had. The child would have a safe roof over his or her head, plenty of food on the table, paid utility bills, good healthcare, and if Georgia so chose, the best education available. All the things he never had.

Hell, he didn't even have a college degree, and he'd barely graduated from high school. Unlike Georgia, life had been his classroom. Three years in prison had been his rite of passage. And after he sold his IT security company, the world had been his university.

No, this child might not have a father, but he would have everything else he could ever need. In other words, everything Liam didn't.

A FEW DAYS LATER, Liam's phone buzzed with an incoming text. Georgia had found a short-term rental for him in Northridge. She could show it to him on Thursday. Perfect.

The thought of seeing her again after her revelation filled him with some trepidation. How should he act around her? Should he act as if nothing had changed? Then again, what was the point of behaving any other way? They were getting divorced and he was leaving. She'd agreed. Nothing changed that. Not even a child.

Filming for *Battle of the Heart* would start the following week, and the B&B where he was staying would be filled with production crew while also serving as a set for the film. As he'd told Georgia initially, Atlanta was too far to drive every day, and Northridge didn't offer much in the way of hotels, so a rental house was his only option.

Speaking of his real-estate-agent wife, he looked up when the bell over the café door tinkled and saw her grandfather come in. MacKinnon called a greeting to people seated around the café, but upon spotting Liam, he turned his feet in that direction. *Uh-oh.* Was he angry over the dunking? Had Georgia told him about the marriage? Or worse, the pregnancy?

He stopped at Liam's table and thrust out a hand. "Just the man I was looking for."

Looking for him? Liam's stomach dropped. This couldn't be good.

Liam rose with some trepidation to shake the man's hand but found the man's grip was firm but friendly. "Sorry I, uh, dunked you."

MacKinnon laughed, a jovial sound. "Well done! Please, sit," he gestured at Liam's vacated seat. "Mind if I join you?"

"Please." Liam resumed his seat while the gentleman took the chair across from him.

"My granddaughter tells me you're being evicted from the B&B for the movie production and you're looking for a place to stay while the mill is under restoration."

Liam released a pent-up breath in relief. "I am."

Calypso arrived at the table and set a cup of coffee in front of MacKinnon. "Ah, Callie, thank you. How's that beautiful daughter of yours?"

"She's hit the terrible twos," she said with a roll of her eyes.

MacKinnon chuckled, a warm sincere sound. "This too shall pass," he said with an empathetic smile.

"Not soon enough," Calypso muttered, as she turned to clear the four-top next to them.

Marshall shook his head. "Kids. They're a joy and a terror. Any kids of your own?"

"No, sir." Not yet anyway, but in about seven months . . .

Marshall waved a hand at him. "Marshall, please." He took a sip of the coffee and sighed in satisfaction. "Back to our previous conversation—a place to lay your head at night."

"Your granddaughter just texted me about a rental

house, so I don't have to sleep in my car," he replied with a wry grin.

"Well now, I have a guesthouse—used to be the carriage house back in the day—but my late wife converted it into what she called a guest cottage shortly before she died. It might use some updating now, but it's clean and comfortable. Two bedroom, two bath. Nice kitchen. Wi-Fi installed a couple of years ago when a niece from North Carolina moved in for a bit."

Liam could just see Georgia's reaction if she knew about this offer. "Thank you, but I wouldn't want to put you out."

"Nonsense. The place sits empty." He rose, taking his cup. "It's settled then. Move in now, or wait until Carter Watson kicks you out. You can pick up the key from my secretary when it's convenient."

And before Liam could protest further, Marshall was out the door, waving goodbye.

No wonder he's such a formidable lawyer. He could talk a judge out of his gavel.

GEORGIA DROPPED her tote bag onto the bench in the mudroom and slipped off her heels. How much longer would she be able to wear them? she wondered. Male voices drifted to her from the kitchen. Her grandfather's and . . . *Liam's*? Oh, God! He wasn't telling her grandfather, was he?

"What the—"

"Ah. Georgia. We're just sitting down to dinner. Margie made enough chicken and dumplings and butter beans to feed the town, so I asked Liam to join us."

She lifted a brow at Liam, silently asking the question she didn't finish. *What the heck?*

He gave a subtle shoulder shrug.

"Sit," her grandfather directed her, "and I'll pour you a glass of this crisp chardonnay." He lifted the dripping bottle from the old-fashioned silver ice bucket.

"Oh. No. Thank you." She cut a glance at Liam and went to the cabinet and took down a glass. "I . . . don't drink . . . much."

She looked away, knowing that admission would bring a shadow over her grandfather's face and a look of confusion to Liam's. Her grandfather's because it would recall the reason for his daughter's death. And Liam's because she'd had quite a bit to drink at his friend's wedding. Case in point. Which is why she was better off being a teetotaler than even an occasional drinker.

"Besides, I have a headache. Probably just a little dehydrated, so I'm just going to stick with water." She filled her glass from the water dispenser in the refrigerator door.

"All right. More for us," he said as he poured more wine into his and Liam's glasses. "Let's toast!" He lifted a glass once she was settled at the table.

Her stomach dropped and she shot a look at Liam, and he gave a subtle shake of his head. She picked up her water glass, confused. "What are we toasting? Did you win a big case?"

"No. To our guest. Liam needed a place to stay, so I offered the guest cottage."

"The guest—" She couldn't even finish the sentence. "But I told you I found a rental I was going to show you Thursday." She narrowed her eyes at Liam in silent protest. "A restored Craftsman. Three-three, study, even a workout room."

"Nonsense. It's all settled." Grandad set down his glass and shook out the napkin before placing it in his lap. "Why should he pay to rent a house when the cottage sits empty?"

She resisted a derisive snort. Like a billionaire couldn't afford to rent a place. Her gaze ping-ponged between her grandfather and Liam. "But—"

"No buts. He'll settle in after dinner." Her grandfather dug into the meal, effectively ending the conversation.

For his part, Liam rubbed the tip of his nose, trying to hide his smile, and she glared at him. It was a conspiracy, that's what it was. Life was conspiring against her, and her grandfather and Liam were co-conspirators.

She let their dinner conversation flow around her like water around a rock in a stream as her mind raced. What was she going to do? She knew once her grandfather made up his mind, there was no changing it. She'd have to work on Liam. Make him see how awkward it would be for him, as well as for her, to have him living here as her belly grew with his child.

"I'M SORRY. Your grandfather doesn't take no for an answer," Liam said, once Marshall had left them alone in the kitchen.

She huffed out a laugh. "No, he doesn't." Then she threw up her hands. "This is going to become very awkward as my baby bump grows bigger." She placed a hand over her still-flat stomach then pointed a finger at him. "You promised to keep this a secret."

"I did, and I will. But before long there'll be no hiding it." He nodded at her stomach. "I may not have much experience at this, but I'm pretty sure after about the fifth month it will be quite obvious." He had witnessed his mother's two pregnancies, but he'd only been three and five at the time.

"Ha-ha," she mocked a laugh as she strode away from him. "I'll think of something before then."

"Immaculate conception?"

She gave him a look that would melt a glacier. "No. I'll just say it's my ex's and we decided that I would raise the child."

Why did that idea make him want to punch something? His hands curled into fists. "Your ex's? I thought you said you two broke up two months before we, uh . . . met. That would make you four months pregnant right now."

"I know, I know." She closed her eyes in frustration.

"Would it be so terrible to tell him the truth? About everything?"

"Yes, it would." Clearly she saw something in his expression that had her softening. "You don't understand. This is a small town. People talk."

"And? They aren't going to talk when they think you're pregnant and not married?"

"Better than the truth!" She paced the floor. "That I not only fell into bed with the first guy I met after . . . well, after . . . ," she waved a hand, "but that I married him, and now I'm carrying his baby! Oh! And by the way, we're getting divorced as soon as legally possible. It sounds like a soap opera plot."

"Calm down. This can't be good for the baby." He rested his hands on her shoulders in the hopes of calming her down, only to find touching her had the opposite effect on him.

A frown crossed her face and she shook him off. "Don't."

Did she feel it too? That hum of energy between them? The one that had gotten them where they were now?

She lifted a hand to her forehead, as if it ached. "I'll

figure something out. Just . . . please, don't say anything until I do."

He recalled her lie about drinking. "Why did you tell your grandfather you don't drink? Trying to cover the pregnancy? I guess one lie is just as good as another."

She winced. "I didn't lie. I don't drink."

He just lifted a brow at her and waited.

"Okay. So Vegas was the first time I'd ever had a full drink. And clearly I can't even handle champagne."

"The first?" Dumbstruck, he blinked. "Why then if never before?"

A sarcastic laugh escaped as she leaned back against the counter. "Because, I told you, I wanted—*no needed*—to blow off some steam. To—" She stopped, bit her lip, then continued, "To be reckless and irresponsible, just once. And what better place to do that than Vegas?" Her eyes filled, but she blinked away the tears. "And look where that got me," she muttered, as her hands drifted to her stomach.

He resisted the urge to take her into his arms and hold her. He wasn't pleased about their situation, but he could admit it was much worse for her than it was for him. "And why not before?"

She gazed out the window, her face in profile. The high cheekbones, the pert nose, the full lips displayed to perfection in the waning summer light. "My mother. She died in a single-car crash. When I was thirteen. Car versus telephone pole. She had a blood-alcohol level of point two-three."

Ah. "I'm sorry. That must have been a very difficult time for you." The need to embrace her intensified. The need to take her in his arms and hold her until the bleak expression on her face dissolved. Until the tightly wound muscles in her neck and shoulders relaxed under his touch.

"At least she didn't take anyone with her," she said as if that brought her any solace.

A silence descended. The only sound the ticking of the wall clock by the mudroom door.

Leaning against the kitchen counter studying her, a thought occurred to him. "Do you remember anything about that night? The night we got married?" he clarified, lest she think he meant the night her mother was killed. There was no way he wanted her to relive *that* experience.

Georgia hadn't looked or behaved as if she were drunk. No slurred speech, no loss of balance, no glassy-eyed stare. Tipsy maybe, but not memory-stealing drunk.

"Of course. I remember the wedding—dancing, drinking. I remember catching the bouquet. I remember the limousine ride to the chapel and what we did on the way." She blushed at that, a charming deepening of the peachy color of her cheeks and, yes, he remembered that *very* well.

"Do you remember the bargain?"

"Yes," she whispered.

"Then why did you run away?" He crossed his arms over his chest in annoyance. Though in reality, he didn't know why. Even if she hadn't run away and they'd been granted an annulment, it wouldn't change their current situation. Regardless, he would have come to Northridge to buy the mill, and she would still be pregnant.

"I don't know!" She threw her hands up in the air. "I panicked!"

Releasing a pent-up breath, he dropped his arms by his sides. "Water under the bridge now," he muttered.

"Can't you just tell my grandfather you changed your mind? The rental house I found for you is very nice. It's larger than the cottage. More private."

He searched her face before answering. "I know you

think this will be awkward, but I'll be busy with the mill. Up and out early in the morning, home late at the end of the day. I even have a few business trips. It'll be fine."

As fine as living fifty yards from his secret pregnant wife could be. And with that, he left to settle into the cottage before he did something foolish, like haul her into his arms and kiss her.

11

Liam found the light switch on the interior wall beside the door and flipped it on. Instead of the glare of an overhead light fixture like he'd expected, the switch turned on two pale-blue lamps flanking a deep-cushioned sofa in a soft gray. A few throw pillows in blues, whites, and grays lay on the sofa. The icy-blue walls and soft lighting lent the living room a calming, peaceful atmosphere. Art decorated the walls, and books stood on a console table next to a large window overlooking the pool.

To the left he could see the open kitchen, and to the right a door that apparently led to the two bedrooms. Straight ahead stood a glass dinner table with seating for four. Overall, a very comfortable, well-thought-out design.

Picking up the rolling duffle he'd left by the door, he went in search of the master bedroom and bath, appreciating the heart pine flooring throughout. Bone tired, he looked forward to a hot shower and a comfortable bed.

The first bedroom he came to held a queen bed, a set of nightstands, and an armoire. The bath was across the hall.

While tastefully furnished, he hoped there was a larger en-suite bedroom.

Continuing on, he came to what was clearly the master. A king-size bed stood centered between two windows, the upholstered headboard in taupes and grays offered a soothing centerpiece to the neutral colors of the decor.

Lifting his duffle onto the bench at the foot of the bed, he unzipped it and rifled through the bag for a T-shirt and gym shorts, his mind wandering to the conversation with Georgia, wondering how the loss of her mother in such a tragic accident had shaped her. It had clearly impacted how she lived her life—never having had a "full" drink until Vegas. If he'd known, he wouldn't have frequently offered her glasses of champagne at the wedding. But she'd appeared to have enjoyed it.

He snorted. Maybe a little too much.

Vegas is where people went to cut loose—whether that was by partying, gambling, or indulging a sexual fantasy— you could find it all. Georgia had said, repeatedly, that she took her honeymoon to blow off steam after calling off her wedding, but he'd wondered then, as he wondered now, if that was all there was to it.

And here he was, living (albeit temporarily) fifty yards from her. How would he feel watching her belly grow knowing it's his child? And how could he offer her support without giving her the impression he would actually be a father to their child? It would be a delicate balance.

As he flipped on the shower, he thought that, if she knew the truth about his two brothers, she wouldn't want him in the same state with their child, much less the same town.

~

THE FOLLOWING SATURDAY, Georgia nibbled on a soda cracker. Part of her new morning routine, thanks to Alyssa's advice. She found if she ate a cracker or two before ever setting her feet on the floor in the morning, she could avoid the worst of the nausea. At the very least, she wouldn't vomit.

And she had to get through Olivia's wedding this afternoon without turning green. It wouldn't take much to start tongues wagging. She glided a hand across her stomach, feeling the slight rise there. No one else would notice. Yet.

Aside from the death of her mother, she'd had a wonderful adolescence. Sadly, the death of her mother may have made her adolescence better. At least more stable. Georgia never understood why her mother gave her that name—the name of a state her mother had despised. The whole time she was growing up in Macon, her mother would weave tales of the two of them jetting off to New York, getting away from the "narrow-minded people" she swore sat in constant judgment of her. And while the stories had always included Georgia, she often thought, if given the chance, her mother would have left her behind without a backward glance.

Her grandparents had been total strangers the night they'd picked her up from the Macon hospital where her mother had died. An indulgent grandfather and a warm but stern grandmother kept her balanced during those tumultuous years of puberty.

But she'd seen the anguish of her mother's sudden death on the faces of her grandparents, overheard the whispers about her mother's reckless behavior. Later, she swore she would never give her grandparents cause to fret over her like they had her mother. She would do what she was told and ignore the baser instincts of most teenagers.

An excellent student in school, a volunteer student-librarian, and a member of the debate team, she was determined to make her grandparents proud. While her classmates were experimenting with sex, weed, and alcohol, she was studying for her SATs and researching colleges. She didn't go into Atlanta to see movies or stroll the shopping malls to pick up boys. She didn't even get her driver's license until she was eighteen and ready to leave for college. Even in college, she'd avoided the sorority and fraternity parties, choosing to cloister herself in the campus library instead.

After graduating from law school, she had been focused on passing the bar exam and the real estate exam. Dating continued to sit on the back burner and, as a result, she had little experience with men.

So was it any surprise that when Not-Erik came along she fell for him—and hard?

She liked to think of herself as naïve but not gullible. After all, she had a degree in business from UC San Diego, and a law degree from Stanford. She was smart, and well educated.

Yet she'd never seen it coming.

She turned her attention to the bedroom window overlooking the pool and the carriage house where her husband and the father of her child now resided. As promised, she hadn't seen much of Liam since he'd moved in. She should be grateful but instead felt a little bereft. According to her grandfather, Liam had flown to New York for some business meetings. When she'd casually asked when he would return, her grandfather had said yesterday, but she still hadn't laid eyes on the man.

Good, she told herself as she tested the nausea waters by rising from the bed. Maybe his living in the carriage house wouldn't be the awkward arrangement she'd thought it would be. She'd go her way, and he'd go his.

Placing her feet on the floor, she waited a moment for the room to right itself. When the floor no longer tilted beneath her, she rose to start her day, purposefully putting Liam Dunbar out of her mind. Until, that is, she heard the carriage house door shut and the voice of Liam calling good morning to her grandfather.

Rushing to the window like a lovesick teenager, she clutched the desk chair, leaning forward and catching a glimpse of Liam's dark hair just has he caught her movement in the window and looked up.

"Fiddlesticks." She drew back as the heat of embarrassment filled her face. So much for avoiding him.

GEORGIA FELT a twinge of envy watching Zach and Olivia slow dancing. She'd dreamed of her wedding since she was a teenager, and their wedding was everything she'd wanted hers to be.

A beautiful dress, a handsome, smitten groom, and a romantic setting surrounded by friends and family. Instead, she'd called off one wedding only to have a quickie wedding in Vegas with a man she'd only just met. A wedding that should have been annulled as planned, had she not let her cowardice overcome her good sense.

Now, here she was pregnant, married to a man who didn't love her, counting the days until she could file for divorce. The trip to Vegas had been the dumbest thing she'd ever done. And she'd pay for it the rest of her life. Sighing, she took a sip of her cranberry and soda with a twist of lime —at least it *looked* like an adult beverage.

The restored barn made a perfect setting for a rustic but elegant wedding. The worn, unpainted wood of the building contrasted with the sparkling crystal chandeliers, and the elegant place settings on tables dressed in silver linens accented with navy-blue runners. Centerpieces of icy-pink roses, dusky blue hydrangeas, and dusty miller accents followed the wedding's color scheme of icy pink, navy blue, and silvery gray.

Olivia looked every inch the ballerina, tall and elegant in a lace gown of the iciest of pinks. The dress hugged the graceful curves of her body, ending in a chapel-length train appliquéd with the finest lace and a smattering of crystals that winked beneath the glittering chandeliers overhead. She'd pulled her chestnut hair up in a mass of loose waves, so when she turned, she revealed miles of bare skin framed with more of the delicate lace.

Now, she and her groom were wrapped in each other's arms, gazing at one another like the hundred-some-odd guests didn't exist. As if they were the only two people in the world.

From her wedding, Olivia got a life partner. From her wedding, Georgia got great sex and an unplanned pregnancy.

Someone sat in the empty chair next to her. Speak of the devil.

She frowned at him. "What are *you* doing here?"

He shrugged. "Zach invited me."

Annoyed, she returned her attention to the happy couple.

"Weddings seems to be our thing," he said.

She could feel his eyes on her. She snorted. Yeah. Right.

"Let's dance." He took her hand in his and tugged a little.

She shook her head.

"Come on. You can't sit here alone and sullen all night. You'll scare the guests." He lifted a chin toward the dance floor. "Even your grandfather is getting in on the action."

Grandad had Jennie Low, Olivia's stepmother, in his arms, smiling and laughing and looking distinguished in his navy-blue suit.

She exhaled and rose. "Fine. But," she held up a finger, "don't get frisky during our dance."

He chuckled. "Frisky?"

"You know what I mean." She looked down at her barely-there baby bump.

He held up his hands in surrender.

Preceding him, his big warm hand on the small of her back, they wove their way through the tables. When they reached the dance floor, he reeled her in until his arm wrapped around her waist, his other hand holding hers in a bent-arm position, very formal and proper, the space between them acceptable even by Victorian standards.

She rolled her eyes at his antics and wrapped her free arm around his back, and they began to move to the music, rocking slowly to and fro. As the emotion of the song built, she found herself moving closer, inch by inch, as if gravity were drawing the two of them closer, until they were a breath apart.

Sighing, she gave in and laid her hand on his chest and her head on his shoulder. It felt so good to be in his arms, gathered into his warmth. She resisted the urge to stand on tiptoe and bury her nose in his neck to inhale his musky cologne. His hand glided up and down her back, making her relax for the first time since she'd arrived for the wedding.

"You look beautiful tonight." The sound of his voice rumbled in his chest against her ear.

"Thank you." She'd worn one of the few designer dresses she hadn't sold to repay her creditors. A deep-coral Tory Burch cocktail dress she once wore to Lenny Kravtiz's open house for the Bel Air mansion she'd sold him.

"And I recognize those shoes."

"What?" She looked down at her feet.

"Those shoes. You were wearing them the night we met. And at the weddings.

She pulled away to look up into his face. "You remember what shoes I was wearing when we met?"

He pulled her back in. "I remember everything about you that night. And the night after that."

"Why?" she asked incredulous.

"Because you were the most beautiful woman in the club."

～

SHE SNORTED IN RESPONSE.

"You were," Liam insisted.

"Right. Definitely not with Audrey Turner there too."

"Audrey is a beautiful woman, I'll give you that. If you like that polished-perfection look. But you, you glowed like one of those candles on the tables." He indicated the candles in their glass globes lining the bridal party's table.

"Pfft."

He lifted his hand to finger one of the curls she'd left down from her up-do. "Your hair was curly that night, like it is now. And you wore a silver sequin dress with a back so low I could swear your ass would be visible at your slightest movement."

"It was *not*." She slapped at his chest, and he caught her hand and brought it to his mouth. Her pupils dilated and her lips parted, but then she pulled away, glancing around to see if anyone was looking.

Annoyed, he released her hand but kept his arm firm around her waist.

She might not have seen him tonight until he'd sat down at her table, but he'd seen her the moment she walked in on her grandfather's arm and took her seat beside him, with her hair twisted up in some intricate style, shimmering curly tendrils framing her face. The short flowy dress the color of a Southern sunset set off her skin to perfection.

Holding her close, the scent of jasmine filling his head brought back memories of their two nights in Las Vegas, and he grew hard at the memory. Her breasts seemed larger, fuller than he remembered—the pregnancy he supposed— and the slight swell of her abdomen brushed against him.

She gasped, and he knew she could feel the evidence of his desire for her, but she didn't step back. Her breath became shallow, her body a little tense. She wanted him.

And God knew he wanted her. He ached with it. Knowing she was but fifty yards away every day and every night was pure torture.

She lifted her chin and searched his face, questioning, then licked her lips. He lowered his mouth to hers, but before he could make contact, a hand slapped him on the back.

"Great wedding, isn't it?"

He and Georgia both turned to see Marshall's grinning face.

Georgia stepped back as if he were contagious. "Yes." She licked her lips again and tucked a strand of hair behind her ear. "You and Jennie looked like you were having a good time."

"We were." He looked between Liam and Georgia, gaze

intent. "I'm not the only one enjoying the dancing. I'll leave you to it." With a wave of his hand, he headed for one of the bars set up in the corner.

She shook her head when Liam held out his hand for another dance. "We can't. People will talk."

"Let them."

Her gaze shot to his. "You don't understand. This is my *home*. This is where I *live*. I can't give people a reason to talk."

He felt the eyes of the couples nearest them and reached out to snag her around the waist. "You're creating more of a disturbance by arguing with me than you would by just dancing."

She huffed out an exasperated sigh but relented and let him lead her in another slow dance.

Voice lowered, she continued her argument, "In a few months, everyone in town will know I'm pregnant. They see us together and they will likely think you're the father—"

"I *am* the father."

"You know what I mean. And if I use the story that it's my ex's baby, they'll think even worse of me—pregnant by one man, having an affair with another."

The song came to an end, and Georgia drew away. "It's best if we keep our relationship business only." She looked up at him with those sea-blue eyes, pleading for his understanding.

He nodded. She was right about one thing—it was best to stick with their business relationship. He'd be gone by the time the baby came and nothing would be gained by becoming otherwise entangled.

But as he watched her walk away, hips swaying with each step, he wondered if he could keep that promise.

12

Ever since Olivia and Zach's wedding, Liam had been nothing but a gentleman—doing as she'd asked, keeping their relationship focused solely on their business transaction. And she hated it.

Sitting at the desk in her bedroom, she tried to concentrate on the closing documents for the warehouse in preparation for the meeting later in the week, but her mind drifted to their dances at Olivia's wedding. The way his hands had felt on her waist, the warmth of his breath against her cheek, the hard ridge pressed against her belly . . .

"Stop that!" She needed to focus. The fat commission check she'd receive would cover the expenses of Luis's renovation and redecoration and allow him to tackle the other rooms in the office. It would also provide her with a financial cushion she hadn't had since she learned of Not-Erik's embezzlement. Really, even before that, since she hadn't known what he'd been up to.

She should be excited by the prospect, but once they closed the deal, there would be no legitimate reason to spend time with Liam. They would be done. Of course, she'd run into him. Northridge was a small town. But she would turn her attention to other listings, and he would turn his to the restoration of the mill.

The thought left a hollow feeling in her chest.

A splash from the pool below startled her out of her pity party and she looked out the window to see Liam's head pop up from underneath the water, his dark hair slick and shining in the sunlight.

He shoved the hair out of his face then swam to the ladder to get out. He rose from the water like an actor in one of those sexy cologne ads. Water ran down his hard body, his olive skin smooth and slick, and she nearly swallowed her tongue. "Holy—"

She shivered, remembering the carnal knowledge she had of that body. She'd spent two days and nights kissing, stroking, and otherwise worshipping that body, and her girlie parts were saying, "Yes, please" to more of the same.

He walked over to the lounge chair where he'd tossed a towel, and her gaze slid from his washboard abs down the dark line of hair that disappeared beneath his waistband and to his legs, solid and firm in his swim trunks. She felt like a voyeur as he reached for the towel and scrubbed his wet hair with it, his actions leaving it sticking up in all directions. He should have look ridiculous but instead just looked tousled and . . . lip-smacking good. Wrapping the towel around his waist, he bent to pick up the T-shirt that lay on the chair then headed in the direction of the carriage house.

As she fanned her heated cheeks with a notepad, she thought maybe it was for the best that their paths would not cross any more than necessary, otherwise she might not be able to resist the temptation he presented.

Liam Dunbar was a dangerous man.

A WEEK LATER, Georgia walked into the office to see a new sofa and two new chairs in the reception area.

The sofa, with a sleek wood frame upholstered in a rose gray, was arts-and-crafts style with a twist—the wood had been painted a glossy navy. The navy set off the soft gray-green walls, just as Luis had said it would. He'd paired it with two mid-century modern chairs in striped fabric boasting tones of gray-green, rose gray, and navy. Luis had painted the room's baseboards, window frames, doors, and door frames a creamy white, creating a nice contrast between light and dark.

The designer extraordinaire himself appeared from the direction of the office kitchen, wiping his hands with a paper towel.

"Well?" he asked, a brow lifted.

"They're great. But I thought you were getting second-hand furniture. How much are these going to set me back?"

"They *are* secondhand. Maybe even third-hand, considering the shape they were in." He gave the furniture a critical look. "I found them in an antique store in Atlanta while waiting for Jonathan to finish a case so we could meet for dinner. It was our anniversary," he said with a wistful sigh.

"Oh! Happy anniversary!"

"Thanks." He indicated the furniture. "The sofa was covered in a hideous green crushed velvet. Something out of a nightmare. The chairs weren't too bad but needed refreshing."

"You mean you did that? Painted? And reupholstered?"

"Of course. Didn't I say I could?"

She grabbed his face and kissed him on the mouth. "You're a genius!"

He lifted his fingertips to his lips and a blush bloomed beneath his swarthy skin. "Thanks."

"I hesitate to say this because I wouldn't want to part with you, but you're in the wrong line of work."

"It *is* a passion." He blew on his nails then rubbed them against his chest. "But no worries. You need me, so I'll stay."

"So, what's next?"

"Window treatments." He looked toward the two windows in the reception area. The small windows let in little light and made the office look like barracks.

"Short of knocking out part of the wall and installing bigger windows, we'll use full-height drapes from ceiling to floor. They'll make the small windows feel taller. And I'd suggest hanging a tall mirror between the windows to give the illusion that there is a third window and to reflect light." He folded his arms, satisfied with his decision. "But . . ." He tapped his lip in thought.

"What?" She could see her moderate bank account shrinking even more.

"We need art."

"Yeah, right," she said, not hiding the skepticism in her voice. Like she could afford good art.

"I can try my hand at some abstract paintings. See what you think. Something big and bold."

She shrugged. "Sure. Why not?" She wouldn't count him out on that skill either.

"Then the side pieces. Haven't found anything yet that's called to me." He tapped his lips with this finger. "I'd also like to update the fireplace, but that would cost a pretty penny. I think we can get away with updating the mantle and maybe painting the brick." He tapped his lips again in thought. "The same color as the walls. The monochromatic scheme will give the illusion that the room is bigger. Paint the mantle the same glossy navy."

"Really?"

He thought another moment. "Yes."

She couldn't see it but said, "All right. I trust your eye for design."

"A new reception desk wouldn't be remiss either. Something sleek with clean lines, I think."

"It's your desk, pick out what you like. As long as it's cheap."

"No, not cheap." He held up his finger to make his point. "Inexpensive, a good buy."

"Whatever," she said with a roll of the eyes.

"The reception area was the priority, but your office is next, sunshine. You need to look like the successful real estate broker you are, and that," he jabbed his finger in the direction of her dingy office, "does *not* say successful. It says *un*successful."

"No argument there. I have nightmares I'm working in the basement of some military installation."

"We can fix that."

THE NEXT MORNING, Georgia entered the office kitchen trying not to grimace at the knotty pine cabinets with their black iron hardware, the harvest-gold appliances, Formica countertops, and torn linoleum floor. She'd love a new kitchen with sleek modern cabinets, maybe concrete, with state-of-the-art stainless-steel appliances and a new floor. She'd consider a stained concrete floor like in the reception area. But even Luis couldn't work his magic and deliver a shiny new kitchen on the cheap.

She stashed her chicken noodle soup in the fridge, along with a bottle of ginger ale, in case the queasies hit after lunch like they sometimes did.

"Before you return these phone calls, take a look at these mockups." Luis entered the kitchen and handed her several messages. He set out a couple business cards with two different designs, as well as a brochure with two different layouts. "I've also designed a logo. Tell me what you think. Be brutally honest. About everything," he said as he circled his hands to encompass the display he'd created on the countertop.

The logo, business cards, and brochures were all designed in a color scheme matching the paint colors he'd selected for the reception area—the gray-green of the walls and navy accents. Somehow that had become her brand. The gray-green background for the business cards would stand out among the more common whites and creams of most businesses cards.

The logo depicted a gabled roof and two windows of a home in navy on a background the color of her gray-green walls, with lettering in the same navy that read: MACK-INNON REALTY. Beneath that was the tagline: YOUR DREAM HOME AWAITS.

Elegant and simple. They were . . . perfect. "Did you come up with the tagline?"

"I can't take all the credit. Jonathan threw in an idea or two."

"I love them. Truly. Make a business card for yourself too while you're at it."

"Yes, boss. I found a great deal on printing online. The brochures should go in some of the local establishments in case visitors fall in love with Northridge and realize they *have* to move here in order for life to be perfect."

"Whatever you think." She had been so busy with transferring her law license and real estate license and trying to sell the current listings she'd acquired as part of the business's purchase that she was ashamed to admit she hadn't given much thought to marketing. She'd had a marketing department in her previous business. Which Not-Erik had managed, along with other things . . . like the business's finances.

"Next, I'm working on your website and social media platforms. I thought we'd go with Facebook and Instagram for now. We can always add Twitter and Pinterest later. I should have a draft of the website ready to look at tomorrow."

She'd had a fancy website in California maintained by a top PR firm in L.A. She hadn't given thought to a website for her new business either. And she certainly couldn't pay an Atlanta firm to handle it for her. "How did I ever find you?"

"I found *you*, but just lucky, I guess."

The office telephone rang, startling them both—it was such a rare occurrence.

Luis scooped up the receiver on the wall and in a smooth masculine voice said, "MacKinnon Realty, where your dream home awaits."

Georgia smiled and shook her head.

"Yes." Luis glanced up. "Ms. MacKinnon is here. I'll transfer you." He punched hold then held the receiver out to her.

"I thought you were transferring the call."

"I am." He stuck the receiver out again. "I'm transferring the receiver to you."

She rolled her eyes. "Who is it? Never mind, I don't care

at this point, as long as it's a potential client." Lifting the phone to her ear, she nodded at Luis to take the call off hold. "This is Georgia," she said in her best professional voice.

"Georgia, this is Carl Schneider."

Carl was the chair of the Town Council. They'd made their rezoning determination? She wished she was on the other side of Luis's desk so she could sink into a chair. "Yes, Carl."

"The Town Council voted this morning to grant the rezoning request for Mr. Dunbar's mill site. We look forward to the positive economic impact projected in the rezoning request."

"Wonderful news," she said in a measured tone, but her hips wiggled as she did a little happy dance.

Luis shook his head at her antics.

"You'll inform Mr. Dunbar?"

"Yes, I'll let him know." Grinning from ear to ear, she set the phone in its cradle then let out a whoop.

"Good news, I gather?"

"The best! The mill property is now zoned light industrial, which means the contract contingency with Mr. Dunbar has been met and the sale can be finalized." Her relief was palpable. Her first sale with her new business. The nice commission check she'd get soon would relieve some of the financial pressure she'd been under.

"We should celebrate," Luis said, raising a hand for a high five.

"Lunch is on me," Georgia said, slapping his hand with hers.

"This is Liam," he said into the phone as he left his meeting with the contractor.

"Hi, it's Georgia. The rezoning request was approved."

"Yes!" Liam did a little fist pump with this empty hand. "Great work."

"It wasn't just me. Your proven business model and economic projections, along with your commitment to the environment, clearly convinced the council."

"We make a good team." Now why had he said that? He'd worked with many real estate brokers and lawyers in the development of his fourteen other mills and succeeded in getting rezoning approved where it was needed.

"Uh, thanks."

"We should go out and celebrate." He also never asked the other realtors or lawyers out to celebrate.

The offer was met with silence. Thinking the call had dropped, he prompted, "Georgia?"

"I'm here. Thanks, but it's really not necessary."

Disappointed but not surprised, he rubbed his forehead. Right. Probably for the best anyway. "When can we close on the property?" Since he was paying cash, there was no reason to wait.

"Friday?"

"Friday it is. What time?"

"I'll check with the seller, but let's say ten o'clock."

"See you then. I look forward to it." And he wondered, once again, where that had come from.

13

Georgia stood beneath the welcome shade of the tent that served as her booth at the annual Northridge Fourth of July celebration. Other local businesses were setting up as well, including Pints and Paints, the 1885 B&B, and the Secret Garden Nursery. The food vendors were setting up on the other side of the aisle created by the tents, and she could see the banner for Beans 'n Books, and next to it, the Firehouse Brews' tent.

Luis had already arrived and set up tables, complete with red tablecloths and red-white-and-blue bunting. An American flag flew from a pole mounted on the tent frame. With all her bad luck lately, she counted herself lucky to have hired him.

In honor of the holiday, Georgia wore a navy sleeveless sheath with side shearing to accommodate (aka hide) the slight baby bump. She'd finished off the look with a chunky red-and-white bead necklace and red ballet flats.

"Looking very patriotic chic," Luis said as he organized the business fliers and business cards he'd designed, along with fliers of a few of the properties Georgia had listed.

"Is that a thing?"

"It is now," he said with a cheeky smile.

He'd also set out a basket of chocolates and the new keychains he'd bought that featured her logo.

The scents of kettle corn, roasting hotdogs, and funnel cake blended into a nauseating miasma and she swallowed hard. Darn morning sickness. Her doctor had said some women get over morning sickness after their first trimester. She sure hoped she'd be one of them, but she had another two or three weeks to go.

"Hey," Luis said in alarm. "You look a little green. Maybe you should sit down." He pulled out a folding chair for her.

She'd thought to refuse, then another wave of nausea struck and she took him up on his offer.

"Can I get you something? A Coke? Ginger ale?" he asked, his tone solicitous.

"Uh, do you think you can find a ginger ale?"

"You got it. Just leave the rest of the setup. I'll be right back."

She nodded. Working so closely with Luis, it would only be a matter of time before she either told him about her conundrum or he figured it out. She snorted. Wait another three weeks, and he and everyone else would figure it out with one look at her growing belly.

She took a deep breath then regretted it, as another waft of the mingled scents made the bile rise again. "I am not going to throw up, I am not going to throw up," she muttered, closing her eyes in concentration.

"Meditating?"

Her eyes flew open to see the man who'd gotten her in this situation with a curious expression on his face.

"Morning sickness," she said with enough scorn to scorch everything within ten feet of her.

"Ah. What can I do to help?"

"You've done enough, haven't you?" Her hand settled on her stomach.

He leaned in and whispered, "I believe you were there too, sweetheart, and you weren't complaining at the time."

Her face heated, and she gave his shoulder a shove. "Go away." But the request didn't hold any rancor.

He laughed. "Seriously, what can I do?"

She sighed. "Nothing. Luis went in search of a ginger ale."

"That should help." He nodded. "Does he know?"

"No. You, me, Alyssa, and my doctor, are the only ones on this planet who know, and I'd like to keep it that way for as long as possible."

"So you've said."

She glanced at him then looked away. She knew he didn't agree with her, but he had no idea what it was like to live in a small town, especially after her mother's behavior. People always wondering when she would screw up and judge her more harshly for it.

And she finally had. In spectacular fashion. Hoping to change to subject, she asked, "Are you setting up a tent?"

"Yes." He looked down the row of tents, presumably in the direction of American Threads' tent. "Two of my Chicago employees are manning it. Sabrina from HR and Malik from operations. We hope to start the hiring process soon. This will be a good opportunity to introduce ourselves to the community."

"*Et voilà!* Ginger ale with lots of crushed ice." Luis presented the cup to her and she took a tentative sip. "Thanks, Luis."

"Luis." Liam nodded.

"Liam." Luis eyed him with some speculation then

looked at Georgia, and she felt the urge to twitch. But he returned his attention to arranging items on the table, apparently deciding he didn't like the original arrangement.

"Walk with me." Liam extended a hand in her direction.

Cutting a glance at Luis, she nodded. Taking another sip of the ginger ale, she closed her eyes in momentary bliss then rose.

Liam led her away from the food tents, and once she got upwind of them, she drew a deep, cleansing breath. "Thank you."

He turned to her, studying her. "You feeling okay?"

"Yes, it was just the mingled scent of food that made me sick. The ginger ale and fresh air is helping."

"Will you have that the entire pregnancy?" he asked, his brow furrowed.

"God, I hope not! Most women don't, so I'm crossing my fingers that I'm in that category."

"You are not *most* women, Georgia, though I hope for your sake you fall into that particular category."

She didn't know whether to take the 'most women' comment as a compliment or insult, but she disregarded it. "I really should get back. Did you need something?"

A frown crossed his face. "No. I just thought you could use some fresh air."

"Oh. Thank you," she said with some surprise at his solicitousness.

"Despite our situation, I'm not indifferent to your well-being." He rubbed his forehead then said, "I do worry about you," he looked down at her stomach, "and the baby."

"I appreciate it, but I told you I'm willing to do this alone."

"But that doesn't mean I can't help you now . . . while I'm here."

She searched his face, for what she didn't know, then nodded. "I need to go." She lifted her hand in the direction of the tent.

"Just . . . take it easy. It's going to be a warm day. Can't have you falling or anything."

Confused by his concern, she headed back to the tent. If he kept that up, she'd find herself thinking he cared more about her than he actually did.

And that couldn't happen.

A COUPLE DAYS LATER, Liam did a double take, resisting the urge to rub his eyes, unsure of what he was seeing. No, he wasn't seeing things. Marshall MacKinnon was indeed strolling down the sidewalk in early Victorian clothes, complete with top hat, walking stick, and gloves.

"Did I step back in time?" Liam asked, his brow furrowed.

Marshall laughed. "No. I've been cast as Lawyer Gibson Haynes in the film."

"I didn't know you acted."

"Well, I suppose every lawyer acts, especially in a courtroom," he added with a wink. "Besides, it's not such a stretch, since I *am* a lawyer, after all."

Liam couldn't help the broad grin that spread over his face. "You'll make a fine Lawyer Haynes."

"Pfft. I only have two lines. Doubt I'll be receiving any Oscar nominations."

"Well, you look very distinguished."

Marshall tugged on his embroidered vest and grinned. "I do like the costume. I feel a little like my great-grandfather Thaddeus MacKinnon."

"How far back does your family go?"

"My great-great-grandfather, Alistair Caldwell MacKinnon, was one of the town's founding fathers. He built the house we live in now."

"Were they all lawyers?"

"Alistair was a banker. He built what was the Bank of Northridge. His sons and grandsons ran the bank until a larger Atlanta-based bank bought it. Thaddeus was the first lawyer in the family."

To be able to trace his lineage had never really occurred to Liam, but listening to Marshall speak about his ancestors struck a chord with him.

Liam opened the café door for Marshall, who preceded him in. A harried looking fellow stood at the counter where Kristen reviewed a rather large order.

"Twenty-five breakfast muffins, thirty chocolate croissants, and thirty danishes in a variety of flavors, as well as the setups. Calypso is getting the carafes of coffee, hot water, tea bags, and the setups for those. Did I miss anything?" Kristen blew a tendril of hair out of her face.

He had ticked items off his list as she rattled them off. "That looks like it should be it."

"Calypso will meet you at the curb and help load your car."

He nodded. "Thanks."

Kristen yanked a paper towel from the dispenser and dabbed at the sweat on her brow.

"Catering order?" Liam surmised.

"Yeah. Fifth one this week." She flashed him a tired smile. "Not that I'm complaining. It's good for business, just bad for my blood pressure." She stretched her back, moaning a little, then waved across the street. "They're filming at the train station today."

Liam had noticed the lights, cameras, directors' chairs, and other film-making impedimenta when he'd run into Marshall.

"This film will have a positive economic impact on the town."

"Kristen is being modest," Marshall put in. "She and Tyler were the primary proponents of the film license. Northridge didn't even have a film permit process when this all started. She and Tyler helped put everything in place."

Liam glanced at Kristen, whose face was now tinged with a becoming blush. She and Tyler were additional examples of why Liam was so impressed with Northridge and its citizenry. He'd dealt with many small-town citizens and councils who were stuck in the past, afraid to move forward, which was why they were in such dire economic straits. For some, even the possibility of the jobs his mills would create weren't enough to support change.

Again, the thought of relocating crossed Liam's mind. He would be closer to his projects, which meant he might actually be able to go home occasionally.

Home. He hadn't had a place he could really call home for over a decade.

He'd have to buy a home first. And a home in Northridge appealed to him more than any other small town he'd invested in.

And then there was Georgia—the woman, not the state. And their child. He grimaced. It was one thing to say he wouldn't be a part of their lives, but living here, seeing the child—his child—would make it impossible to keep both his physical and emotional distance.

No. On second thought, Northridge could not be his home.

GEORGIA PLUNKED the chilled bottle of non-alcoholic sparkling cider down on Luis's desk.

"What's this?"

"A celebration, that's what."

"With *that*?" He raised a dubious brow. "What are we celebrating? Your Sweet Sixteen? Where's the real stuff?"

"Well, it *is* the middle of the work day." No reason to go into a whole no-alcohol explanation.

He just rolled his eyes. "I'll get some cups," he said with a resigned sigh and headed for the kitchen.

When he returned, she poured cider into the two paper cups and handed him one while she lifted the other in a toast. "Cheers!"

"Wait." His hand on her forearm halted the progress of the cup to her mouth. "What are we toasting to?"

"Oh, right! I made a huge sale!"

"Congratulations!" He took a sip of the cider and shuddered, making a face. "Next time there's a celebration, let me do the honors." He nodded toward the half-empty bottle.

Ignoring his comment, she continued. "You know that fifteen-hundred-acre property with the forty-thousand-square-foot early-twentieth-century mansion just outside Northridge? Well, I sold it—for cash!"

Luis choked on the mouthful of cider he'd just drank. Once able to catch his breath, he repeated, "Cash?"

"Yup. And they want to close right away. As in next week."

She was already spending *some* of the money in her head. With the six-digit commission on the sale, maybe could afford a house of her own before the baby was born.

She loved her grandfather, but she wanted a place of her own where she would raise her baby.

"Who's the buyer?"

"I can't say. It's being purchased through an agent." She had a great deal of experience with the need for discretion. In L.A., she'd sold property to movie stars, rock stars, sports stars, and other celebrities, and she didn't kiss and tell. But this one was the most interesting of any of her sales. From what she could gather, the buyer was a disaffected royal prince or something. Very mysterious.

"You can't say or you don't know?"

"I can't say. Well, I don't really know for sure either." She picked up the bottle, poured the remainder into her cup, and took another sip.

Luis sat on the edge of his desk. "Well, that is *very* interesting."

"And *very* lucrative." She looked around the office. "What else do we need to do to get this place presentable?"

"You mean besides a bulldozer? Well, there's the Mamie-pink tile bathroom, the paneled den," he visibly shuddered, "and the other office space. Then the exterior could use a complete makeover—pressure washing, painting, new land-scaping, a sign ..."

She gnawed on her lower lip a moment. In addition to a place for herself, she needed to set aside a chunk of money for the baby. And give Luis a much-deserved bonus—and maybe a raise. "Do it."

"Thank goodness," Luis breathed.

"But," she held up a cautionary finger, "with the same eye to a modest budget. The fewer expensive options we can get away with and still make the place look ..."

"Like it's not condemned?" Luis offered.

She snorted. "I was going to say appealing."

LIAM ENTERED BEANS 'N BOOKS, intent on one of Kristen's iced americanos. But before he could make it to the bar to place his order, an all-too-familiar laugh caught his attention. Scanning the café tables, he spotted Georgia seated next to a clean-cut guy in a white button-down—and she had her hand on his forearm, smiling up into his face.

Liam's first instinct was *oh, hell no.* Then his higher brain kicked in and he pulled up short. He had no right to this reaction. Sure, he and Georgia were married. And yes, she was having his child. But they weren't really together, nor were they even in love. It wasn't a *real* marriage.

She leaned close and showed him something on her phone, and Liam's caveman instinct made another appearance. Contradictory thoughts and reactions warred inside him—irrational jealousy did battle with rational awareness while his amygdala clashed with his cerebral cortex. Nevertheless, the next thing he knew, his feet were moving in their direction.

"Georgia," he winced at the accusatory tone in his voice.

Her head snapped up. "Oh, Liam. Hi." She gave him a bright, guilt-free smile.

Of course it was guilt-free—she wasn't doing anything wrong, he had to remind himself. He glanced over at Mr. Clean-Cut then back at Georgia, his brows lifting expectantly.

"Oh, right. Where are my manners? Stuart, this is Liam Dunbar. Liam is renovating the old Redmond Mill to manufacture apparel."

"Really?" Stuart said, a look of surprise on his movie-star face. Liam stared him down until Stuart's brow furrowed in confusion. *Careful there, Stu, you could end up with permanent brow lines in that pretty face.*

"Stuart and I were went to high school together. We were just reminiscing." Again with her hand on his forearm. "He and his wife," she lifted her hand to indicate a petite and very pregnant brunette browsing the bookshelves, "are moving back to Georgia and they want to settle here. I'm showing them a few houses."

His wife. Okay then. Didn't Liam feel all kinds of stupid now? "Ah. Well. I'm sure Georgia will find something perfect for you, your wife, and your, uh, child."

Georgia gave him a funny look and he decided it was time to cut and run. "Well, I've got to go. Nice meeting you, Stuart. Best of luck with the relocation. Georgia." He nodded.

He almost made it to the door when Georgia called out, "Liam?" He turned with reluctance.

"Were you here for coffee or something?"

"Uh, yes. But I'm running late for a meeting with the, uh, contractor." *Smooth. Real smooth.*

"Oh. Well, I won't keep you then."

He stepped outside, took a few steps out of the view of the café, then stopped. What the hell had that been all about? He'd never had a jealous bone in his body. And now he sees his Vegas fling with another man and he transforms into a Neanderthal.

He looked back in the direction of the café with longing. *Damn.* He'd really wanted an iced coffee. But there was no way in hell he was going back in there. He'd already made a fool of himself once.

He didn't know why, but his short-term wife was turning his life inside out.

It seemed every day Georgia entered the office to find something new. Luis was making incredible progress. Today it was drapes and lamps. Yesterday it was an area rug. She had to admit, the room was coming together better than she could have imagined. Luis really had an eye. The art he'd created for the walls was perfect. Just bold strokes of complimentary colors on two large canvases, but they really made the room look rich and inviting.

The designer—and now painter—extraordinaire sat at the desk typing something on the laptop she'd bought him for scheduling and communicating with clients.

"Morning, sunshine."

She couldn't hold back the smile. "Why do you call me that?"

"Your sunny personality?"

"Pfft. Right."

"Your golden-blond hair then?"

"That makes more sense."

Luis studied her and she resisted the urge to cover the baby bump with her hand. "Either someone's been indulging in too many of Kristen's cocoa caramel mochas or there's a cinnamon bun in the oven."

She actually felt the blood drain from her face. "How . . . ? Never mind." She waved a hand. "I give up trying to understand how you know what you know."

"*Carina*, I'm uncle to my three older sisters' *bambinos*. I think I know a pregnant woman when I see one."

Georgia sighed and rubbed her neck. "Okay. I'm pregnant." She pointed a finger at him. "But you have to keep it a secret." A twinge of guilt that others knew before she'd told her grandfather struck her. Yet the thought of telling him made her queasy.

He eyed her bulge with some skepticism and jutted his chin in its general direction. "That's not staying a secret too much longer."

"I know, I know. Just—let me break the news, okay?"

"Of course." He mimed zipping his lips shut. "They won't hear it from me. But I wouldn't wait too long to tell whoever you need to. Soon your stomach will be speaking for itself."

"You're not going to ask me who the father is?"

"No. Though I won't lie, I'm dying to know."

"No?" She lifted a brow in surprise.

He waved her off. "No. If you want to tell me, I'll listen. If not, you'll tell me when you're ready."

"Thank you." She set a hand on his arm, and he shrugged, as if to say it's no big deal.

"But I do have my suspicions . . ." He covered his mouth and coughed, "Liam."

Georgia stepped back as if struck.

"Oh please. I've seen you two together. The chemistry between you two is combustible. Trust me, you're not hiding that secret too long either." At her continued stunned silence, he said, "Don't worry. That secret's safe with me too." He handed her some messages then took a sip of his coffee that smelled like vanilla and hazelnuts.

The tantalizing scent jolted her from her stupor and she groaned. "God, I really want coffee."

He cast a glance at the cup he'd just set on the desk. "Sorry—there's a lot I would do for you but giving up coffee in solidarity of your abstinence is not one of them."

She waived him off. "Wouldn't dream of asking. And thank you."

"For what?" He looked up from the keyboard where he'd resumed typing.

"For being a confidant."

"Say nothing of it."

Scanning the room again, she asked, "Do you have a fleet of fairies who work all night? How do you manage to get all this done?"

"A fleet of fairies? Hmm. That's not a bad idea. But no, Jonathan sometimes doesn't get home until late, so I work in the evenings."

"I really wish you would keep track of those hours so I could pay you for them."

"Pfft. Why pay me to have fun? It would be like paying kids to play on the playground."

With a snort, she glanced at the messages. Nothing earth shattering. But no potential new client listings or buyers either. The cash from the sale of the mill and the mansion would hold her for a while, but new business would give her peace of mind. "Well, thanks. For everything." Sighing, she hoisted her tote bag up a little higher and looked around the reception area again. "Is this done?"

Luis shrugged. "For now. If I find some accent pieces that work, I may add those. You know, a vase here, a bowl there.

But," he stood and waved her into her office, "what do you think about this?"

Gone was the ugly steel-gray metal desk and in its place stood a sleek, yet feminine desk in glossy navy. The rich navy, a color she never would have considered, looked beautiful and classy against the cool gray walls Luis had painted the previous week.

"It's beautiful!" She traced the brushed pewter hardware on the drawers.

"Jonathan and I wandered around Duluth last weekend and I found this in a secondhand store. A little paint and a change in hardware, *et voilà!*"

"I love it! Thank you."

"My pleasure. We'll need to get you a decent office chair, one that's ergonomical, especially with a little one on the way. Sorry, but my mad skills can't help you there."

"Right. Maybe do a little research?" she asked, hopeful. She didn't want to thumb through a catalog or scroll through a website for an office chair.

"Sure. Otherwise, a couple of guest chairs, maybe a small conference table and chairs over there along that wall, and something for the walls, and we'll be in business."

"Receipts?"

He handed them over, neatly folded inside an envelope.

The new desk sat in front of the window. The floors had been stripped of the hideous carpet, but Luis was still considering what to do with them that wouldn't break the bank. "And the floor?" she reminded him with a lifted brow.

"Don't rush me." He waved her away. "I need time to consider the possibilities."

"Why not just stain it like the other one?"

"No. Your office calls for something special. I just don't know what that is yet," he said with a wink.

A STRANGE PHONE number popped up on Liam's smartphone. He hesitated to answer it, thinking it was likely spam, but it was Cole's area code. Not again.

With a sinking feeling in his stomach, he answered, "Hello?"

"Hey, man."

"Cole? Where are you? Whose number is this?"

"Well, it's a funny story—"

"Cut the shit, Cole. Tell me what happened."

Liam dropped onto the bed, rubbing his forehead, for he had no doubt this call wasn't good news.

"I'm in the L.A. county jail. Busted for buying coke."

"Fuuuck." Liam dropped his chin to his chest. "And rehab?"

"I left. Couldn't take all their rules and shit."

Son of a bitch. "Do you have bail money? A lawyer?"

"Neither. I'll just get a P.D."

"Hell no. No public defender. Sit tight, I'll get you a lawyer. And the bail money." He heaved a heavy sigh of anger and frustration.

"I—" silence followed, then Cole continued, sounding contrite. "Thanks, man."

Liam ended the call and resisted the urge to throw his phone against the wall.

What the hell was Liam going to do with Cole? Many would say he should just walk away and let Cole sink or swim. But Liam couldn't do that. Not when he was the reason Cole was a drug addict.

THE FIRST THING Liam spotted when he drove up to MacKinnon Realty on Saturday was the exterior makeover.

Georgia—or, rather, Luis—had painted the red-brick exterior gray. It appeared they had painted the gutters and downspouts white, as well as the window trim. Luis—for he had no doubt whose decision it had been—had gone with a deep navy for the shutters and painted the door the same gray-green as the reception area walls and Georgia's new logo. The colors were crisp and appealing. Especially after the unoriginal red-brick and black-trimmed exterior.

The second thing Liam spotted when he drove up was his pregnant wife on hands and knees in the dirt. "What the hell?" he growled as he slammed the car door and strode up the sidewalk.

He reached her in three strides and, gripping her arm, hauled her to her feet. She yelped. "What the hell are you doing?"

Shocked by his rough greeting, her eyes narrowed and sparked. "What the hell are *you* doing?" She glanced around and lowered her voice. "It should be quite obvious what *I'm* doing. *I'm* planting plants." She indicated the still-potted plants at her feet waiting to be added to the landscape. "And you made me curse."

Tyler and Kristen, Zach and Olivia, and Alyssa and Dillon, as well as Luis, all stopped what they were doing to look on in confusion. Taking the dirt-covered spade from her hand, he dropped it on the grass and turned her to face him. "You shouldn't be crawling around on hands and knees in your condition."

"My *condition*? I could have sworn I was living in the twenty-first century, not the nineteenth." At his continued glare, she blew out an annoyed breath. "I asked Dr. Grimshaw and she had no issues with it."

She licked her lips—damn if he didn't want to yank her against him and kiss her breathless—and cast a sideways glance toward her friends. "Besides, other than you, Luis, and Alyssa, no one here knows I'm pregnant yet, and I'd really like to keep it that way for the time being." Poking him in the chest, she continued, "And for someone who has no intention of being a parent to our child, you're getting a little proprietary."

She was right. What had come over him? He couldn't take care of Cole, so he'd turned his attention and frustration on Georgia. He dropped his hands from her shoulders and stepped back. "Sorry." Feeling seven pairs of eyes boring into his back, he said with a little less volume, "Luis knows?"

"He figured it out."

Liam gazed down at the subtle bulge. "It won't be long before *everyone* figures it out."

She rolled her eyes, and he sighed. *Fine.* "And what did you mean I made you curse? You don't curse?"

She sniffed and lifted her chin. "No. My grandmother taught me ladies don't curse."

Now that he thought about it, he'd never heard her curse. Shaking his head at her prim expression, he asked. "What can I do to help?"

"Thought you'd never ask," Luis said from behind him, a note of relief in his voice. "We could use another set of strong arms to pull up that hideous overgrown shrub at the corner of the house. Let's go, boys!"

Dirty and exhausted, Georgia stood in the street and admired the change she and her friends had wrought. The new paint colors were gorgeous and the landscaping added much-needed curb appeal. The commission on the sale of the fourteen-hundred-acre property easily covered the cost of the materials, and her friends covered the labor.

Luis had created sweeping landscape beds filled with pine straw from Georgia pines. One bed around the elm in the front would be reserved for seasonal flowers like mums and marigolds in the fall and pansies in the winter. For summer, they'd planted colorful petunias. The guys had the backbreaking job of laying fresh sod in the remaining areas of the property.

They had lined the freshly pressure-washed sidewalk with fluffy mounds of mondo grass, what she'd been planting when Liam arrived. The men had ripped out the overgrown and misshapen shrubs and replaced them with variegated boxwoods and Burford hollies. Then they'd loaded the yard waste onto a trailer Tyler would take to the nearby waste-management facility.

One area she'd splurged on was her sign. It needed to make a statement and it did with the logo Luis had designed. And the simple elegant landscaping around it didn't detract.

Her throat filled with tears at the sight. She'd never had to work so hard for her business, and she was proud of what she'd accomplished in a few short months. She owed a good bit of it to her friends and she intended to thank them with a dinner at the Big House, but the thought of doing another thing had her biting back a groan.

Luis stood back, taking photos from different angles to add to the website and social media.

An arm slipped around her waist, and Alyssa laid her head on Georgia's shoulder. "It looks amazing."

"It really does. Thank you," Georgia said, emotion clogging her throat again. Baby hormones.

Just then a car pulled up, and Alyssa's mother got out. She'd been keeping the kids so Alyssa and Dillon could help with the landscaping. As soon as Mrs. Campbell set Delilah on her feet, the little girl ran up the sidewalk. Only she ran straight to Liam, who had his back to her. Grabbing his legs, she yelled, "Daddy!"

A look of utter surprise crossed Liam's face, and Georgia couldn't help but laugh. Twisting around, he looked down at the curly haired little munchkin, and something happened Georgia never expected . . . a grin split his face. "Well, hello there."

Delilah looked up at him with a confused look on her face, as if to say "you're not my daddy."

Georgia could understand the girl's mistaking Liam for Dillon. Liam's build was similar to Dillon's and his hair was close in color. And since Dillon had gone inside to use the bathroom, of all the men outside, Liam most closely resembled her father.

Liam bent to pick her up then balanced her on his hip, and she gazed at him as if mesmerized, and he did the same in return.

Clearly they each knew a beautiful human when they saw one. Delilah had her mother's moss-green eyes and pale-blond hair. And as for Liam, well, any red-blooded female would see the beauty in that face with its day-old scruff, square jaw, and coffee-colored eyes. Delilah laid her hands on either side of Liam's face and grinned, and Georgia's heart puddled at her feet.

Clearly, Liam didn't *dislike* children, so why was he so adamant about having nothing to do with their child? She sighed heavily, which Alyssa must have taken as an expression of fatigue, but then again she wasn't wrong on that count either. "You're tired. You should get some rest."

"But—"

"No buts. We can do dinner another night. Go home, take a hot bath, and put your feet up." She held her hands out for Delilah, who went to her with a smile. "Mommy!"

"She's right," Kristen said, joining them. "It's been a long day of hard labor and I, for one, plan to do just that, while Tyler orders pizza and opens a nice bottle of red."

"What is Tyler doing?" he asked as he stepped up behind his fiancée, laying his hands on her shoulders.

"You're going to rub my feet," she replied with a wink at Georgia and Alyssa.

"Oh. I can do that."

At the moment, Georgia thought, a foot rub—along with a shoulder and back rub—sounded like the most hedonistic pleasure ever.

"Guys," Alyssa announced, "we're going to take a rain check on dinner and let Georgia go home and crash."

"Agreed," Zach chimed in, taking Olivia's hand.

Everyone said their goodbyes. Georgia was not only grateful for their help but for their understanding about dinner. Not that she would admit it to him, but Liam was right. She had exhausted herself.

And speak of the devil. After relinquishing Delilah to Alyssa, Liam had doused himself with the hose, washing off most of the day's grime, and his damp hair curled around his ears. Dang, he was sex on a stick.

Running his hands through his wet hair, he sauntered down the sidewalk toward her like a cat stalking its prey. "You okay?" he asked, an expression of concern on his face.

"I'm tired," she admitted.

"Come on then." He held out a hand to her, and she eyed it.

"Where are we going?"

"Home."

That one syllable word from him made her shiver.

Home. If only.

If only they were married because they were madly in love and not because of some half-baked whim. If only they were anxiously awaiting the birth of their first child. If only they were planning their future together.

But they weren't.

"You can take a hot bath and I'll make something for dinner."

"Oh, but—"

"No buts."

Her grandfather was in Charlotte for the weekend, so she had the Big House to herself. The thought of being alone with Liam in that house, her soaking in a bath while he made dinner, struck her as more intimate than anything they had done that fateful weekend in Las Vegas.

"I'm not a great cook, but I can throw something on the grill and put a decent salad together."

"I'm too tired to argue, so I'll take you up on that offer." She took his hand and they walked to their cars.

As Liam put potatoes in the oven to bake, he tried his best to forget that Georgia was upstairs, right now, naked.

And as he chopped tomato for a salad, he also tried his best to forget what her body had looked like in the shower in Vegas with water coursing down it, following every subtle curve.

And as he sliced a loaf of sour dough bread, he tried his best not to think about how she would look when she stepped glowing and wet from the tub, her breasts flushed from the heat. Breasts that were now more lush and full with her pregnancy.

"Shit!" He stuck the forefinger he'd just cut into his mouth. "Pay attention." Setting the knife aside, we poked around in the cabinets hoping for a Band-Aid. He scored a small first aid kit in a cabinet next to the glasses.

Finger taken care of, he tossed the sliced bread into a basket he'd found and set it on the table. Taking the two steaks out of the fridge—a four-ounce filet mignon for Georgia, an eight-ounce for him—he tried to put his bandaged finger on why he was more attracted to Georgia now than he had been in Vegas. And that was saying something since his attraction to her in Vegas had been pretty intense.

He'd wanted to protect her then and give her everything she'd wanted—including a Las Vegas wedding. Now he wanted to wrap her up in bubble wrap and give her even more.

Except a father for her child, a voice reminded him.

But that was because he'd make a lousy father, he rationalized. Their child, his child, would be better off without him.

He recalled his interaction Delilah. The sound of that diminutive voice yelling "Daddy" just before she'd wrapped her arms around his legs sent a jolt through him. It wasn't a jolt of alarm but rather of elation. For one one-hundredth of a second, he'd imagined she was his. And when she laid her tiny hands against his face and grinned up at him, his heart had melted.

"Hi."

Georgia's voice snapped him out of his reverie, and he nearly dropped the steaks on the floor. Her damp hair curled around her face and shoulders. Her beautiful face devoid of makeup. This was Georgia at her most appealing. Open, comfortable, unguarded.

She'd put on a gauzy loose-fitting dress in a soft blue that reminded him of the summer sky in Provence. He could see the subtle bulge through the thin fabric. The dress fell almost to her ankles, but the spaghetti straps that held it up dialed up the sexy. He imagined if he lifted those straps from her shoulders the dress would whisper down her body and pool at her bare feet, leaving nothing to obstruct his view of her.

He finally found his tongue. "Hi. I was just about to put the steaks on. The salad's ready, and the potatoes are warming in the oven. Hope the menu sounds okay." Suddenly, her good opinion of the menu meant everything to him.

"Sounds delicious." She glanced around, now seemingly shy and unsure of herself.

"Sit. You need to rest. Can I get you a glass of water?"

"I won't argue with you there. Water, with a slice of lemon?"

"Sure."

When he set the glass of ice water on the table, the subtle scent of her soap or shampoo filled his senses and he had to resist the urge to nuzzle her behind the ear and breathe deep.

"I'll just . . ." he pointed to the summer kitchen where the grill awaited the steaks, and he beat a hasty retreat.

CLEAN, sated, and exhausted, Georgia leaned back in her chair and took another sip of water. Liam's dinner had hit the spot. She hadn't been that hungry until Liam set the steak and baked potato in front of her, and suddenly she'd been ravenous.

He must have been starving too because they'd spoken little during dinner, too focused on the food. But it hadn't been an awkward silence. It had felt oddly . . . comfortable.

Sitting back in his chair with his glass of red wine, he broke the silence. "Do you regret it? Meeting? Spending the weekend together? Getting married?" He hesitated. "Getting pregnant?"

Her gaze shot to his. The questions surprised her, and

she worried her bottom lip with her teeth, thinking as she turned her water glass in a circle on the table. Did she? If she had to do it over again, would she change anything? Even getting pregnant?

Skimming a hand over her baby bump she knew the answer.

"No." His shoulders visibly relaxed, and that surprised her too. From all indications, he regretted it. At least the marriage and the pregnancy. Maybe not the weekend-long hookup.

"No?" he asked again.

"No. Maybe I wish it had happened differently." She shrugged. "You know, the more traditional route. The big white wedding, the honeymoon, then the pregnancy."

"Instead we had the honeymoon, a small Las Vegas wedding, and an almost immediate pregnancy, to be followed soon by a divorce." His voice held a note of . . . regret? Sadness?

"Yeah. Just a *tad* out of order." She held up her thumb and forefinger a half-inch apart then dropped her hand to her stomach. "But I could never regret the little butterbean."

He chuckled. "Butterbean?"

She lifted a shoulder, too tired to do more than that. "Yeah." Then she shifted in her seat and moaned. She knew tomorrow she'd feel like one of the trains that still rolled through town had hit her. She hadn't had much opportunity to work out since she'd returned to Northridge, and her body clearly missed the Pilates routine.

"You okay?"

"Just getting tight and sore. Gym workouts aren't the same as hard labor. And my feet feel like I've been standing on a bed of nails all day."

He rose from his seat and knelt at her bare feet. Taking

one of them into his hands, he kneaded the arch of her foot and she resisted the urge to pull away. Not because it didn't feel good. It felt like heaven. But because it was too personal. Too intimate. When he pressed his fingers into the top of her foot, she noticed the Band-Aid on his left forefinger. "What did you do to your finger?"

He looked at it as if he'd forgotten about it. "Oh, the knife slipped when I was slicing the bread."

"Poor baby. Want me to kiss it?" As soon as the words left her lips, she wanted to take them back. How silly! As if the virile and masculine man at her feet needed her to kiss away his booboo.

But apparently he didn't think them silly at all, because his pupils dilated and the air between them crackled with unspent energy. When he lifted it to her, she bent to kiss it, drawn by the heat in his eyes. Then he shook his head and chuckled, making her feel silly all over again, and she sat back with a huff.

"You're going to make a great mom." His gaze locked with hers, and his mouth lifted at the corner.

"I hope so."

"I know so." His hands continued to work their magic on her right foot and calf, and she bit back a moan that bordered on sexual. His big warm hands massaged her calf then back down to her foot. Then he set that foot on the floor and picked up the other one, devoting the same attention to it.

Gazing down on the top of his dark head, a wave of tenderness swept through her and she wanted to place her hand there and stroke his hair. "How do you know? You don't know me. Not really."

"I know you better than you think."

"Pfft."

"You're kind. You love and care for your grandfather and your friends. You work hard. You're going to teach your child to be kind and compassionate, to work hard, to set goals. You're going to teach your child to be just like you."

She blinked back tears, touched by his words. "Thank you." She wondered once again why, given the way he'd interacted with Delilah, he had no intention, or apparently even any desire, to be involved with their child.

Before she could say anything, he patted her foot. "You should go to bed."

Kneeling at Georgia's feet, looking up into her face, so many contradictory emotions ran through him. Tenderness, contentment, lust, fear, regret. He could almost imagine a life with her. A life where he wasn't alone. Where he could call a place home. A place where he could run *to* instead of away *from*.

Almost.

Rising to his feet, he said, "I'll clean up the kitchen and let you get to bed."

"You cooked, I should clean up." She made to rise.

"No. Go to bed, Georgia. I'll lock up when I leave."

She studied his face another moment then nodded in resignation. "Good night, Liam. And thank you. For helping today, for making dinner." A smile touched her lips. "And for the foot rub."

"Good night."

He gathered the dishes from the table and set them on the counter. Bracing his hands on the cold granite, he dropped his head. Georgia was dangerous. She made him feel things he had no business feeling. Made him want things he didn't deserve.

He'd regretted the look of disappointment on her face, but it was for the best. It was clear that she wanted the long haul. What's more, she deserved it. In which case, he wasn't her man. Despite their weekend in Vegas, the impetuous wedding, the baby, it was better for everyone if he didn't get involved with her.

They would follow through on the divorce in November, he'd leave after the mill was operational, and he'd turn his attention to his next endeavor. And maybe someday she would meet the long-haul guy she deserved.

Why did that thought leave him as cold as the granite beneath his hands?

A FEW DAYS LATER, Georgia sat at the breakfast table when her grandad pulled out a chair to join her. "I'm glad to see you're putting on a little weight," he said as he sat.

She nearly spewed her mouthful of orange juice across the table. Swallowing, she glanced down at her slight baby bump then back at her grandfather. "What?"

"When you came back from California you were a might too thin. But since you've been home you've put on a few pounds. They look good on you."

She mentally shook her head.

He wagged a grapefruit spoon at her, as he continued, "And you've got a glow about you. Clearly being back in Northridge suits you."

If he only knew it wasn't Northridge that brought on that glow and those "few pounds," as he'd called them. Her breasts were larger too. Since puberty, she'd been a member of the thirty-four B club. Not too small, but certainly not the kind of breasts one would call spectacular. She'd gone up a cup size and had had to order some new bras. She hadn't even had this baby yet, and it was already costing her.

Recent sales notwithstanding, between the business expenses, the doctor's visits, and the new clothes, she'd be living in her grandfather's house until the kid was in college and she was old and gray. But she was getting ahead or herself. How was she going to afford diapers and baby food? Clothes and shoes and baby furniture? And what about all the other stuff like car seats, strollers, and toys?

Then there were doctor and dentist appointments. And what if the child needed braces? Or she was such a terrible mother that he needed mental health counseling? The average cost of raising a child to adulthood was almost two hundred fifty thousand dollars. And that was *before* college.

Panic set in, and she was second-guessing her decision that the money Liam offered only be set aside for the child's education. But before she started hyperventilating, she reminded herself that she'd be closing on the fourteen-hundred-acre property next week. *Deep breath. You've got this.*

"Now you look a bit peaked. Breakfast not sitting right with you?"

She realized her grandfather was talking to her. "Huh? Oh, no. Just, um, couldn't sleep last night. The, uh, business is really taking off." If you considered the sale of the mill and the one large property "taking off."

He reached over and patted her hand. "I knew you'd be a success. But don't overdo it."

"Thanks, Grandad." She drew in another deep, cleansing breath. One crisis at a time.

"It's a girl."

"What?" Liam blinked in confusion at Georgia standing outside his door.

She cupped her belly then threw her arms out. "It's a girl. Just thought . . . you'd maybe like to know." She chewed on her lower lip, something he'd come to learn signaled she was either thinking or nervous.

He felt almost weak-kneed at the thought of a girl. *Okay then.* He didn't know why, he'd just assumed it would be a boy. A girl. Again, the universe had a sick sense of humor, giving him a girl. But it wasn't *giving* him anything, because he wouldn't (couldn't) be a parent. He thought again of Delilah and how beautiful she was. Would his daughter be beautiful? If she took after her mother she would.

"Hello?"

He focused on Georgia's face again. "Uh, come in." He held the door open for her and after a brief hesitation, she brushed past him, the scent of her perfume drifting in the air. Closing the door, he followed her into the living room.

"Can I get you something? Water? Milk?" He shoved his hands into his pants pockets, unsure what to do with them.

She gave him a blank look. "Milk?"

"Isn't that something you should be drinking? For the baby?" He dropped his gaze to her blossoming stomach. It was almost as if it grew bigger every day. He supposed it did. It wouldn't be long before the secret would be out. He was surprised her grandfather hadn't noticed yet.

She shook her head with a smile. "I'm drinking milk in the mornings."

He nodded, pulled his hands out of his pockets and crossed his arms, feeling awkward. "So, when did you find out?"

"Today. Do you want to see the sonogram?" She took her phone out of her back pocket, an eager look on her face.

Odd flutterings took up residence in his stomach. "Uh, no. That's fine," he said and watched as her face fell. Ah, hell. He didn't mean to hurt her feelings, it was just . . . he had no business getting drawn in. It would be better for everyone involved if he just provided the financial support he'd promised but wasn't a part of this child's life.

He thought of Ben and Cole and wondered whether, if he'd been more responsible, Ben would still be alive and whether Cole would be living a clean productive life without a criminal record and drug addiction. Hell, *Liam* had a criminal record for that matter. It was Liam's crime that had landed Cole in the mess he was in now.

"Look, I'm sorry." He approached her. "I just think, since I'll be leaving, it would be best I not get . . . attached."

"No. You're right. I understand."

SHE BLINKED BACK tears and tried to shake off the pall that had settled over her like a dark cloud following Liam's comments. He was right. The last thing she wanted was to develop a relationship with him, only to have him leave. They would be filing for a divorce, she reminded herself, in less than four months. But God, she longed to see him interact with their daughter the way he did with Delilah.

To distract herself, she looked around the carriage house for the first time since entering.

When she'd lived with her grandparents, the building had been filled with junk—old furniture, boxes of old clothes, books, family china that had been handed down but not used. Absently, she wondered what her grandmother had done with all that junk.

Now, the carriage house welcomed guests with inviting, comfortable furnishings. She supposed it would have made more sense for her to settle here for the time being rather than in her old room. She could have moved here permanently—raised her daughter here.

"Why didn't you move in here when you came back to Northridge?" Liam asked as if reading her thoughts.

She'd turned at his question and shrugged. "I thought Grandad would like the company until I found a house of my own. Are you comfortable here?"

"Yeah. Beats living in a B&B for the next few months. It gives me more peace and privacy than the B&B as well."

She nodded absentmindedly. Her attention returned to the news she'd received today. When the sonographer had glided the wand over her burgeoning belly and stopped, her heart had stuttered, thinking something was wrong. Then the tech's face had broadened into a grin. "You have a girl." Tears sprang to her eyes again at the memory of that moment. The moment the baby became real to her.

"Hey, you okay?" Liam took her by the shoulders, studying her face.

She nodded, unable to speak. Unable to express her feelings. Unable to confess that she wished she had someone by her side to go through this with her. To feel the same joy and awe. Someone to love. And to love her.

Liam gathered her into his arms, setting his chin on top of her head, and it felt so good. So . . . right. Why did he have to be so nice to her?

"A little overwhelmed?" he asked, surprising her.

"Yeah," she muttered against his chest, resisting the urge to nuzzle his neck and breathe in the spicy, musky smell of him. His big, warm hands glided up and down her back in soothing motions and she relaxed against him. The slight bulge of her belly pressed into him, and her breasts grew heavy as her thoughts turned from his comforting embrace to something more carnal.

His thoughts must have been following hers, because his breath shallowed, and the ridge of his growing erection nudged at her baby bump. He drew back and lifted her chin, inching toward her as if she would flee if he moved too fast. Her breath hitched, and he stopped millimeters from her mouth. "I want to kiss you," he murmured.

"I want you to kiss me," she whispered back, her eyes focused on his lips.

He closed the minuscule distance between them and touched his lips to hers in a tender kiss, like a butterfly lighting on a flower. Her arms lifted of their own volition to wrap around his neck and pull him closer.

He complied and the kiss went from tender to hot in zero-point-eight seconds. Rising on tiptoes, she opened her mouth to his tongue, and he groaned, his fingers digging into the flesh at her hips. Rotating them, he backed her up to the foyer wall. Releasing her mouth, he dragged his lips along her jawline to the tender spot where her earlobe met her neck, and she shivered at the wet heat of his mouth.

"God, I want you," he growled against her skin, and she went weak in the knees.

"Oh!" She gasped as something vibrated against her overly sensitive body.

"Shit." He stepped back and dug into the front pocket of his jeans. "Sorry." He looked at the screen and a frown creased his brows. "I, uh ... I have to take this."

"Of course," she panted, her heart beating in double time. And though her body cried out in frustration, her head said the interruption was fortuitous. "I should—" she pointed toward the front door.

"No. Stay."

HE COULDN'T EXPLAIN why he wanted Georgia to stay when he knew this was going to be a difficult conversation. Ordinarily, he wouldn't want anyone around as he aired his dirty laundry.

"This is Liam," he answered. His gazed landed on Georgia's kiss-swollen lips and he reminded himself to focus on the conversation at hand. He wandered over to the wall of windows that looked out over the vast backyard to put some distance between them.

"Mr. Dunbar, this is Sam Haynes."

"Yes, Mr. Haynes. What's the word on Cole?"

"We've been trying to get Cole into a rehab facility, but—"

"But he's got a bad rap at the local facilities."

"In a word, yes. He reluctantly told me he'd been kicked out of the last facility."

"Yeah. Failure to follow facility policies." Turning his back on the view, he sighed, and rubbed the spot between his brows where a headache waited to pounce. "I'd like to get him into Shadow Mountain."

At the mention of the facility, Georgia's head snapped up from her smartphone where she'd been looking at what appeared to be the sonogram she'd wanted to show him. So she knew the facility. He wondered why.

Mr. Haynes snorted into the phone. "Yeah. Good luck with that. They have a waiting list over six months long."

"I know. How much time is the prosecutor going to give you to get him admitted?"

"A week, maybe two if I tell her we're working on it."

"Okay. Let me see what I can do."

"Mr. Dunbar, you do know Shadow Mountain is one of the most expensive rehab facilities in California."

"I do. I'll be in touch." He ended the call and lifted his eyes to Georgia's face. "How do you know about Shadow Mountain?"

"Hello, Realtor to the Stars here." She pointed to herself with both hands. "Plus, I sold the director a house in Lake Tahoe." She hesitated then came to him, placing her hand on his arm. "Who is Cole?"

"My younger brother." He clenched his jaw.

"And he was busted for buying?"

"Yes. He's been addicted to drugs since he was a teenager." Liam had already revealed more of his private life than he normally would, and he had no intention of confessing his role in Cole's addiction.

"I can call the director. See what I can do," she offered.

Liam didn't like asking for help, but he'd do anything for Cole. "I'd appreciate it."

"I can't make any guarantees . . ."

"I know. I just appreciate your help. More than I can say."

She nodded. "I should go. I promised to eat dinner with Grandad, and he'll be wondering where I am."

"Right." He watched her as she walked to the door. "Georgia?"

She turned. "Yes?"

"Please keep this between us."

"Of course." She gave him a sad smile. "You keep my secrets. I'll keep yours."

"So?" Alyssa asked as soon as Georgia sat down at the table on the patio at the Whistle Stop Pub."

"It's a girl."

Alyssa squealed then clamped a hand over her mouth, glancing about her at the other patrons. "Aw, a girl." She sighed, a dreamy look on her face. "I remember when we learned Delilah was a girl. Dillon panicked, saying he knew nothing about raising a little girl. I reminded him we didn't know anything about raising a little boy either. Now the sun rises and sets with her."

A flash of envy went straight to Georgia's heart, threatening to dampen her buzz.

"Have you told Liam?"

"Yeah." She shrugged. "I thought he might like to know."

"And?"

"And . . . he congratulated me but said it was best that he not get . . . attached . . . since he'll be leaving."

A frown creased Alyssa's brow. "So he's not going to be . . . involved?"

Georgia glanced down and shook her head. "It's for the best really." When she looked up again, the expression of sympathy on Alyssa's face had tears clogging her throat.

"Oh, honey." She laid a hand over Georgia's.

"Can we just not talk about it right now?" *Or ever?*

Alyssa nodded then changed the subject. "How are you feeling? Everything else going okay?"

"I'm fine. Starving actually. Can we go ahead and order?"

After placing their orders, Alyssa reached for a small duffle bag Georgia hadn't noticed when she'd arrived. "I brought a few things. Some shorts, a sundress, and some tops."

"Great. This should tide me over until I can get into Atlanta to buy some clothes. I'd buy online, but I don't know what size."

"Abigail's on Main Street carries some maternity clothes—"

"Shh." Georgia looked around to see if anyone was in earshot.

"You know, it's going to become rather obvious at some point, especially in those St. John sheath dresses you're so fond of. You can't hide the pregnancy until the baby is born. And then what? You tell everyone the stork brought her?"

Georgia had gone with a floral green-and-white shirt-waist dress, so she could tie the sash a tad higher than her waist. The pattern also helped camouflage the bulge. "I know. I know. I just want to wait."

Alyssa shook her head in disapproval. "It's your story to tell, but I think you need to tell it sooner rather than later. You need to tell it before someone else does?"

"Who do you mean? Liam?"

"No, I mean the gossips. If you don't tell your story, they'll tell their own, and it won't be very flattering."

"Like the *true* story is any more flattering?"

"At least you control the message. Just sayin'."

Georgia knew Alyssa was right, but she shuddered to think of telling her grandfather. After his comments the other morning, it was clear the time to confess was fast approaching. She just needed the right time. And place. And to visit the Wizard of Oz for some courage.

GEORGIA SETTLED back against the pillows and pulled the blanket up, sighing in relief. The long days that sometimes merged into long evenings of paperwork, the need to tiptoe around her grandfather's speculative glances, the close encounters with Liam, the looming public revelation, and the pregnancy itself were wearing her out.

She reached over and turned off the lamp. Closing her eyes, she concentrated on her breathing the way her favorite L.A. yoga instructor taught her.

"Oh!" Her eyes sprang open at a flutter in her belly so subtle she thought she'd imagined it. She waited. Maybe she *had* imagined it. Another one, this one stronger, had her gasping again. "You *are* real," she muttered in wonder, as her hands glided across her belly.

For the first time, she wondered who her child would resemble. Would she have the strong MacKinnon jaw and blue eyes? Or would she have Liam's dark-brown waves and brown-black eyes? Would she have his full mouth and dimpled chin? She didn't care either way, she thought, as long as her baby was healthy.

The baby moved again, and Georgia laughed with the

shock of it and pressed her hand to the mound, receiving another kick in response. A shiver of pure delight ran down her spine.

Having children had been on her life-list for many years. She had planned to wait a year or so after she and Not-Erik were married to try, but it wasn't something she dwelled on. It would happen when the time was right. She snorted at life's many ironies. The time couldn't be more wrong. And despite that, her excitement grew at the thought of holding the child in her arms, looking into her face, and . . . loving her.

A tremor of fear also ran down her spine. This creature would be totally reliant on Georgia—for everything. Was Georgia up to the task? Would she be a good mom? A good *single* mom, which would require her to juggle her business and her child. And she'd never been very good at juggling. She liked to think she could count on her grandfather's support.

Her grandfather.

A wave of dread came over her when she thought about telling him. Disappointing him. Just like her mother. But she would have to tell him, and soon. He'd already noticed her weight-gain. There was no way she could continue to keep her secret in the next two weeks, when she'd be a full five months pregnant.

The baby lay quiet now, no more kicks, but she knew she was there, safe in her warm cocoon, and Georgia had to believe everything would work out for them both. It had to.

LIAM OPENED the door to the knock, knowing it was either Marshall or Georgia. No one else ever just showed up at his door.

"Hi." She gave him a small smile, and his stomach dropped like it does when you lift off the ground in a jet. "Are you busy?"

"No. What's up?"

She held up a sheaf of papers. "I have some forms you'll need to complete for the divorce."

Ah. Right. The divorce. A ridiculous feeling of disappointment filled him.

"We still have time, but I thought I'd give these to you since you might want your lawyers or accountants to provide some of the information, like the financial affidavit."

"Come in."

She breezed past him, the light scent of her perfume following in her wake, and his abdomen tightened. Jesus. She was here with divorce papers and all he could think about was taking her to bed. Or the sofa. Or the chair. Hell, even the floor would do.

She laid the papers on the bar and he stepped up beside her. Flipping through the pages, she stopped on a page that read: DOMESTIC RELATIONS FINANCIAL AFFIDAVIT OF DEFENDANT.

"The baby has complicated things," she said almost apologetically, like it was somehow her fault. "Otherwise we wouldn't need to complete the forms."

"It's not a problem, Georgia," he said, a note of resignation in his voice that said, *not getting the annulment we agreed upon complicated things.*

She looked up at him, her blue eyes studying his face, and he couldn't help his gaze dropping to her lips. And any annoyance he had over their tangled legal affairs dissipated.

"Georgia, I—"

She licked her lips, eyes wide and unblinking. "Is it weird that we're talking about divorce, and I want you to kiss me?"

His breath caught, he shook his head, unable to speak.

She lifted her face to his and that was it. Raising his hand to her face, he lowered his mouth to hers. Their lips touched and it was like setting a match to a stick of dynamite. He hauled her against him, breasts to thighs and everything in between. She moaned as his tongue swept into her mouth, tangling with hers. Gripping his hair, she took control of the kiss, ramping up the heat and sending what little blood was still in his brain to parts south.

He broke the kiss, almost smiling at her whimper of disappointment. But when he moved to her neck and the tender spot near her ear, the whimper turned into a gasp. Lifting her chin, she gave him better access to her soft, heated skin.

When she pressed into his erection, he hissed out a breath. "Georgia," her name came out husky, "I want you. Bad." It took everything he had, but he released her and stepped back. "But if you don't want this, tell me now."

She didn't say anything, just stepped into him, wrapped her arms around his neck, and standing on tiptoe kissed him again.

17

Georgia had come to the carriage house to drop off paperwork for the divorce, and now she was kissing Liam like he was her food, water, and oxygen rolled into one. Her brain poked at her, but her body told it to buzz off.

His hands skimmed her rib cage from hip to breast, each pass feeding the fire and need. As his mouth found her collar bone, nipping and licking the skin, his hands drifted lower until they'd reached the hem of the simple A-line dress she wore. Lifting the hem, he stepped back and pulled the dress over her head, leaving her in nothing but her blue lace bra and panties.

They both looked down at the swell of her abdomen, and she wondered what he was thinking, but she was afraid to ask. Did it turn him off? Did he think it hideous? The last time he saw her naked, her stomach had been flat and tight, thanks to all the Pilates she'd been doing in L.A.

He placed a tentative hand on her stomach and she almost leaned into it. "Will this be okay?"

She tipped her forehead against his chest and nodded,

mesmerized by the image of his big tanned hand against the pale bulge of her flesh.

He scooped her up in his arms and she gasped in surprise. Looping her arms around his neck, she pressed her mouth against the heat of his throat while he carried her to what she presumed was the bedroom. Placing her gently on the bed, he gazed down at her and she shivered with desire. He wanted her. The erection straining against the front of his jeans a rather obvious indication.

He sat beside her on the bed then reached out a finger to trace the lace lines of her bra along the swell of her breasts, sending shivers along her spine. "You are so beautiful, Georgia. So fucking beautiful." Then, as if he could no longer resist, he bent over her and traced the same line with his tongue.

When he pressed his mouth to her hardened nipple through her bra, she arched off the bed with a cry of shock and desire. "Liam!" Her breasts had become even more sensitive with the pregnancy, as if the nerve endings had increased tenfold. She felt his smile against her breasts, then he flicked open the front clasp of her bra and took a bared nipple into his hot, wet mouth.

Grasping his hair, she kept him there until she was writhing with need. "Please, Liam. Now."

He rose and made quick work of her panties and his own clothes, until he was standing naked in all his sexually aroused glory. Opening the nightstand drawer, he took out a condom and knelt on the bed.

But she stayed his hand before he could open it. "Have you been with anyone since Vegas?"

"No." His response almost indignant. "Why?"

She gave a little shrug. "I'm already pregnant and I know we're both clean because my doctor tested me for everything under the sun." Heat rose to her face as she whispered the next words. "I want to feel you."

He growled then tossed the condom onto the nightstand. Opening her legs, he knelt between them, but instead of entering her, he slid a finger inside her, making her hips buck at the sweet invasion. Groaning, he closed his eyes for a moment then opened them again to watch as he stroked her. She'd never experienced anything so erotic. All his attention centered on her core.

The tension built to such an intensity that she thought she might burst if she didn't obtain release. Just as she climaxed, Liam plunged into her, sending her up, up, up until she thought she might shatter.

LIAM GROANED as he entered her, the spasms from her orgasm squeezing him, sending him into paroxysms of desire. "Jesus, Georgia," he panted, clamping down on his need to find his own release. He was thirty-five years old, and this was the first time in his life he'd ever had sex without a condom. The feeling was . . . indescribable and his body screamed for more.

But he held still inside her until the spasms eased. He wanted to send her flying again before he found his own satisfaction.

Georgia gripped his ass, urging him to move, and he complied with extreme pleasure. He slid out and back in in a tortuous slow motion, prolonging the pleasurable feel of her wet hot heat around him. But as her breathy pants increased and her nails dug into his flesh, he could no longer hold himself in check.

Driving into her faster and harder, her hips thrusting to

meet his, he sailed over the precipice with her this time, her name on his lips.

LIAM ROLLED off her then pulled her to him, tucking her against his side. He all but sighed in contentment when she draped her arm across his body and laid her head on his chest. They lay that way for a few minutes, no sound in the room but their breath returning to normal.

"I'll go slower next time." Assuming there would be a next time. He stroked her arm then smiled at her husky "Mmm."

"Good?" He couldn't help himself—he had to ask.

"*Very* good," she murmured.

He'd never been a cuddler. He didn't date. He didn't do relationships. They complicated an already-complicated life. One that required he move on every few months. He held back a snort as Georgia's arm slid across his belly—case in point. Although he didn't believe he used women—he always made sure there was a mutual understanding—he was more of a wham, bam, thank you ma'am kind of guy.

Georgia had been the first woman to spend the night with him. And now the first woman he'd enjoyed without a condom. Add to that list the first woman he'd married, the first woman he'd impregnated, and the first woman he'd divorce, and this woman was fast becoming a lot of firsts for him. And he really didn't know that much about her. He recalled what she'd said when she offered to speak to the director of Shadow Mountain—*Hello, Realtor to the Stars.* What had she meant by that?

"Tell me about L.A. About being Realtor to the Stars."

"What?" She lifted her head, her eyes glazed with a post-coital fog.

"I want to know about your life in L.A."

She sat up, shoving the mass of tangled curls out of her face. She'd never looked more adorable. Or sexier. Then she pulled the covers up over her breasts and he nearly sighed in disappointment.

She shrugged and said, "I sold real estate in Southern California, primarily L.A. and Malibu."

He eyed her then rolled his hand as if to say, *and what else*.

Frowning, she gnawed on her lower lip. Her *tell* that she was nervous. Why would that be? he wondered. When she didn't offer more information, he tried an easier question. "Why California?"

"I went to college at Berkley, then law school at Stanford, and I just . . . stayed."

He whistled his appreciation. "A smart cookie then."

"I enjoyed real estate law, so I got my real estate license then learned the business as a junior agent at a high-profile real estate agency." She adjusted her position, careful to keep the sheet covering her, more's the pity. "I thought I'd stay and work my way up, but . . ."

"But?"

"I met Erik and we started dating."

"The ex, I take it?

"Um, yeah."

"What does he have to do with your job at the real estate agency?"

"He was also a junior agent, but my sales far eclipsed his. He talked me into striking out on our own. He made it sound so . . . exciting."

"And was it?"

"It was. At first. We left and started Beverly Hills Realty. I had a trust fund from my grandparents. We used most of that for the startup costs. Erik said we needed to look successful if we were going to sell multi-million dollar Bel Air mansions."

"And did Erik put in money?" He already didn't like the sound of this.

She shrugged. "He did. Just not as much." Her expression turned thoughtful for a moment, then she continued. "We had different but complementary personalities. Erik relied on my law degree and knowledge of mortgages and contracts. He knew if he had to deal with those aspects of the business he would never make it. Also, where I was the hand-holder—the nurturer—Erik was the rainmaker. He loved rubbing elbows with the rich and famous. But for whatever reason he couldn't close the sale."

She shrugged again. "I didn't mind. He brought in the business and I sold the property. We became L.A. power brokers in the high-end real estate market. Two years after we started the business, we were named best brokers in L.A. We had more business than we could handle. We hired more agents and more support staff. Moved to our own four-story building."

"We earned a reputation. Celebrities trusted me—us—to buy and sell their multi-million-dollar homes. My clients knew I wouldn't kiss and tell. I became friends with many of them. That's how I came to be in Las Vegas with Audrey Turner. I sold her a house on Malibu Beach and she became one of my closest friends. Erik and I had succeeded beyond my wildest dreams."

But her sad smile said quite the opposite. She stopped, and he got a sinking feeling in his gut, and he remembered what she'd said in Vegas the night he met her. *I learned he wasn't the man I thought he was.* "Georgia, it sounds like you were a tremendous success. It didn't all end just because you and Erik broke up. What happened?"

SHE RAN a finger through her mussed hair and grimaced. "To be honest, the California scene was beginning to wear on me. I had clients use coke right in front of me."

He shook his head. "For a teetotaler, that had to be quite a shock."

"One time was while I was in the same car. All I could think about was getting pulled over with coke in the car."

Not-Erik often called her too sanctimonious. Told her she was lucky to have him around. If it weren't for him, she would either still be working as an agent or she'd be a quaint little real estate office. He'd made her big-time. Which wasn't true. She knew people sought her out because she was not only a good salesperson but because she was honest and trustworthy. People respected her. Which was also why it had been so important to pay off her creditors despite the personal sacrifices she had to make after Not-Erik was arrested and she learned he'd stolen almost everything from her.

"Georgia, there's more," his quiet voice brought tears to her eyes. Baby hormones, she thought, as she blinked them back. He took her hand in his and lifted it to his lips, and she looked at him, seeing nothing but compassion and understanding on his face.

With a shuddering breath, she said, "Erik was arrested for fraud and money laundering. A prior crime. But as it turned out, he'd also cooked the books. My books."

"Son of a bitch," he muttered.

"It's partly my fault—"

"Bullshit."

She shook her head. "It is. I should have paid more attention. When I received that first phone call from American Express saying the previous month's bill hadn't been paid, I should have checked into it. But Erik handled the finances—he was an accounting major—he assured me it had merely been an oversight. That he would talk to the woman in accounts payable."

Squeezing her eyes shut, she continued. "The reputation I worked so hard to build was gone almost overnight. Not only because of his arrest. Erik took almost every dime I had, leaving me and the business deep in debt."

"Mother fucker," he ground out.

"Erik wasn't even his real name. I was about to take the name of a man that wasn't his to give."

"Are you serious?" Liam asked, disbelief in his voice.

"Yep. It was one of several aliases he used. Alyssa and I renamed him Not-Erik. Anyway, he knew his current scheme was coming to an end. He hadn't been paying the bills for over six months, or only paying the bare minimum to avoid the collections calls. And yet, he was going to marry me. Or at least I thought he was. Who knows? He may have left me at the altar instead. The FBI said he was planning his exit."

"You really dodged a bullet."

"I did. I know I did, but it doesn't assuage the pain of betrayal. Before the trip to Vegas, I sold just about every thing I owned to pay off the debts. My house in Malibu, the real estate office, furniture, computers, everything. When it was all said and done, I paid every single creditor, some-thing I'm proud of, despite the loss of my business. I may have lost everything, but at least I could hold my head high knowing I had done the right thing by the people with whom I did business."

He squeezed her to him for a moment but didn't speak.

"As for my employees, well, I hadn't been in a position to help them. I'd had to lay off every one of them, but I helped as many as I could find work in other agencies." It was one of the toughest times of her life, besides when her mother died, but she'd pressed on and made it out the other side. Sort of. Now she faced another tough road ahead.

"You *should* be proud of yourself. Most people would have declared bankruptcy and washed their hands of the mess."

Those words coming from Liam were a balm to her.

"No wonder you needed a weekend in Las Vegas."

She laughed at that. "Yeah."

"And you returned to Northridge."

"I had enough money left in my trust fund to buy the real estate business here and to get back to Northridge. I did manage to keep my car, and some of my designer shoes and clothes. But everything else . . ." she shrugged.

"Did you report it to the police?"

"Of course."

"And?"

"They're investigating. I turned over all my records." She groaned. "I was such an idiot."

He shifted to face her and took her by the shoulders. "You're not an idiot. You trusted that asshole because you are, by nature, a trusting person."

"If I'd been honest with myself, I would have realized I'd settled for Erik. It happened so gradually that I didn't notice that I began letting go of the things that were important to who I was." She rambled on, unsure why she was telling him all this, but it felt good to get it out. "I'd overlooked his dabbling in designer drugs, his companions from the seedier side of Hollywood, and his extravagant spending habits, which became more extravagant over the years."

"Then there were the parties at my Malibu beach house. Yes, many of my own friends were there, but gradually, my friends were outnumbered by his 'friends,' if you could even call them that. And though I'd made Erik promise there would be no drugs at the parties, I found paraphernalia on more than one occasion."

When she'd confronted him about it, he'd told her it was no big deal. Everyone in Hollywood did it. Except her. Except many of her friends. But even with all that, she'd never have expected him to do what he did. Because she *had* trusted him.

"I put up with his judgment of me. It took his arrest and his theft to make me realize I felt less-than with him. I'll never do that again. I'll never settle for less than I deserve."

"You shouldn't have to settle. You deserve to be respected and admired. You're the strongest woman I know."

His heart ached for her. If he could get his hands on this Erik, or whatever his name was, he'd gladly make him pay. He felt her shake her head in disagreement against his shoulder.

"You are. And you're going to make a success of your new business."

She snorted. "Without the sale of the mill to you, I don't know what I would have done. I just couldn't tell my grandfather."

"Then I'm glad I could help."

"Me too."

"But you should tell him. He'll understand."

She shook her head. "I don't want to disappoint him."

"I don't think he will be disappointed. I think he'll be proud."

After a few moments of silence, he said, "Come here." He pulled her back into his arms and slid down into bed, cradling her to him.

Exhausted after reliving the events of the last year, she fell asleep.

18

Hot and hungry, Georgia breezed into the office intent on the salad she had in the refrigerator.

"Honey, is that you?" Luis called from the direction of her office.

"Yes, dear. Be right there." She giggled at their antics then headed for the kitchen. Grabbing the salad and a bottle of Perrier out of the fridge, she stopped by Luis's desk to check for messages before entering her office.

"Surprise!" Luis held his hands out, gameshow-model style.

On the wall directly behind him he'd created a photo collage of what appeared to be black-and-white photos of Northridge from the nineteen-hundreds.

"Wow. That looks amazing."

"I found them in the antique store on Oak Street. They were taken by a photographer at the now-defunct *Northridge Gazette*."

Setting her lunch on her desk, she approached the display.

The black-and-white photos of the town were all the

same size and taken from various angles, making them perfect for a grouping on the wall above the small conference table he'd found last week. He'd purchased basic white frames trimmed with a fine strip of silver so that the images were the focal point.

It was interesting to see the old photos of characteristic Northridge buildings like the Old Bank, the livery stable that now housed Firehouse Brews Tap Room, the Northridge Hotel which was home to her grandfather's law offices, and the First Bank of Northridge, now the chic wine bar and restaurant. There were also photos of the old ice cream parlor that was now Sweet Creams Ice Cream, the hardware store where Pints and Paints was currently located, the General Store that was now Beans 'n Books, and the train station, now the Whistle Stop Pub.

She peered closely at the photo of the train station and gasped.

"What?" Luis asked, sounding alarmed. "Did the little princess kick?"

Luis had taken to calling the baby that since he found out it was a girl, and Georgia was charmed. The baby may not have a father in her life, but she would have lots of people who loved her.

"No." She lifted a finger to the photo of a dapper gentleman with a cane standing outside the train station. "This is my third-great-grandfather, Alistair Calder MacKinnon."

"Get out." Luis leaned in to get a better look. "Handsome devil," he muttered. "What are the odds I'd buy a photo with your great-great-great-grandfather in it?"

"Right?" She turned and saw another surprise. "What's this?"

"An area for the little princess," Luis said as if it was obvious. And, of course, it was.

A white wicker bassinet stood in the corner next to a matching changing table. On the wall above the changing table, Luis had hung colorful cloth letters that spelled out "Little Princess."

"Oh, Luis." She blinked away the tears in her eyes. "That is the most thoughtful idea. Thank you."

"Don't get all misty on me," he muttered.

"Can I get all mushy on you instead?" she asked, right before giving him a big fat kiss on the mouth.

"Hi."

Liam glanced up from the blueprints on the makeshift table of sawhorses and plywood to see Georgia standing in the doorway of the mill looking as fresh as a ripe peach.

"Hi." Pregnancy suited her, he thought, then shook his head at the foolishness of the thought.

She shrugged, looking a little sheepish. "I was driving by and decided to stop and check on the progress."

Liam liked that she wanted to stop by. Probably liked it more than he should have. "Here." He picked up a hardhat and handed it to her.

"Thanks." She set it on her head and grinned. "How do I look?"

He chuckled. "Adorable." He lifted the hat from her head and readjusted the strap before returning it with a snugger fit.

Georgia's face flushed and she surveyed the stacks of building supplies. The sound of nail guns and shouts punctuated the air. "Love what you've done with the place," she shouted to be heard over the din.

Liam chuckled. "Yeah. Not much to see yet but," he pointed upward, "we do have brand new trusses and the rest of the roof will go on this week."

"That's progress." She joined him at the table and the light scent of her perfume filled the air, a pleasant distraction from the smell of sawdust, treated wood, and sweat from the construction workers.

He eyed her belly. At this point, how could anyone not notice her pregnancy? Least of all her grandfather. "Have you told him yet?" He didn't need to specify. She knew exactly who he was talking about.

She sighed as her finger traced the lines of the roof on the blueprint. "No. I'm telling him this afternoon."

Liam saw the worry in her eyes and a surge of guilt washed over him. He was the reason she was in this situation. He should have walked away that night. Should never have taken her to his room. To his bed. And yet, the time with Georgia had been special. Something he would never forget. Knowing that, would he change that if he could? Seeing the concern etched on her face, he thought, yes, he would. If it would make Georgia's life easier. But despite her concern, she'd said she had no regrets.

"I'll go with you."

"No. Thank you, but no. This is something I have to do alone."

A thought struck him. One he didn't like and he didn't know why. "And will you tell him I'm the father, or will you tell him it's your ex's?" His insides clenched, waiting for her response.

She stared at him, her gaze steady on his, as if searching his face for the answer. "If I'm telling him I'm pregnant, I'm going to tell him the truth. All of it." She hesitated. "Unless you don't want me to." The last was said in a whisper.

"No. I want you to tell him it's mine. I don't run from my responsibilities." As long as that responsibility doesn't extend to actual parenting. As promised, he will ensure the child has the best of everything, from toys to clothes, health-care to education. Be he could not be a father to this child, he reminded himself. Not with his track record.

"And the marriage?"

She shook her head. "No. I can't tell him that. It would break his heart if he knew we were married but getting a divorce before the baby was born."

"I understand."

Sighing, she looked forlorn and friendless, though he knew she wasn't. He had the strongest urge to take her in his arms, kiss her on the head, and tell her everything would be all right. But how could he do that when he wasn't sure it was the truth?

GEORGIA'S GRANDFATHER sat in the swing on the back porch, a glass of lemonade in his hand. "Mind if I join you?" she asked.

He slid over and patted the seat next to him. "I'd love it."

The sun was setting and a light breeze stirred in the pine trees, lifting the scent of pinesap in the heavy September air, eliciting memories of her childhood. She and her grandad would often sit and swing discussing her school day as dusk turned to evening. She'd often shared her hopes and dreams with him, cherishing his unwavering support.

But the moment of reckoning had come, and it was as good a time as any.

Grandad wrapped an arm across her shoulder and pulled her in to kiss her forehead. Tears clogged her throat. God, why did she have to disappoint him?

Taking a deep breath, she said, "I need to tell you something."

"Well, that sounds ominous."

It is. "I'm pregnant."

"It's about time," he said, followed by a gusty sigh.

"What?" She squeaked and spun to face him.

"Do I look like I just fell off the turnip truck?" he asked with a snort.

"Uh, no, but . . . how did you know?"

His gaze dropped to her belly. "I'd have to be blind not to know."

She lifted a hand then dropped it in her lap. "Then why didn't you say something?"

"Not my place to say anything. *You* needed to be the one to tell *me*."

She sat there dumbfounded a few moments.

"Is it Erik's, sugar?" His voice held a note of disappointment.

She could understand this reaction because it would mean she'd been with Not-Erik even after his arrest. She cleared her throat. "No."

"Thank goodness," he muttered. "Then whose?" he asked, his voice soft but with an edge to it.

"It's Liam's."

This time her grandfather spun to face her in shock. "Liam? But I thought you two just met?"

"Well, no. Remember I told you I decided to take my, er, honeymoon since it was non-refundable? I met Liam in Vegas." Heat crept into her face. There was no denying what she'd done in Vegas. With Liam.

"And did he follow you here?"

She had to tread carefully here. "That was a coincidence really." It kind of was. "Apparently, he was interested in the mill property before we met in Vegas, so it was not out of the question that we would meet again." Georgia resisted the urge to squirm beneath her grandfather's inquisitive gaze. She could practically see the cogs turning as they analyzed the information she'd given him, searching for any flaws in the story.

He leaned back in the swing, folding his arms over his chest, careful not to spill the lemonade. "Is that man going to do right by you and the child or do I have to have a talking-to with him?"

"It's . . . complicated." Before he could interrupt, she held up her hands, stopping him and said, "But he's doing enough."

Her grandfather frowned. "I'm not suggesting he marry you, after all it *is* the twenty-first century, but he *is* the child's father."

She gulped. Should she tell him the truth while she's spilling her guts? No. It would only hurt him to know that they were already married but getting a divorce as soon as possible despite her pregnancy. And an impulsive marriage to a stranger would go against his sensibilities, twenty-first century notwithstanding. *And sleeping with a stranger didn't?* a voice asked.

"He needs to take some responsibility," her grandfather continued. "After all, it takes two to make a baby."

Heat rose in her face again. "Um, yes. Well, he's setting up a trust for the baby. He's a man of his word, and he's said the child will lack for nothing."

"Except a father."

"And a grandfather," she said quietly. "I never had a

father, but I had the best grandfather in the world. And she'll have the best great-grandfather in the world."

His face softened, his eyes filled, and he smiled. "It's a she?"

"It is." She slid a hand over her growing abdomen. She'd been playing with names and had finally landed on one. "Lillian Charlotte MacKinnon." By the time the baby was born, Georgia would be divorced, so Dunbar wasn't an option.

He lifted his gaze to hers. "For your mother and grand-mother," he said, his voice choked with emotion.

"Lily for short." She gave him a moment to compose himself, but before she could say anything else, he spoke. "Why didn't you tell me sooner?"

"I didn't want to disappoint you." Tears filled her own eyes.

"As if you could ever disappoint me." He wrapped an arm around her again and she leaned against his chest.

"But I know how much my mother disappointed you, and here I am practically following in her footsteps."

A quizzical look came over his face. "Disappointed? Why would you ever think that?"

"Well, she didn't exactly live the life you wanted for her."

"No one can ever live the life someone else wants for them. Everyone has to live their own life. If I'd lived the life my father wanted for me, I'd be in the Georgia state legisla-ture, or maybe the governor's mansion." He shuddered.

Her grandfather was much more at home helping the people of Northridge than standing behind a podium making political speeches.

He reached down and squeezed her hand. "My only disappointment for your mother was that she never found happiness. It was as if she was always searching for . . .

something, and it stayed just out of her reach." He was silent a moment, clearly thinking back. Then he shook his head and released her hand.

"You're hardly following in her footsteps. You're thirty-two, where she was eighteen. You have your education, a profession, a business. You can provide a stable home. Besides, if anyone is to blame for your mother's actions, it's me and your grandmother. We were overindulgent. Enablers is what they call them these days. We let her get away with too much. But she was our only child." A sad smile crossed his face. "A gift. We thought we'd never be blessed with a child of our own. So we spoiled her."

He paused, took a sip of his lemonade, and then continued. "They say if you raise your child, you can spoil your grandchildren, but if you spoil your child, you'll raise your grandchildren." Another sad smile touched his face. "Truer words were never spoken. Not that I have any regrets about raising you. You were never a burden to me or your grandmother. You know that, right?"

He gave her shoulder a squeeze and she nodded, swallowing hard. Other than the marriage, it was time to tell him everything. "There's something else." The thought of telling her grandfather about her own stupidity filled her with dread.

He dropped his arm from around her shoulders and gripped her hand. "The baby? Everything is okay? She's healthy?"

She glided her hands over her sleeping child. "She's healthy. No, it's something I should have told you after Erik was arrested. But let me finish before you ask any questions."

He hesitated then nodded.

When she'd finished her story, her grandfather sat in

silence, his brow furrowed, his free hand clasped in fists where it rested on his thigh, and she felt heartsick.

"I've made so many stupid mistakes. Erik, getting swindled, an unplanned pregnancy . . ." he started to speak, but she shook her head. "All I ever wanted to do was make you proud. And I've failed utterly."

Tears trickled down her cheeks, but before she could wipe them away, her spry grandfather was kneeling in front of her, his hands on either side of her face, his thumbs capturing the tears. "Listen to me, Georgia. You must listen. You have not failed. You have not embarrassed me. You have not ruined your life." He pressed his forehead to hers. "I could never be more proud of you than I am now. You have handled adversity with such grace, such tenacity . . . you should be proud."

"Anyone can succeed in life when everything goes smoothly, but it takes someone special to succeed despite the obstacles, and you've done just that. Your business is growing, you're gaining a reputation as an excellent realtor, I think Luis worships at your feet, and now you're going to make me a great-grandfather!" He beamed and slapped himself on the knee. "How about that? And you know what else? You're going to be a great mom, single or not."

She leaned over and hugged him, blinking back more tears. "Thank you." She kissed his cheek. "I love you."

"I love you too, sugar." He stood and reclaimed his seat next to her on the swing. "Now, when can I expect to see my great-granddaughter?"

"My due date is January twenty-fourth."

He chuckled. "Maybe we'll get lucky and she'll be born a few days early—on your grandmother's birthday."

The heavy weight on her heart had lifted. Despite the

mess she had made of her life, her grandfather loved her, and she laughed with the relief of it. "Maybe we will."

LIAM KNOCKED at the backdoor to the Big House. Marshall opened the door and gestured for him to come in, a grim expression on his face. "We'll meet in my office."

Uh-oh. So this wasn't going to be a casual sit-down.

When he'd returned to the carriage house that afternoon, he'd found a note from Marshall taped to the front door saying he wished to meet with him. He didn't need a crystal ball to know what the meeting would be about. Georgia had clearly told him.

He followed Marshall down a hall to an office facing the vast backyard. Richly furnished in dark masculine furniture —antiques from the looks of it, the office exuded wealth and stature. Above the fireplace hung an enormous oil portrait of a man dressed in the style of the late eighteen-hundreds, complete with a pocket watch chain draped from his vest button to a pocket. He stared down his nose at the room's occupants, sure of his place in the world.

Liam couldn't imagine what it was like growing up in your ancestral home, sure in the knowledge of your family and their history. Sure in the knowledge of who your father was.

Marshall indicated Liam should sit in the guest chair while he sat behind the imposing desk. A power play then. Okay. Liam got it. Georgia was his beloved granddaughter, and Marshall was going to make Liam pay for putting her in this situation.

"You got my granddaughter pregnant," Marshall began, pulling no punches.

"All due respect, sir, Georgia was an active participant as well."

Marshall's cheeks flushed a bright red, and he cleared his throat. He clasped his hands and set them on the desk in front of him. "Yes, well, the question now is what do you plan to do about it?"

Marshall clearly wanted to keep this interaction formal, so Liam acquiesced. "Georgia and I have discussed it. I will ensure the child is financially secure. She will want for nothing. If Georgia is so inclined, the child can attend the finest schools, participate in whatever extracurricular activities she desires, travel, attend college without acquiring debt, and any monies left in the trust after her needs have been met will be hers to do with as she pleases once she turns twenty-five."

"And what about you?"

"Me, sir?"

"Yes. I'm not suggesting you marry Georgia—"

Oh, the irony. If he only knew . . .

"But it seems you would want to be involved with your daughter's life."

"Georgia and I believe it is best if I am not involved. My business ventures take me all over the world. American Threads is just one of my companies. I'll be leaving Northridge as soon as the mill is up and running, and at this point, I see no reason to return on a regular basis. The Redmond Mill is the last of the properties I'll restore for American Threads. We already have fourteen factories making textiles and clothing, more than enough to meet the market demand. I'll be moving on to my next venture."

"So, my great-granddaughter will be raised by a single mother?"

"Sir, Georgia and I have agreed it is best for all

concerned. And while Georgia will be a single mom, I have no doubt she will be an amazing mom."

He studied Liam as one would study a bug under a microscope, and for the first time in a very long time, Liam felt like a reprimanded child. And he felt like he'd disappointed the man, which bothered him more than he thought it would. To have the respect of a man like Marshall MacKinnon was priceless, but if the man had had any respect for him, it was surely gone now.

At last, Marshall spoke again. "I only want what is best for Georgia and the child. She has assured me that she is fully prepared to raise the child herself. I don't like it, but I will accept it. It is, after all, the twenty-first century. The last thing I want is for her to be in an unhappy marriage undertaken for the sole purpose of providing the child with a father."

Liam resisted the urge to shift uncomfortably in his seat. And what about a marriage undertaken on a whim? he thought. How would Marshall feel about that?

The gentleman held up a hand. "But hear this, if you fail to follow through on your promise to financially support my great-granddaughter, I will come after you with all the power of the laws of the State of Georgia. Do I make myself clear?"

The reputed formidable advocate drove his point home by jabbing his finger into the top of his desk with every word.

"Yes, sir." And Liam had no doubt he was a man of his word.

With the weight of (most of) her secrets off her shoulders, Georgia entered the office with big plans. Plans she hoped Luis would be on board with.

"Morning, sunshine." Luis said from behind his desk. He always managed to make it into the office before she did.

"Morning."

He tilted his head and studied her. "How are you feeling? Any more queasiness?"

"No. Thank goodness!" She'd escaped morning sickness almost immediately after the end of her first trimester.

"Good. But there's something." He waved a finger in front of her face. "What's cooking in that brain of yours?"

She laughed and shook her head. Luis was probably the most perceptive person she'd ever met. "Funny you should ask." She slapped the multiple listing service printout onto the desk in front of Luis. "Want to flip a house?"

He pulled the pages toward him, reading the details.

"It's a foreclosure and we can get it for a song," she said as he read. She had all the details memorized. A twenty-five-hundred-square-foot two-story American Craftsman cottage, three-bedroom two-and-a-half-bath on a half-acre lot.

She tapped her foot with nervous energy. She couldn't do this without Luis, especially now. If he wasn't game, she'd have to pass on it.

"Could be promising. We should look at it."

"Really? You'd be willing to partner on this?"

"Sure. We can go in halfsies and split the profit when it sells."

"Yes!" She gave a little fist-pump. "Do you want to see it?"

"Now?"

She held up her hand dangling a key. "Yes."

Less than five minutes later they pulled up in front of the house. And less than thirty seconds after that her shoulders sagged in disappointment. The exterior wasn't bad. It needed a fresh coat of paint but otherwise appeared sound. The yard needed work, of course. But the interior—one look after opening the front door was all it took. And after touring the house, picking their way around debris, Georgia groaned. "It's a real fixer-upper, isn't it?" She wrinkled her nose. The previous owners had trashed the place when they left, ripping out toilets and appliances, tearing out the carpet, even removing what must have been granite countertops in the kitchen.

"Who does this to a defenseless house?" Luis muttered. He stood, hands on his lean hips, and surveyed the wreckage. But instead of the destruction, she hoped he was visualizing the possibilities. "Well, absconding with the countertops and appliances actually helps us."

"How's that?"

"Because, now there's nothing stopping me from completely revamping the kitchen."

"Other than cost, you mean?"

"We'd have to replace everything anyway. This way we can replace it with our own vision."

"You mean *your* vision."

"Of course!" He kicked a broken floor tile. "Let's do it."

"You sure? It's going to be a lot of work." She looked down at her protruding stomach. "And I'm not going to be much help."

He nodded without glancing at her, and she could see the wheels turning behind his eyes as he studies the space. "Yes."

THAT NIGHT, standing in the checkout line at Smith's, Georgia overheard her name from one register over.

"Yeah, have you seen her stomach? There's no question she's pregnant."

"I wonder who the father is?"

"She just moved back to Northridge from Hollywood. Maybe it's some movie star's."

The other woman snorted. "Or maybe some rock star's."

"I heard she was having an affair with a married man," yet another woman said.

Georgia gasped. Where did *that* ugly rumor come from? Heat rose to her face as she glanced up at the young man scanning her groceries. With any luck, he either didn't hear them or didn't know she was the subject of the gossips.

"No! Really?"

"You're not old enough to remember her mother, but she got pregnant at eighteen. No one ever knew who the father was then either."

"Didn't she die in a car accident?"

"Yes, and left her an orphan."

Georgia blinked back tears. Come on, Georgia thought, can't we get these groceries scanned and bagged quicker? She didn't even know who was speaking, but she'd just try to get out of the store without running into them.

"Will there be anything else?"

Georgia glanced up at the checkout clerk. "Huh? Oh, no. Thanks." She quickly swiped her credit card and turned to the shopping cart and headed for the exit.

"Ma'am. Ma'am?"

Stopping, she peered over her shoulder. "What?"

"Your receipt?"

She shook her head and fled for the parking lot.

"Wʜᴀᴛ's ᴜᴘ?" Alyssa asked, a breathless note in her voice. "Is it the baby?" She'd called almost the moment Georgia sent her the text.

"No. Yes. Well, no. I'm fine. We're fine." *Stop babbling.* "It's just . . . you were right."

"Nice to know. About what?"

"About the gossips."

"Uh-oh. What happened?"

Georgia told Alyssa about the three anonymous women in the grocery store and the lie about an affair with a married man.

"No, they did not!"

"Yes, they did. You said the gossips will tell their own story and that it wouldn't be flattering. I should have listened."

"Oh, honey. I'm so sorry. What are you going to do?"

"I don't know. What *can* I do? I have no idea who they were."

"You can tell your own story—at least the story you want to tell. Come out about it. The more you try to hide it, the more elaborate and vicious the stories will become."

Georgia rubbed her forehead, hoping to forestall the headache developing there.

"You need to own it, Kristen-style. To face people down until they think twice about gossiping about you."

"What do you mean?"

"When word got out about Tyler being Seth's father, and how Kristen kept it from them both for seventeen years, Kristen went into preemptive mode. She told anyone and everyone who would listen. And if she caught anyone gossiping about her, she made them regret it. It eventually become old news, and the gossips moved on to the next poor soul."

Georgia gnawed on her lower lip. "And it worked?"

"Would you want to go up against Kristen?"

"Definitely not."

"I rest my case. Next time someone starts gossiping about you, stare them down and make them regret it."

Liam had just finished up a takeout pizza from Dominick's when there was a knock on the door.

"Hi." Georgia wore a shy smile and short shorts. Really short shorts.

"Hi. Everything okay?" Why was it every time he saw her now his first concern was for her and the baby?

Before she could answer, a distant rumble of thunder

rolled over them. Sounded like a much-needed summer storm was coming.

"Yes. I just have some news. Can I come in?"

"Sure." He stepped back then closed the door behind her, holding back a groan. He'd never seen her in shorts, and they did wonders for her legs. Wonders like revealing their silky smooth skin and firm, lean muscles. Legs that he'd like wrapped around him about now.

Whoa there, caveman. Get your lizard brain under control. "Uh, can I get you something to drink?"

"Water would be great. I'm making an effort to get my ninety-six ounces a day."

"Ninety-six ounces?" he asked as he directed her to the kitchen, happy to have a benign topic to take his mind off her legs.

"Yeah. It's recommended pregnant women get eight to twelve cups a day." She leaned against the counter, studying the kitchen, and he remembered she hadn't seen the carriage house renovations until he'd moved in. "Which explains why we have to pee so often."

He laughed and shook his head, unsure how to respond to that. "Uh . . . okay then." Taking two glasses down from the cabinet, he said, "You said you have news?"

"Oh! Cole is in."

"What?" He stared at her a moment, glasses still poised in mid-air, before it hit him. "Wait. He's in Shadow Mountain?"

"Yes. The director, Sally Moran, is willing to admit him. They expect him on Monday."

"That's amazing! Thank you!" He set the glasses on the counter then hauled her into him for a hug. She had no idea how much this meant to him. Not just for Cole but because no one had ever gone out of their way to help him like this. Ever.

She stepped out of his embrace with a laugh. "You're welcome. But," she held up a finger, "he breaks one rule, and he's out."

"Understood." He checked his watch. "Do you mind if I call his lawyer and let him know."

"No, go ahead."

Taking his phone off the dining table where he'd set up his office, he dialed the attorney and watched as Georgia wandered the living room, picking things up and setting them down. He wondered if she remembered any of the knick-knacks that sat around the room. Were they moved from the Big House when the carriage house was renovated?

Finished with the call, he joined Georgia. "The wheels are in motion. The attorney will ensure Cole is at the facility Monday morning."

She nodded.

"I can't thank you enough," he said, his voice quiet with emotion.

"Liam, it's—oh!" Georgia's hand flew to her stomach.

"What is it? Is everything okay?" The panic surprised him, and he took her by the shoulders.

She beamed. "It's fine. Maybe this butterbean is going to be another Mia Hamm."

At his puzzled expression, she continued. "She just kicked. Hard. Oh." She looked down and he could see her stomach rippling beneath her T-shirt.

She grabbed his hand and place it on the bulge. Liam's eyes widened and his heart skipped a beat at the feel of the baby undulating beneath his hand. He'd never felt anything like it, and he couldn't explain how it affected him.

"Amazing, huh?" she asked as she gazed up at him, her beautiful blue eyes alight with awe.

He kept his hand there, even as the motion stilled. Elation filled him. As did fear.

"Liam, it's okay."

He wasn't sure what she referred to. The baby? His emotions? The situation?

She reached up and laid a hand on his cheek and, inexplicably, he turned into her soft palm and placed a kiss there. It had been meant as a gesture of tenderness, but at her intake of breath, his blood headed south, and the mood shifted from one of tenderness to one of desire.

Reaching out, she tucked a hand into the front waistband of his jeans and tugged.

She'd get no resistance from him. He went willingly, wrapping his arm around her waist, molding her to him until they were touching from chest to thighs.

Nuzzling her neck, he inhaled. "So sweet," he muttered. "You smell so sweet."

He wanted her. So damn bad. And good to know the feeling was mutual. He'd been thinking about their last encounter, and reliving all their encounters in Vegas, unable to stop the memories. "I've been thinking about you. And this." He lifted a hand to her breast and stroked her nipple until it hardened beneath his touch.

"Have you?" She pressed a kiss to his neck, then her tongue darted out to get in on the game.

"Uh-huh." He closed his eyes, reveling in the sensation.

"I've been thinking of about you too. And of this." She put her hand against his erection and squeezed.

"Dear God," he groaned, pressing into her hand like an inexperienced adolescent.

"What else have you been thinking about?" she asked as she sucked his earlobe into her hot mouth.

Two could play that game. Her shorts were so short, he had better access to the goods from the hem than the waist. He skimmed his fingers along an inner thigh, enjoying the short indrawn breath it elicited. Sliding two fingers into her shorts he touched her wet panties. "This." He stroked her through her underwear and she swayed toward him, moaning.

Grasping his shoulder, she hitched a leg around his waist, giving him better access, her breath coming in pants.

"Fuck, Georgia." His hands slid along her thighs, then he lifted them up and open, sliding her onto the island behind them before stepping between them. "I want you right here, right now."

Apparently she was on board with that because she opened the fly of his jeans and shoved them down around his hips. "Yes. Now. Please."

Once she'd finished with his pants, she worked on her own, raising her hips, tugging them down her thighs.

The countertop put her at just the right height. She opened her legs to him and he nearly lost it right there.

Taking matters into her own hands, so to speak, she wrapped a hand around his length and drew him into her. "Now, Liam."

He slid into her and she could have wept with the sensation. She couldn't get enough of him. Wrapping her legs around his waist, she gazed down at where they were joined, watching as he pulled out, slow and steady, then slid back inside her. She gripped the edge of the countertop, and with each slow thrust, the tension built. He scooped his hands under her butt, lifting her, and she gasped as he plunged deeper into her.

"Too much?"

"No! Don't stop!"

His pace quickened until they were both breathless and sweating. "Now, Georgia." He growled. "Now. I can't wait any longer." He kissed her then, his tongue mimicking his thrusts and, before she knew it, she exploded.

It wasn't until their breathing returned to normal that they noticed the approaching storm was almost upon them. They both looked up at the ceiling as thunder boomed overhead.

"Sounds like you might be here a while," Liam said as he pressed a kiss to her forehead.

"Sounds like it. Pity. What ever will we do?" She wiggled her hips and he released a masculine growl.

"I can think of a few things."

"Perhaps there's a deck of cards around here somewhere," she said with a cheeky grin.

"Not exactly what I had in mind."

"No? Well, what *did* you have in mind?"

He gripped her still-parted thighs as she wrapped her arms around his neck and carried her to the bedroom.

"Now, why didn't I think of that?" she asked as she plowed her fingers into his hair and pressed her lips to his.

GEORGIA WOKE to a gray dawn with Liam's front to her back and his warm hand cupping her stomach. Her heart squeezed at the intimate touch of his hand where their child slept. As if her thoughts had awakened Lily, the baby rolled and stretched in response, rippling the surface of Georgia's skin. Liam's hand pressed into her and he snuggled closer, kissing her bare shoulder. She wanted him again.

Apparently he wanted her too because his hand drifted lower until he found the moist apex of her thighs. She moaned and he growled. Parting her, he slid inside, slow and easy, filling her. He seemed content to remain still inside her, but she had other ideas. When she wiggled her hips in encouragement, he chuckled, his breath hot on the back of her neck.

"Move," Georgia said between gritted teeth.

"My, aren't we bossy this morning," Liam said as his hand rose to cup her breast, but he complied with her demand and began a lazy rhythm that had her panting with desire in no time.

While his thrusts grew harder, he never quickened the pace, and she felt the tension building like a tightly wound spring. And when he slipped his hands between her legs, that spring released in a burst of energy. With a deep-throated growl, he found his own release moments later.

They must have dozed off because, when Georgia woke again, the gray dawn had given way to watery sunshine. Releasing a disappointed sigh, she lifted Liam's heavy arm from her and sat up.

"Where are you going?" he asked in a sleepy voice.

"I need to go. I have a meeting this morning, and I'd really like to get back to my room before Grandad is up and about."

"Want to avoid the walk of shame?" he asked with a smirk.

"Uh, yeah. Especially with my grandfather."

He propped himself up on his elbow. "Actually, I'd appreciate that. He might come over and cut my balls off if he saw you now, lips swollen, hair mussed, a satisfied smile on your face. There would be no doubt what you've been up to."

"What *we've* been up to."

"What *we've* been up to." He tugged her down for another kiss then sat up too. "Do you want to shower?"

"Um, no. We both know where that will lead." She pulled her T-shirt on then scanned the room for her panties and shorts.

"In the kitchen," Liam pointed out helpfully, as his heated gaze landed on her naked lower half.

"Oh yeah." She bent over the bed for one last kiss, and with all the aplomb she could muster, walked butt-naked out of the bedroom to the kitchen. She found her clothes laying on the floor by the island and blushed as she shimmied into them. Did they really have sex on the island?

Turning to exit the kitchen, she saw an all-too-familiar book cover on the counter tucked up near the coffee maker: *What to Expect When You're Expecting.* The book lay open face-down. She pressed a hand to her mouth in surprise. Why did Liam have a book about pregnancy when he'd made it clear to her on more than one occasion that he would not be involved?

Glancing in the direction of the bedroom and finding the coast clear, she picked up the book. It was open to the chapter on the fifth month, specifically the section on "Your Baby This Month."

She didn't know what to think about this. Was he changing his mind? Would he decide to be part of Lily's life and, by extension, Georgia's? She couldn't let her heart hope. Setting the book back down in the same position, she quietly closed the door behind her in case Liam had gone back to sleep.

She gingerly pushed open the mudroom door to the Big House, hoping it wouldn't squeak like it always did. But of course it squeaked. It always did. Cringing, she closed it and tiptoed into the kitchen—

"Morning."

She gasped and jumped like a frightened cat. Pressing a hand to her racing heart, she exclaimed, "Gracious! You scared me!"

"Guilty conscience?" He studied her with a raised eyebrow.

She decided to take the same tack she now would with gossipers—brazen it out—and, mustering the same aplomb it took to walk butt-naked from Liam's bedroom, she said as she walked through the kitchen toward the back stairs, "What? I'm *already* pregnant."

"Georgia."

She winced at the tone in his voice. It was the same tone he used to disconcert a hostile witness. She turned. "Yes?"

He reached out a hand to her and she took a couple of reluctant steps in his direction and took his hand. His brow was furrowed as he speared her with his gaze. She resisted the urge to fidget.

"Is he trifling with your affections?"

She almost laugh-snorted. "What?"

"I don't want to see you hurt. If he has no intention of being a father to his child, or of participating in your life in any meaningful way, he should leave you be. Do you want me to evict him? Would that help?"

"No!" She pulled her hand from his. "Don't . . . don't do that. Don't take this out on Liam. I'm an adult—"

"Yes, you are. But you are behaving in an uncharacteristic manner. Are you sure your physical attraction to him hasn't clouded your thinking?"

Heat rose to her face at his reference to "physical attraction." And no, she wasn't sure that attraction hadn't clouded her thinking. But darn it, she was having fun. She'd already paid the piper for her impulsive actions in Las Vegas. She couldn't get any more pregnant than she was now. What else was there?

He could break your heart, a voice reminded her.

"Grandad, I appreciate your concern. But I went into this with my eyes open."

He frowned at her again. "Just be careful, Georgia. Your father, whoever he was, broke your mother's heart, and she was never the same again. I don't want to see that happen to you."

Georgia swallowed past the lump in her throat. This was the first time her grandfather had mentioned her anonymous father—or shared that a broken heart was at the root of her mother's erratic behavior.

She leaned down and pressed a kiss to her grandfather's forehead then rose. "I'll be careful, Grandad. I promise."

As Liam massaged shampoo into his hair, he recalled every moment of the previous night and that morning. Every breathy sigh from Georgia's lips, every mewl of desire, every passionate kiss. But the memories didn't stop there. He recalled how it felt to wake with her wrapped in his arms, to feel the bulge of their child, and the rippling of her belly as the child moved. Last night, and this morning, when he'd been with Georgia, there had been not just a physical connection but an emotional one.

He paused, dropping his sudsy hands by his sides, and stared, unseeing, at the spray from the showerhead. What the hell was happening? How had Georgia winnowed her way past his defenses? Defenses he'd spent a lifetime building?

No one had ever gotten this close to him. Not even his brothers. What was it about her that encouraged him to drop his guard? Was it her kindness toward him? Was it the enormous favor she had bestowed on him for the benefit of his brother? Was it her determination to overcome the obstacles in her life? And despite those obstacles, to remain optimistic? Or that she knew his criminal past and was willing to overlook it and give him another chance?

She had every reason not to trust people, specifically men. But it wasn't in her DNA. She trusted. She welcomed people into her life. She loved.

He could learn a thing or two from Georgia. About forgiving himself. About letting people in. About letting himself love. But it terrified him down to the marrow in his bones.

20

That afternoon, Georgia rose from her seat at the coffee bar.

"Whoa. Okay. Where did *that* come from?" Olivia asked as she eyed Georgia's belly.

"Olivia, if you're married and you don't know where that comes from, we should talk." Kristen said, a smirk on her face.

Olivia stuck her tongue out at Kristen then asked, "Where have I been?"

"Uh, Europe?" Kristen offered helpfully. "Too much married sex addled your brain?"

Zach and Olivia had taken a delayed honeymoon since she was scheduled to teach a master class for the American Ballet Theater two weeks after their wedding. They'd traveled to Europe, and she'd stayed after the honeymoon to give a special performance with the Paris Ballet and teach a master class there.

Olivia rolled her eyes and looked back at Georgia. "You know what I mean. I go away for my honeymoon and come back to find you, what? Five? Six months pregnant?"

"Five and a half."

"Who's the lucky father? Anyone I know? Or was it man-in-a-can?"

"I *cannot* believe you just asked that," Kristen said, smacking the countertop, a note of reprimand in her voice.

"What? We all know it wasn't immaculate conception, so I ask a reasonable question."

Georgia supposed it was a reasonable question, especially since she wasn't dating anyone. A hysterical laugh almost escaped. Dating? No she wasn't *dating* anyone because she was *married*. She chewed her lower lip. Currently, only three people—four, if you counted her—knew who the father was. Should she keep it that way? Or pretend it's her ex's?

Olivia laid a hand on Georgia's arm, drawing her attention. "I'm sorry. It was a rude question."

Georgia studied Olivia's contrite face. "It's okay. It isn't an unexpected question, especially since there's no man in my life." Glancing around and seeing the café all but empty in the late afternoon, she leaned in. "It's Liam Dunbar's."

"Who?" Olivia asked, confusion crinkling her smooth brow.

"Oh!" came Kristen's response. "You know, the hot guy renovating the Redmond Mill."

"Oh. Ohhh." Olivia eyed Georgia, speculation on her face. "But he only arrived in May, and your five and a half months pregnant."

"Yeah, so we met, um, earlier." She waved a hand behind her, indicating they had a history.

"Uh-huh. I'd say you did more than just meet . . . earlier." Olivia's gaze flicked to Georgia's bulge.

Kristen gasped. "Damn, girl, marriage has removed any filter you once had."

Olivia flushed then turned on Kristen. "Kettle, meet Pot."

"Yeah, but I've always been that way."

"So, are you two a thing then?" Olivia asked.

"Oh, uh, no." A wave of heat swept over Georgia. "We're not a thing. He'll be leaving after the mill is completed."

Kristen's knowing gazed settled on Georgia's face. "Well, if you're good with that, then so are we. I raised a pretty great kid by myself, and you will too. Don't let anyone make you think otherwise."

Georgia skimmed her hand over her belly. "Thanks. I think it's for the best."

"I'll be here to help anytime you have questions—or just need someone to talk to."

Tears clogged Georgia's throat. "Thanks." Between her grandfather and her friends, she could do this.

What choice did she have?

THE FOLLOWING SATURDAY, Liam parked in front of the house Georgia and Luis had bought. Even from the street, he could hear the scream of table saws and the staccato of hammers.

Luis was in the kitchen directing the placement of an island with the help of Zach and Tyler. "She's upstairs," he said to Liam.

Following the sound of feminine voices, he found Alyssa and Georgia in what appeared to be the master bedroom holding up paint swatches. Georgia's hair was up in a messy bun, curls spilling out randomly. From behind, you'd never know she was pregnant.

"Hi."

They both turned, startled.

"Seems things are coming along." He took in the new drywall near the bedroom closet.

"Yeah. What brings you by?"

He shrugged then stuck his hands in his pants pockets. "Just wanted to see your investment." *And you.*

"Doesn't look like much now, but Luis's plans are terrific."

He started rolling up his sleeves. "What can I do? Put me to work."

Her brows lifted. "Really?"

"What? I've renovated fourteen mills. I've learned a thing or two about construction."

"Okay then. The guys could probably use some help with the heavy work. Especially the upper cabinets."

"On it." He left the room, but before he'd stepped into the hall, her voice stopped him.

"Thanks."

"Of course."

~

GEORGIA COULD FEEL Alyssa's eyes on her.

"What?"

Alyssa shrugged. "Nothing."

"It's not nothing. Spill it."

Alyssa fanned out the paint swatches. "Liam seems like a good guy," the casual tone belying her intent.

"He is. But don't go there. It's not going to happen." She took the paint swatches from Alyssa and held up the collection of soft blues. "I think I'm going with robin's egg then vanilla cream for the trim."

"Good choice." Alyssa wandered over to the window where the men's voices could be heard and looked out. "If you go ahead with the divorce, does he plan to be involved with Lily?"

"Uh. No."

"Why not?" Turning, Alyssa leaned against the window sill, arms folded across her chest.

"He's leaving. And his business requires extensive travel."

Alyssa tilted her head, eyes narrowed. "And what do you want?"

Swallowing past a knot in her throat, Georgia set the paint swatches on a box. "I'd like him to be involved."

"And you think that's a good idea?"

"You don't?" Georgia went on the defensive. Why wouldn't having her father in her life be good for Lily?

"Children need stability. Consistency. A routine. Having a man in and out of her life could be confusing for Lily."

"He could be an uncle."

"So you won't tell her who her father is?"

"I—" Why hadn't that question occurred to her? Georgia's gaze flew to Alyssa's face, and she sank onto the box containing the new bathroom vanity. "I hadn't honestly thought about it."

"You need to. Is Liam a doting uncle? Or is he her father? And if he is her father, will he be involved in her life—on a regular basis—not when the whim strikes him?"

"You're right. I have some decisions to make. But he does have his rights as the father."

"He does," Alyssa conceded. "But you need to think about what's best for Lily. She's the most important figure in this equation."

∼

"UNMARRIED AND PREGNANT. You know what they say—the apple doesn't fall far from the tree."

At first, Georgia tensed at the snide comment coming from the older women one table over. Not the same ones gossiping at the grocery store last week, she didn't think. They had sounded younger. So word—or her belly—was spreading fast.

"You would think she'd want to stay away from Northridge instead of coming home pregnant. What must her poor grandfather think?"

The other woman chimed in, "First his daughter gets pregnant at eighteen, then she's killed in a car accident. Drinking, you know. It's not enough that he had to raise his grandchild. Now he might have to raise his great-grandchild."

By the tension in his shoulders, Liam heard it too.

"Just ignore it," she said, her voice low. "I'll take care of it." It was time to take Alyssa's advice.

The incident in Smith's had been like diving into the deep end of the pool and getting it over with. She'd known it would happen, and though she had dreaded it, now that it had happened, it didn't bother her as much. And the two women were known in the town for their narrow-minded, holier-than-thou attitude and penchant for gossip.

Forget them. She had the support of her grandfather and her friends. That's all she needed.

Liam's mouth formed a straight line and she knew he wanted to say something more. "Would it be so bad to say we're married, since—oh, by the way—we are?" he whispered.

"And the fact that we don't live together as a married couple now?"

"They don't know that. I *am* living in your grandfather's

carriage house. How would they know you're not in the carriage house with me?"

"And when we get divorced in November?"

He shrugged. "You say it didn't work out."

She shook her head. "No. I may be the object of ridicule from those two ol' biddies, but I won't be the object of pity. After you leave, it will be 'poor Georgia, a single mom who couldn't hold on to her husband.' I'll take the derision over the pity any day."

After her mother died and she'd come to live with her grandparents, for the first couple of years, wherever she went she received sad faces, pitying glances, and shakes of the head. Poor orphan Georgia—her mother didn't care enough about her not to drink and drive. This time she wouldn't be the object of pity. She owed that much to her daughter.

"You're impossible," he snapped.

A retort was on the tip of her tongue, but the server appeared with her personal veggie pizza—extra cheese—and her stomach took command. "Ooh, pizza!"

LIAM CHUCKLED, despite his annoyance, then sat back so the server could place his plate of lasagna in front of him. He eyed the slice of pizza she lifted to her mouth. "No more nausea?"

"No, thank God," she mumbled around her mouthful. She washed it down with a sip of water. "Now I can truly eat for two."

He chuckled, glad she was over that particular hump. He didn't like seeing the dark circles and the slight grayish green cast to her complexion. In fact, she was the radiant picture of health. Eyes shining, cheeks flushed. She'd bloomed in the last few weeks. He tilted his head. She might even be more beautiful now than the night he'd met her.

"What?" she asked, a slice of pizza halfway to her mouth.

"You're adorable." Where had that come from? he wondered.

"Pfft." Taking another bite of her pizza, she appeared to ponder him. Swallowing, she continued, "You're just saying that. Trying to humor an ungainly pregnant woman."

He leaned over the table and said, "A woman I impregnated." He relished watching the heat suffuse her face to enhance the color in her cheeks. "And I enjoyed every minute of it."

Her mouth formed an O, and he longed to kiss that mouth.

She squirmed in her seat and, just as he was basking in his ability to elicit a sexual reaction, she set down her napkin before saying, "I have to pee."

He barked out a laugh at her timing, trying to ignore the blow to his ego, and rose from his chair to assist her, feeling the censorious gazes of the two old biddies.

But before Georgia turned in the direction of the bathroom, she leaned over the women's table with a bright smile on her face and said, "Yes, I had sex. Lots of it, in fact. And as for my grandfather, he's thrilled that he'll soon have a granddaughter to bounce on his knee."

Bravo! Their shocked faces were all the reward he needed.

～

"So, word is you knocked up Georgia," Zach supplied, hands on his hips.

Liam choked on a mouthful of beer, coughing and sputtering. Tyler helpfully pounded him on the back—maybe a bit harder than was necessary under the circumstances. Boy, news traveled fast. It had just been that afternoon that he and Georgia had encountered the two gossips in Dominick's.

He walked over to a side table and picked up a glass of water. When he got his breath back and cleared his watering eyes, he looked across the billiard table into the questioning gaze of two very fit men, arms crossed over their chests, the game of cutthroat they'd been playing momentarily forgotten.

Well, shit. Was he about to get another comeuppance from these two? "Yeah, I did. But," he held up a finger, "she was an active participant in the, uh . . . process."

"At least you remember your, er . . . encounter," Tyler muttered.

"Encounters," Liam corrected. "It was a weekend, not a one-night stand."

"Well, that makes *all* the difference," Zach said with an eye roll and a note of sarcasm in his voice.

Tyler snorted and the corner of Zach's mouth lifted. They were just jerking his chain. Assholes.

"So, are you going to marry her?" Tyler asked as he lined up his shot.

And the beer went down the wrong way again.

"Dude, you have some sort of drinking problem?" Tyler asked as he again pounded him on the back.

When he could speak again, he croaked, "No. I have some sort of asshat problem."

Zach chuckled then picked up his own beer for a sip, never taking his eyes off Liam.

"Not that it's any of your business but, no, we aren't

getting married." *We already are, if you must know. But we're getting a divorce.*

Tyler sank Zach's ball, making Zach groan.

Liam circled the table looking for a shot then sent Tyler's five-ball into the side pocket, earning him a muttered "shit" from Tyler.

"What did you mean 'at least I remembered my encounter'?" Liam asked.

There was a marked silence from both men, making Liam look up from the table. Tyler wore a sheepish expression, and Zach nudged him. "You brought it up, man."

Tyler nodded. "I have some sort of alcohol-induced amnesia." He held up his beer. "I can drink beer and wine, but you give me liquor, and I'm toast. I appear to function normally, but I can't remember anything that happens after a couple of drinks."

"And?" Liam prodded.

Tyler glanced at Zach again then leaned his pool cue against the wall behind him.

"And for seventeen years I had a son I never knew I had."

"Wow." Liam settled his hip on the pool table and folded his arms, ready for a good story.

Tyler told him about his encounter with Kristen when they were just teenagers. He'd left the next day for Princeton with no memory of their time together. When he returned to Northridge after seventeen years away, he and Kristen developed a relationship, only for him to learn her son Seth was his. It caused a rift between them, but it didn't take Tyler long to realize the gift Kristen had given him.

A bout with cancer as an adult had left Tyler sterile and facing the sad prospect of having been too late to have children. Seth changed all that. Now Kristen and Tyler would be getting married later that year, Seth had a father, and Tyler had a son. A happy ending all the way around.

Liam could see how much this meant to Tyler. "That's great, man. Truly." He reached for his beer and raised it in Tyler's direction. "Congratulations."

Tyler accepted the toast with a grin. "Thanks."

"But back to you and Georgia," Zach said as he lifted his pool cue, taking aim at Tyler's ball. "What are your plans?"

"Again, not that it's any of your business, but Georgia and I are in agreement that I will provide financial support for the child." Life's cruel irony wasn't lost on him. Tyler had desperately wanted a child and had thought he couldn't have one. Here, Liam was having a child when he was adamantly opposed to being a parent.

"That's it?"

Liam bristled. "That's it. I'll be leaving once the mill is up and running. Now, are we here to play pool or to have an inquisition?"

"An inquisition," Zach responded.

"Definitely an inquisition," Tyler agreed with a nod.

Then they both cracked up.

"You guys are assholes."

"Seriously though." Zach frowned. "We just don't want to see Georgia hurt."

Liam nodded. He appreciated that. He appreciated that Zach and Tyler were good guys and cared about those in their orbit.

"I promise, I won't hurt Georgia. We are agreed on the arrangements. She doesn't want anything more from me than that."

At least he was pretty sure she didn't.

Georgia glanced at her watch. "Gotta run. I've got a . . . thing." She picked up her cup of herbal tea and chugged the rest of it.

"Does this *thing* involve your baby daddy?"

Georgia shrugged. "We have a meeting about the divorce."

"You have a meeting for sex." At Georgia's snort, Alyssa circled a finger in front of Georgia's face. "That glow isn't just pregnancy. That's the face of a sexually satisfied woman."

Georgia placed her hands on her belly. "How do you think I got this way?"

"A *recently* sexually satisfied woman."

A flush crept up Georgia's already heated face. "Well, we *are* married. And I don't have to worry about getting pregnant."

"But you do have to worry about breaking your heart," she added, her voice soft with concern.

"Pfft. We're just having fun—enjoying it while it lasts. I have no illusions about our relationship. We're getting a divorce in November, and he's leaving as soon as the mill is operational. Period."

Then why did the thought of him leaving fill her with dread?

"So you're still planning to get a divorce then?"

"Of course. I mean, it's not like we're in love or anything."

She wasn't anyway. At least not yet.

21

"So you climbed Mt. Everest. What was it like?"

He'd been about to doze off, Georgia's warm body tucked up against him, when she asked her question. "How'd you—? Did you Google me?"

"Google *is* an amazing source of information," she said by way of explanation.

He shifted, pulling her onto his chest. She settled into him, and he sighed in contentment. Had he ever been this content? he wondered.

"What was it like?" he repeated her question. "Insane."

She propped herself up on her elbow and gazed down at him. "Then why did you do it?"

How could he tell her he did it to both run away from his demons and to punish himself for his failures. How could he tell her it's why he undertook all the risky adventures he had before he started American Threads. The company and its mission gave him a purpose again after he sold his IT security firm. "Would you believe I did it, in the words of George Mallory, 'because it's there'?"

She snorted and rolled her eyes. "Fine. Don't tell me the real reason, but tell me what it was like."

"Freezing, grueling, sleep-depriving, oxygen-depriving, exhilarating, frustrating, terrifying, and . . . humbling. Nothing like the world's highest mountain to make you—and your problems—feel insignificant."

"Hmm."

He thought she dozed off, then she took a deep breath. "How'd you know how to hack the utility company's computers?"

It was his turn to take a deep breath. "With more smarts than most and too much time on my hands, I became a computer nerd using the school's computers."

She giggled. "You? I can't see you as any kind of nerd."

"True story." He lifted his hand as if swearing to it. "I took a couple of computer classes, then I tried my hand at hacking. First it was innocent stuff like hacking into the school's grading system to see my classmate's grades. Then, I'm not proud to admit, I started taking money to change grades." He and his family needed all the money they could get, and he couldn't find a legitimate job in his neighborhood. The only other option was selling drugs, and he wasn't going there. "IT security at the school and the utility company was rudimentary at the time, otherwise I never would have gotten in."

He paused, wondering if he should reveal more. Why not? He'd already told her some of the worst parts. "I told you about the utility bill, but I didn't tell you that not only couldn't we pay that bill, we were on the brink of eviction. Losing the electricity in the middle of winter was bad enough, but being out on the street was unthinkable. Eliminating the past-due electric bills allowed us to pay the rent."

"Oh, Liam." She pressed a kiss to his bare shoulder. "Where was your mother?"

"Dead."

She stilled but didn't say anything. He was glad. He didn't want to get into that.

"I used my time in prison to earn a degree in computer science and learn how to protect information systems from hackers like me."

His mouth lifted in a rueful smile she couldn't see. "While the three years in prison were probably the best thing to happen to me, they were the worst thing to happen to Cole. With no adult to take care of him, he was placed in foster care, where he was handed off from one family to the next. One of his older foster brothers introduced him to drugs. Cole eventually ran away, living on the streets. It took a couple of years for me to find him."

"I'm so sorry—for you, for Cole. What did you do after you got out of prison?"

"I worked two jobs, one selling computers in a big-box store, another one programming from home. Cole and I lived in a shitty one-bedroom apartment, and I did my best to get him cleaned up. It would work for a while, then Cole would go back to the drugs and the streets."

"Even so, I saved as much as I could and finally started my own IT security company at the age of twenty-four. I knew our impoverished circumstances weren't helping. I had to find a way to make more money and take control of my life and help him take control of his. Seven years later I sold that company for more money than I thought existed. Unfortunately, no amount of money seemed to help Cole."

"What did you do after that?"

He shrugged. "I was burned out from burning the

candle at both ends for so long. I took some time, traveled the world—"

"Climbed mountains," she interjected.

"Climbed mountains," he agreed. He'd been a rolling stone. He'd tried to bring Cole along, get him away from the drugs, hoping the adrenaline rush of extreme sports would replace his need for drugs, but Cole hadn't been interested.

"AND AMERICAN THREADS?" She settled on his chest again, enjoying the feel of his hands on her bare skin as they glided in circular motions along her back.

"Through my travels, I'd been enlightened by what I'd seen, and wanted to do more with my life. After seeing the sweatshops in some of the countries I visited, I had the idea to start my own clothing company with an eye to affordable American-made products backed by American pride and ingenuity, a living wage, and sustainability. You know, pie-in-the-sky notions."

"I was in search of another venture. I spent a few months traveling the U.S., meeting with state and local leaders, learning what communities needed, and what they didn't need. When I traveled the South, I came across one abandoned cotton mill after another. By then, I knew I wanted to build something I could see and touch. I wanted to bring good-paying manufacturing jobs back to the U.S. I wanted to build an affordable American brand of clothing using all-American products."

"So, I began buying old textile and clothing mills in depressed areas in the South, renovating them, filling them with state-of-the-art manufacturing equipment, hiring local workers, and paying them a living wage with great benefits."

"And American Threads was born," she put in.

He chuckled, and she felt it rumble in his chest. "Yep. I found beauty in the old mills and wanted to preserve their history while building environmentally friendly facilities. It became a labor of love. I never expected the business to become so successful. I just wanted to create something I could be proud of. I hadn't expected overnight success, but word spread about the company's mission and it resonated with the buying public. Soon, the five mills I had couldn't keep up with demand."

"When you love what you do, success generally follows." She'd had that in L.A. And would hopefully have that again here in Northridge, though she'd be content with half the success she'd had with Beverly Hills Realty.

"I suppose that's right. After the first five mills were operational, I changed up the business plan to include retail outlets alongside the mills, where overruns and other merchandise could be sold to the local community, creating retail jobs in addition to the manufacturing jobs."

"You should be proud of what you've created."

"I am, but I wanted to offer more. My team and I developed a manager training program so that workers could work their way up in the company, giving them upward mobility without having to leave their hometowns and without expensive college tuition.

"So American-grown cotton, American-made fabrics, American-made clothes. Vertical integration, sustainable practices, community involvement. Pretty impressive," she said, pressing her lips to his chest.

"But when the Redmond Mill comes online, I'll have fifteen mills, more than enough to manufacture what the market demands."

"So, what's next?"

"Revitalize the Rust Belt."

"Boy, you don't take the easy road, do you?"

"No. But it's doable." He rolled over onto his side, facing away from her, and reached behind him to compress her front to his back.

She studied the tattoo on his right shoulder blade. She'd seen it in Vegas and a few times since, and finally took advantage of an unusually chatty Liam to satisfy her curiosity. The simple design was not one she would have thought suited him. A heart outline surrounded the initials BLD. It also interested her because it was the only one he had, so it must have a special meaning to him. She ran her fingers over it, feeling puckered, irregular skin beneath the ink. Liam tensed.

"What is this tattoo?"

Without speaking, he reached back and grasped her hand, pulling it away from the tattoo, placing it on his upper arm. Just when she thought he wasn't going to answer her, he said, "It's my brother Ben's initials. He died when I was fourteen."

"I DIDN'T KNOW you had another brother," she continued as she propped herself up on her elbow.

"He was younger than me and Cole."

"How did he die?" Her quiet voice filled with grief for a boy she never knew was practically his undoing.

"A fire." He attempted to clear the emotion from his voice, but the knot in is throat wouldn't subside.

"How old was he?"

"Nine."

"And the skin under the tattoo—you were burned?"

"Yes."

"And Cole? Was he injured too?"

"No." He knew his words were terse, but he couldn't give her more than one-word answers without breaking down and telling her the whole horrific story.

"I'm sorry." Her lips pressed to the reminder of his failure and he had never felt more vulnerable than he did at that moment. He didn't do vulnerable. What he did do was distraction.

He shifted abruptly, turning to face her before pulling her beneath him and kissing her with all the pent-up emotions he couldn't share. Taken by surprise, it took her a moment, but then her arms wrapped around him and she opened her legs to him as if sensing his need for oblivion. He was more than happy to find it inside her.

THE FOLLOWING MONDAY, Georgia moaned and rubbed her back. The dull ache that began yesterday had intensified this morning. Was she in labor? The thought panicked her. It was too soon—only twenty-four weeks.

"This isn't happening. This isn't happening," she muttered to herself as she fidgeted in her chair trying to find a more comfortable position. She closed her eyes as a wave of nausea washed over her and wondered if the morning sickness had returned.

Luis came in, chattering about a new painting technique he wanted to try on the house they were renovating, a cup of herbal tea in his hand, then he stopped abruptly, a scowl on his face. "Girl, you don't look so good."

She shook her head to clear the brain fog. "I don't think I feel so good either." She rubbed her forehead and recognized the heat emanating from it. She rarely got sick, but she recognized a fever when she felt it.

"All right. Let me get Dr. Grimshaw on the phone." He left her office before she could ask how he knew who her doctor was, then realized he'd likely seen the appointments on her calendar. She didn't have the energy to protest. Instead, she laid her head on her desk and cupped a hand around her stomach, hoping the baby was okay. In response, a kick landed that nearly took her breath away, but she smiled. Okay then.

"Dr. Grimshaw's nurse is on line one," Luis yelled from the other room.

Taking a deep breath, she picked up the receiver.

"Good morning, Georgia. What's going on?" The nurse's soothing voice put her at ease almost instantly. Whatever was wrong, she would handle it with calm efficiency.

Georgia described her symptoms and answered the nurse's pointed questions.

"It's likely a kidney infection. Not that unusual in pregnant women. You already have pressure on your bladder, so you don't realize you have a bladder infection until the infection hits your kidneys."

"What do I need to do?"

"Come to the office and let me run a urinalysis. If it's a kidney infection, Dr. Grimshaw will need to admit you to the hospital for a day or two and put you on IV antibiotics and fluids."

Georgia shuddered. She hated needles.

At her silence, the nurse prodded, "Georgia?"

"Yeah, I'm here."

"Okay. Do you have someone to drive you?"

She'd find someone. "Yes."

"Good. I'll see you shortly."

Luis poked his head in the door. "Alyssa's here."

Georgia hung up the phone and blinked in confusion at the two concerned faces. "How? Never mind." When it came to Luis's sixth sense, or more likely his eavesdropping, she stopped asking.

"Let's go, momma," Alyssa said as she picked up Georgia's purse and tote bag and threw them over her shoulder.

LIAM STRODE into the hospital room and stopped short, his heart suddenly trying to climb up his throat. Georgia looked frail in the hospital bed, the small mound of her belly visible beneath the covers. IV tubing ran from the bag on the pole to her arm, and a monitor beeped with what he assumed were her vitals and maybe the baby's. She appeared to be asleep, so he approached her quietly and took her free hand in his. She was warm to the touch.

When he'd gotten the text from Alyssa that morning saying Georgia was on her way to the hospital, panic had filled his chest. Was it her? Was it the baby? Both? It was too soon for the birth. Alyssa had reassured him that it was a kidney infection and that it was common during pregnancy. Even so, he'd broken every speed limit between Macon and Northridge to get there.

He brushed the hair off her forehead, feeling the heat of the fever, and closed his eyes in worry. What if they hadn't caught it in time? What if the antibiotics didn't work?

"Hey."

His eyes flew open to see her gazing at him, glassy-eyed and confused. "Hey."

"You're here."

"Of course I'm here. Where else would I be?"

"Macon," she said with a slight smile. "How did you know?"

"Alyssa texted me."

"Alyssa? How'd she have your number?"

"I gave it to her for just this type of situation."

"You did?" An expression skittered across her face—surprise? And then it was gone. She tried to sit up and winced.

"What's wrong? What can I do?" He leaned over the bed, ready to help.

"It's nothing. Just the IV." She lifted her hand in indication and cringed. "I hate needles."

He snorted. "Me too."

"You? But I thought men were supposed to be tough and stoic when it came to these things."

"Maybe we're *supposed* to be, but I'm not ashamed to admit my dislike of needles."

After he helped her get comfortable again, carefully disentangling the IV tubing from the blankets, he pulled up the chair and took her free hand again. "What did the doctor say?"

"I'll get two rounds of IV antibiotics, and if my fever is gone I can go home tomorrow and finish up the treatment with oral antibiotics. I'll have to have urine cultures once a month until the end of the pregnancy."

Hearing about her urine should have made him twitch, but when it came to her health, nothing seemed to make him uncomfortable.

"They catheterized me," she said, a pained expression crossing her face.

That did make him wince, and he involuntarily crossed his legs. "I'm sorry." He squeezed her hand. "And the baby?" He resisted the urge to lay his hand on her abdomen.

"She's fine." She gazed down at the mound with something akin to adoration, and his throat clogged up.

His shoulders also relaxed, making him aware for the first time of the tension there. "Does your grandfather know?"

"Yes. He and Alyssa are in the cafeteria getting something to eat, then he has a hearing this afternoon, so he has to leave."

He nodded, somewhat relieved that he didn't have to face Marshall right now. Though he was staying in the guesthouse, he rarely crossed paths with him. Liam had been traveling some over the last two weeks. Even so, the invitations to dinner had ceased after Georgia broke the news to her grandfather. Not that Liam blamed him.

"Hello. Time for your blood draw." A young lady in purple scrubs with matching purple stripes in her hair came in carrying what looked like a tote of cleaning supplies.

Georgia groaned. "Do we have to?"

"Ah." The girl set her tote down then drew on a pair of rubber gloves before examining the IV in Georgia's hand. "Don't like needles, huh?" She smiled at Georgia and patted her hand as if she were her grandmother rather than a twenty-something healthcare worker. "I'm sorry. Nobody really likes needles, but my patients tell me I'm the best. You won't feel a thing."

"Ha. That's what the nurse who put the IV in said."

"Want to squeeze my hand?" He didn't relish seeing Georgia in pain, even if it was just from a needle stick. And what about the labor and delivery? a voice asked. But he pushed that aside. He likely wouldn't be here when the baby was born. They'd be divorced and he'd be on to the next project by January when the baby was due.

And the thought of abandoning her made him feel like an asshole.

~

"I'm not feeble," Georgia complained as Liam tucked blankets around her. "I'm fine."

"Humor me." He closed the plantation shutters on her bedroom windows, leaving the room dim despite the afternoon sun. "Sleep a bit, and then I'll bring up some soup."

She snorted. He was fussing over her like she was a doddering old woman. But as he closed the door behind him, she had to admit the ride home from Atlanta and climbing the stairs to her room had left her exhausted.

He'd been so kind and attentive. She couldn't have asked for a better caregiver.

The baby moved as if rolling over for a nap of her own. Georgia followed suit and curled up around her stomach, her hand resting there, falling asleep almost instantly.

~

About an hour later, Liam balanced a bowl of soup on a tray, along with a glass of ice water with a lemon slice, the way Georgia liked it. Opening the door, he saw that she still slept. He took the extra bowl he'd brought up and turned it over on top of the full bowl to keep the soup warm.

Curled on her side, her blond hair spilling across the pillows, she looked like innocence itself. He'd asked her once if she had any regrets. But what about him? Did he have any regrets?

Maybe. But not for himself. For Georgia. Not for the first time, he admonished himself. He never should have seduced her. Never should have indulged her impetuous wedding. Never should have placed her in this position. After their divorce she would be a single mother, raising a child on her own.

And whose fault is that, asshole? a voice inside his head taunted.

He wandered her room, wondering if this was how it had looked when she was growing up, or whether, when she'd left, her grandparents had redecorated the room. The creamy walls, the blues and browns of the linens and upholstery, the polished antiques, and the cut crystal picture frames all held a quiet elegance. On a desk in front of the windows stood one of those frames. In the dim light, he could barely make out what it was. Lifting it to see better, he caught his breath.

The fuzzy black-and-white image revealed a tiny face, the curve of a head, and the minute fingers of a hand raised as if waving hello. "My god," he whispered, and his heart nearly burst from his chest at the realization. This was his daughter. His and Georgia's. The frame was engraved with "LILLIAN CHARLOTTE MACKINNON." Lillian Charlotte? He noted that she hadn't included Dunbar. Was that his daughter's name? She hadn't even spoken to him about it. But then again, why would she? Hadn't he rebuffed her when she'd tried to show him this very photo?

His hand rose of its own volition to skim across the glass-covered image. He couldn't breathe and his chest ached. His vision blurred. Maybe he was having a heart attack. Or maybe it was an emotional epiphany.

Things just got real. Maybe too real.

"Hey."

He almost dropped the photo in his haste to set it back

down. "Hey." His voice came out gruff. He cleared his throat and tried again. "I brought you some soup."

She sat up in bed and fluffed the pillows behind her back. "I could have come downstairs to eat."

"It's no bother." He set the tray in front of her but couldn't meet her gaze.

"Thanks." She gave him a smile, her eyes still heavy-lidded with sleep.

"I, uh, I need to meet with the engineers, so I've got to go." *Liar!* He did have to meet with the engineers but not for another two hours.

"It's okay, Liam. I really appreciate everything, but you have work to do. Go. I'll be fine."

After seeing that tiny image, Liam wondered if *he* would ever be fine again.

Sitting in her car outside the fully renovated cottage, it dawned on her—it was the second of November—the day she could file for divorce. Liam had already given her the financial affidavit she'd needed. The only thing left was his signature on the documents. The documents she'd been carrying around in her tote bag for weeks.

And yet, he hadn't asked about them either. Was he having second thoughts? Was she?

Of course she was. She wanted him to be a father to Lily. She wanted him to be a husband to her. She wanted him to love her. The way she loved him.

How could she not fall in love with a man who took care of her when she had a kidney infection, who admonished her when he found her on hands and knees planting mondo grass, who cooked for her and gave her foot rubs?

She blinked back tears. Alyssa had been right once again. While she'd told Alyssa they were just "having fun," somewhere along the way, Georgia had fallen for Liam. When would she learn to listen to her friend? She always seemed to be right.

"I'll think about that later," she muttered to herself as she got out of the car and inspected the freshly painted exterior of the house with a critical eye. The sweet arts-and-crafts cottage had been painted powder blue with white trim and the single three-window dormer a deeper cornflower blue. The columns and porch railing were painted the same white as the trim. But it was the cheery yellow front door that drew the onlooker's focus and invited visitors to the deep front porch.

As she took the three steps up to that porch, she envisioned a swing in the same cornflower blue, with pillows of yellow, white, and powder blue, and two rockers in white. In the spring, summer, and fall, the flower boxes on the windows would be filled with colorful blooms.

She entered the house for one more walkthrough before putting it on the market.

This adorable little twenty-five-hundred-square-foot cottage was a far cry from the mid-century modern beach house she'd owned in Malibu, with its wall of glass overlooking the Pacific, but the cottage held so much warmth. She felt at peace as whenever she walked the airy open rooms or gazed out at the tidy backyard with its flower gardens filled with orange and yellow mums and the water feature Luis had added at the last minute.

It would make some family a great home.

Then a thought struck her. It would make her and Lily a great home. She stood in the open living-dining-kitchen space. This was all the room she and Lily needed. She would buy her half of the house from Luis. She and Lily would be happy here. Her hands slid along the bulge of her belly, and as if to echo the sentiment, the baby rolled and stretched, making Georgia's stomach move in an undulating motion.

And yet—

When she closed her eyes at night, she saw a different life for herself. One she thought she'd have by now. One with love and companionship. Shared dreams and shared lives. A family.

Maybe someday, with someone. But the sad truth was not now, and not with Liam.

$\sim$

THAT VERY AFTERNOON, Georgia placed a contract on the desk in front of Luis.

"What's this?" he asked as he slid the document toward him.

"It's a contract for the purchase of the house."

"You sold it already?"

"Yep. To me." Once she'd made up her mind, she'd returned to the office and drafted the contract.

His eyes lit up. "Omigod. I had hoped . . ."

"You'd hoped?"

"Yes. Everything I did on that house, I did with you and Lily in mind."

Georgia blinked back tears. "Oh, Luis." She circled the desk as he stood. "I love you!" She wrapped her arms around him and pulled him in for a vise-like hug.

"Love you too." He false-gasped. "But I can't breathe."

She laughed and released him.

"Seriously, you've got a hug like a boa constrictor. Promise me you'll never hug Lily like that."

Georgia brushed at a tear then said, "I'm giving you ten percent over market-price." Before he could protest, she continued, "You did all the work. It's well deserved."

He picked up the pen on his desk. "Then where do I sign?"

She directed him to the signature lines and watched him sign with a flourish.

"Done."

"I have one more favor to ask."

"What's that?" Luis asked, eyebrow raised.

"Will you decorate the nursery?"

"I thought you'd never ask!" He held up a finger. "But it must be a surprise. You can't see it until it's done."

She stuck out her hand. "Deal."

Luis took her outstretched hand and, this time, he reeled her in for an uncharacteristic hug.

"Morning, sunshine," Luis said the Monday after Thanksgiving, with his usual morning cheer. "How was your Thanksgiving?"

"Morning. It was nice, how about yours?"

She and her grandfather had had a quiet, but cozy Thanksgiving. She had invited Liam, but he'd told her he would be out of town. And while she hadn't seen him all weekend, she wondered if that was an excuse. She couldn't help but feel him pulling away from her.

"It was wonderful! We spent Thursday and Friday at the Four Seasons in Atlanta and had the decadent Thanksgiving buffet. I swear, I think I gained twenty pounds!" He patted his flat belly. "I'm as big as you are now."

She just turned sideways and lifted a brow in challenge.

"Okay, maybe not."

She picked up the messages from the desk with the intention of going to her office.

"Wait. I have to show you the conference room."

Georgia stopped in her tracks then faced him in excitement. "It's finished?"

"It is."

Luis had been working on what would become the conference room for a month now and she couldn't wait to see the final product. She followed him into what had once been the dark, depressing paneled den. Opening the door, she gasped. Gone was the paneling, and in its place pale-gray walls, the same color as her office. To help buffer sound, Luis had selected a charcoal smooth-pile carpet. And for the conference table, he had repurposed a trestle table painted a sleek black.

"I think we should use rolling office chairs rather than anything secondhand, for ease of use," he explained.

"I agree."

He'd used the same design idea for the two small windows, using floor-to-ceiling drapes in a medium gray. A long cabinet stood along one wall, where a small under-counter refrigerator would be filled with beverages for clients and visitors. For lighting, he'd chosen recessed cans. Overall, the look was clean and professional.

"We still need art for the walls. I have a photographer friend who could take photos of some of Northridge's historic homes. I'm thinking black and whites? What do you think?"

"I love it."

Luis nodded in satisfaction. "The kitchen is next."

"Oh, thank goodness!"

She preceded him out the door of the conference room, but he outpaced her, racing ahead to her office. "What are you doing?"

"Ta-da!" Luis said with a sweep of his hands.

"What?" Georgia's breath left in a rush as she peered into her office. "The floor! You finished the floor!"

"Do you love it? Hate it? Tell me, tell me. I can't take the suspense anymore."

The bare concrete floor had been replaced with a beautiful terrazzo. Bits of navy, green, gray, and peach tile glinted in the morning sunlight streaming through the window. "I love it!"

"Whew! That's good to know. I took a big risk not asking you first, because if you didn't like it, it would take a jackhammer to remove it."

"When?"

"Over the long weekend, of course."

Before she could step into her office for a better look, Luis said, "You can't go in yet. It's not quite dry, then it needs to be sanded and cleaned."

"But how? Did *you* do this?"

"God, no. I may be uber-talented, but a terrazzo floor requires an expert. A friend owed me a favor."

"I don't know what to say. It's . . . fabulous!"

"Nothing less for you and the princess would do."

A WEEK LATER, Georgia looked up with a start to see Luis, Alyssa, Kristen, and Olivia standing in her office. "God, you're stealthy." She laid a hand over her thundering heart. "How about giving me a little warning next time."

"Sorry, boss," Luis said with a sweep of his hand that said he wasn't really sorry.

The group gathered around her desk, smiles on their faces.

She stared up at them and blinked. "What?"

"We need to talk about your baby shower," Alyssa said, a broad grin on her face. "Fabulous floor, by the way."

Before she could say anything, Luis said, "Thank you."

He did deserve the credit, after all. "I'd almost forgotten about the baby shower." She set aside the contract she'd been reading and gave them her full attention. "So, what's the plan?"

"Well, to start, we thought we'd have it Christmas Eve—make it a Christmas-themed shower," Alyssa said, practically bursting with excitement.

"Why Christmas Eve?"

"Well, it's a month before your due date, wherever we have it will be decorated for Christmas—"

"We thought we'd have it in the café," Kristen interjected.

"Won't that put a damper on your last-minute Christmas sales?" Georgia asked.

"Nah," Kristen said, dismissing the concern. "I usually close at six o'clock on Christmas Eve anyway, so folks know if they need a last-minute gift, they'd better get there before that."

"I have a better idea," Luis put in, and everyone turned to look at him. "Have it in Georgia's new house."

"The house? *My* house?"

"You bought a house?" Alyssa cut in.

Before Georgia could respond, Luis blurted, "She bought *the* house. The one we've been renovating."

Squeals of joy followed his announcement.

"It's perfect," Alyssa said.

"But I have to move in and unpack. It won't be decorated for Christmas . . ."

"Pfft. Leave all that to me. Or to us." Luis turned to the group, seeking encouragement.

"Yes," Olivia said. "You're eight months pregnant, you don't need to be moving and unpacking boxes. And you'll want to be settled before Lily arrives." She shrugged. "We were going to help you anyway." She looked to the group and everyone nodded. "We'll take care of it for you."

"And you know I wasn't going to let you just move in without my expert advice," Luis said, a brow lifted in challenge.

Too tired to argue, and touched by the kindness and support of her friends, she relented. "Okay. Christmas Eve at my house."

"Yay!" Alyssa clapped. "This is going to be such fun!"

FINISHING a new listing for one of Northridge's historic homes, Georgia closed the multiple listing service website and noticed the bookmark from the *Newsweek* article she'd first started reading back in May when she learned that Liam had a criminal record.

Unable to resist, she carried the laptop to her bed and settled back against the pillows to finish it. Scanning the article, she found where she'd left off. After serving his sentence, he'd turned computer security expert and built a multinational IT security firm, which he later sold for a cool billion with a capital B.

In addition to Everest, he'd climbed other big mountains, ran in the grueling Marathon des Sables in the Moroccan Sahara, BASE jumped from Tabletop Mountain in South Africa, and dog sledded to the South Pole.

Sounded like a man running from something rather than *to* something, she thought. But what was he running from? His criminal past?

According to the article, he grew bored and looked for a new venture. That new venture became American Threads. Then the article followed much of what Liam had told her about the company. Scrolling down, she stopped when Ben's name caught her attention.

As she read the story, tears spill over onto her cheeks. "Oh, Liam," she said to the empty room. She thought about the tattoo, the burn scars, and Liam's terse answers to her questions about Ben. It was clear he blamed himself for Cole's addiction. Did he blame himself for Ben's death too?

This article answered a few of her questions, but it also raised many more. Questions he'd likely never answer.

THE MOMENT LIAM woke he felt it. The heavy weight of knowledge, as if his body knew what day it was before his brain did. The anniversary of Ben's death. Unable to hold the memories at bay, Liam relived that night like he had so many times before.

His mother had been working the night shift cleaning office buildings, so Liam had been in charge of his brothers. Getting their supper, scolding them to do their homework, urging them to go to bed since it was a school night. If he'd let them stay up like they'd wanted to, Ben would still be alive. They would have all been in the living room together and could have easily escaped the flames and smoke. But Ben had dutifully fallen asleep in their mother's bed, Cole and Liam in their own.

Liam could smell the acrid smoke, remember the taste of it in his mouth, the burning sensation in his lungs. Then he could feel the heat of it, hear the dull roar as it devoured the apartment's cheap furnishings, peeling wallpaper, and thin carpeting. By the time the smell had yanked him from a sound sleep and he'd gathered his wits enough to realize what was happening, the back of the apartment, where his mom's bedroom was, had been engulfed in flames.

He had bodily carried Cole out of the room, dropped him outside the apartment door, and told him to run downstairs and out of the building.

But Cole kept screaming, "Where's Ben? We have to get Ben."

"Go, now! I'll get Ben. Just go!"

Liam hadn't waited. He'd headed back into the inferno, wrapping a blanket from the sofa around him. The visibility was so poor that he'd become disoriented and at one point had turned in the direction of the kitchen instead of the bedrooms. His eyes, nose, throat, and lungs burned from the smoke. His skin felt as if he were in an oven.

A wall of flames met him in the narrow hallway. Impassable. Inescapable. "Ben! Ben!" he called over and over, his voice hoarse with smoke and anguish, tears of fear and grief streaming down his face. Maybe he'd gotten out. Maybe he was on the fire escape right now. Maybe he'd made it out before Liam and Cole did.

He considered soaking the blanket in the kitchen sink. Maybe it would offer enough protection to get through the flames. He had to know. He had to get to Ben.

A hand clamped down on his shoulder and he screamed. "Ben?" he'd yelled, hopeful.

"Son!" No, a firefighter. "We have to get out. Now!"

"Ben!" Liam yelled to be heard over the roar. "I have to get Ben!"

"No! It's too late! The ceiling is going to collapse any minute." Without another word, the firefighter slung Liam over his shoulder and ran from the apartment. Moments later the groan of something collapsing reached them as the man ran down the stairs, Liam bouncing ignominiously across his shoulder.

His mother had left him in charge and he'd failed. Cole and his mother never blamed him, but they didn't have to. He felt it in every look, every action, every thought. Liam bit back a sob. He didn't even have a picture of Ben. Any photos they'd had had gone up in flames.

Ben had died because Liam didn't save him. It was just that simple. And he would never forgive himself for that.

"AND WE'RE DONE," Luis said as he set a Christmas-themed bouquet of flowers on the coffee table then stepped back, hands on his lean hips.

Liam scanned the welcoming open living room in Georgia's new house and had to admit it had come together well. And quickly, considering how many people had been there to help. Olivia and Zach, Kristen and Tyler, Alyssa and Dillon, Luis and his husband Chase, and of course Liam had been crawling all over the house like ants at a picnic, moving furniture, unpacking boxes, and filling cabinets and closets per Georgia's written instructions. It had been good to have a distraction, but he couldn't shake the heavy weight of grief and guilt.

They had knocked out the move in a day. The only thing left was for Georgia to bring her personal belongings. Even the baby's things had been put away in the nursery. At least what she'd bought so far. In between supervising the furniture placement, Luis and Alyssa had decorated a Christmas tree and the fireplace mantle. There were other holiday touches throughout the house, like candles and floral arrangements, all tasteful and cheerful.

"I just texted Marshall to let him know we're all set." Alyssa pocketed her smartphone as she spoke.

"And Dominick's is delivering the food in about fifteen minutes," Kristen advised.

They'd ordered a hearty Italian meal of lasagna, twisty bread sticks, salad, and cheesecake for dessert. He didn't know about everyone else, but he'd worked up an appetite picking up sofas and chairs, mattresses and box springs, and maneuvering large appliances into place.

Marshall would bring Georgia to the house and blind-fold her before she came in, and they'd have what Alyssa called "The Big Reveal."

Liam looked around at Georgia's group of friends and felt a twinge of regret. Other than his brother Cole, who lived on the other side of the country, Liam had lived a solitary adulthood. His business ventures had taken him around the country and around the world, but he'd never shared his life with anyone. His had been the life of the proverbial rolling stone.

Oh, he had friends—business partners really—whom he'd meet for dinner or drinks when he was in Illinois, New York, or California, but he'd never had anyone . . . close. Anyone he could count on to help him move. He smiled to himself. Not that he'd ever needed that kind of help, but they say you know who your true friends are when they help you move.

Georgia was lucky in that regard. And when he left, it was a comfort to know she wouldn't be alone.

He, however, couldn't say the same, and he was beginning to regret that.

"Put this on," Georgia's grandfather said, holding out a colorful silk scarf that must have been her grandmother's.

"What? Why?"

"Your friends want to have something called 'The Big Reveal'—something about reality TV, I don't know."

She shook her head but complied, tying the scarf over her eyes and securing the ends behind her head.

A blast of cold air entered the car as her grandfather opened his door then closed it. Normally, she'd shiver at the icy temperature, but since she carried her own personal heater twenty-four-seven now, she relished it. When her door opened, her grandfather took her arm and helped her from the car. "God, I'm so ungainly," she sighed then groaned as she pushed her relative bulk from the seat.

"It's only temporary," her grandfather commented. "Before you know it, you'll be holding your precious daughter in your arms, and it will all be worth it."

"You're getting awfully sentimental." She chuckled. "Who would have thought?"

"Who would have thought I'd be having my first great-grandchild?" he replied.

He guided her up the sidewalk. She'd seen the finished product—both interior and exterior—and appreciated Luis's eye for color and detail. Now she would see what the house looked like as a home. Her home. And Lily's.

Her grandfather guided her through the open door until she was standing, she assumed, in the open living room right off the front door. She heard whispers and nervous giggles and thought she recognized Alyssa's "shhh," as if their presence there was a surprise.

At some signal, her grandfather stepped behind her and untied the scarf.

"Surprise!"

She gasped when she saw everyone, all of her friends, new and old, as well as her husband and father of her child, gathered in her now fully furnished living room. Her throat clogged with tears, and she batted her eyelids, blinking away the blurriness. She should be focused on the furnishings, but she was so moved to see everyone there.

"Well, what do you think?" Alyssa said with a sweeping gesture.

Of course she'd seen the furniture when she and Luis had picked it out, but seeing it all put together was something entirely different. Everything came together so well.

Furnished in an eclectic mix of charming cottage furnishings with contemporary touches, it . . . worked. They'd selected two cozy overstuffed sofas covered in denim slipcovers—easy to remove and wash with a baby in the house. Two more overstuffed chairs were also slipcovered in a butter yellow. A jumble of pillows in blues, whites, yellows, and greens lined the sofas. A washed out boho rug in blues and yellows covered the refinished heart pine floors.

"Oh!" Her gaze landed on the Christmas tree in the corner, beside the fireplace. "It's beautiful!" Greenery draped the fireplace mantel, ornaments of green and red and gold nestled into it.

To the left was the bar separating the kitchen from the living room. Up a tidy staircase, were the two bedrooms. The walls of the rooms were a soft skylight, somewhere between a pale blue and a pearl gray, creating a soothing but cheerful warmth.

"You did all this?" She gazed around the house then at her friends.

"Yup," Kristen said. "And let me tell you, my back is feeling every bit of it."

"I'll rub it for you later," Tyler said with a cheeky grin.

"I'm holding you to that," Kristen said as she leveled a look at him.

Georgia grinned at their antics but also felt a twinge of jealousy as her gaze shifted to Liam standing by the bar, a beer in his hand. He smiled at her, but there was a sadness in his eyes. Was he regretting his upcoming departure as much as she was?

"And now, for the *pièce de résistance*," Luis said.

She gave him a confused look.

"Don't you want to see the little princess's nursery?"

"Oh. Yes! Please!" She'd almost forgotten.

Luis led the way with the others in tow. For a moment, he stood outside the closed door, where a sign hung that read "Lily's Room," before opening it with a flourish.

Georgia gasped and laid a hand over her mouth. Tears threatened again, but this time, she let them come. "It's . . . beautiful," she whispered.

Luis had painted the walls the palest pink. "I thought a clean neutral decor would be suitable, at least until Lily hits the terrible teens."

The white crib, which could be converted to a bed when Lily was old enough, stood front and center on the far wall. Above it hung the letter L for "Lily" in the center of a collage of white and silver frames. Two frames were currently empty.

Catching her thoughts, Luis said, "For after the baby comes."

She nodded and entered the room, stepping onto the

plush pearl gray carpeting. In the corner sat an overstuffed chair with ottoman in a pale-gray twill, a white stuffed bear tucked up against a pink pillow. The crib sheets and bumpers were a mix of pink, gray, and white, and a pink ruffled baby blanket lay draped over the side of the crib.

A sparkle caught Georgia's eye and she looked up to find a delicate crystal chandelier hanging where a tacky old ceiling fan had once hung.

"You've outdone yourself. Truly." She turned toward Luis.

"I had help. Liam? Where *is* he? Liam?"

Liam? Liam helped Luis? Well, of course he did. He probably helped move the furniture in.

The crowd parted and Liam stepped into the room, and her breath caught at the mix of pleasure and pain she saw on his face.

"Yeah," Luis continued, "he's the one who picked out the chandelier, the frames, and the chair and ottoman, which rocks by the way. Literally. The chair, not the ottoman."

She locked eyes with Liam's, completely confused, yet touched by this revelation. For someone who didn't want to be a parent, he sure had stepped up. His actions often contradicted his words, leaving her confused and off balance.

"Thank you," she said softly, aware of everyone's attention.

"You're welcome," came his quiet reply.

～

"LET'S EAT! I'M STARVED," Kristen said, and everyone followed her to the kitchen where the food waited.

Liam couldn't move though. He stood rooted in place,

staring at the woman who carried his child. His wife. She'd never looked more beautiful. Radiant with an inner glow no makeup artist could ever recreate.

"Liam, I—"

Afraid of what she was going to say, and afraid of what he might say in return, he interrupted. "You need to eat." He held out his hand indicating she should precede him. Her face held a pleading look, one he couldn't acquiesce to. "Come," he insisted. She nodded and walked out of the nursery. Breathing a sigh of both relief and sadness, he followed her.

The raucous laughter from the kitchen did little to shake him from his mood. Alyssa handed Georgia a plate of food and carried a glass of water over to the table in the kitchen nook, gesturing for her to sit down. He should be the one caring for her, ensuring her comfort, her wellbeing. But he wouldn't be here to do that. She'd looked happy to see her friends, to see the home they'd helped create for her and his daughter. He wanted to be part of that happiness, but he didn't know how.

"Liam." Marshall held out a plate to him. "Better get it while the gettin's good."

Right. Marshall's icy demeanor had thawed a bit over the last few weeks. He wondered if he would ever regain the man's respect. Then he remembered it wouldn't matter. He wouldn't be here for it to matter.

After he filled his plate, he stood at one of the kitchen counters where he could observe the festivities but remain separate, removed from it all.

A clinking of glass quieted the room, and Georgia picked up her glass. "I should probably stand for this, but I can't get up," she said with a laugh, and everyone joined in. "I just wanted to thank you for . . . everything." She blinked away tears. "I couldn't ask for better friends or better family." She lifted her glass in Marshall's direction. "To friends and family."

"To friends and family," everyone echoed.

Yeah. Two things Liam didn't have—and never would.

23

Liam held Georgia close, her back to his front, his hand splayed across her belly. She'd been exhausted after all the evening's excitement and fallen asleep before he could turn out the light and crawl into bed. As for his part, he couldn't sleep. His mind skipped from one thing to the next. The mill. His plans for the Rust Belt. Georgia. Lily. Ben. Cole. Thoughts collided, careening off one another like billiard balls struck by the cue ball.

Georgia sighed in her sleep and snuggled closer to him, and his mind quieted, even if only momentarily. Somehow she had become his world. She'd found a chink in his armor and insinuated herself into his heart. He'd never intended for this to happen. He didn't deserve her. He didn't deserve his daughter. A man like him shouldn't be given another opportunity to wreck someone else's life.

What the . . . a movement, barely perceptible, rippled beneath his hand and his breath caught. *My God.* He waited another moment, scared to breath. This time he felt something sharp—a knee? an elbow?—beneath his hand, and he wondered how Georgia slept through such commotion. *Damn.* Was his daughter trying to tell him something?

"Hi, Lily," he whispered. "You don't know me, but I'm your dad." He felt a bit foolish but continued, "I just want you to know that you'll always be safe and protected. You won't want for anything. And you'll have the best mom in the world, even if I won't be here."

The baby's movements had quieted. She'd probably been rolling over.

He regretted his decision to leave. He regretted his decision not to be part of Lily's life. And Georgia's. Maybe he could visit. See Lily from time to time. That way he could watch her grow, be a part of her life, without the risk of ruining it.

Funny how he hadn't given much thought to the divorce the last few weeks. Georgia hadn't given him the papers, and he hadn't asked. Whether that was intentional or subconscious, he didn't know. They could still come to an agreement if Georgia felt the need for something formal. Content with his decision, he pressed a hand to Georgia's stomach, hoping his daughter could feel his presence.

WHILE LIAM SHOWERED, Georgia went down to the kitchen for her one allotted cup of decaf coffee. As she waited for the Keurig to do its thing, she scrolled through photos on her phone from "The Big Reveal" the night before. The smiling and laughing faces of her friends and grandfather made her smile. She opened a candid group photo of everyone in the kitchen. Liam stood apart from the group, like a stranger looking in.

Is that what he felt like? If so, her heart ached for him.

Or was he just beginning his withdrawal from her in anticipation of his departure? He hadn't been himself last night, but with so many people around she couldn't ask what was wrong. And then she'd fallen asleep.

The mill wasn't quite operational, but he'd told her he had a round of meetings in Detroit, Cincinnati, and Pittsburgh. He'd be back, but only for the ribbon cutting.

Inhaling a shaky breath, she fought back tears. Returning to the photos on her phone, she scrolled through before and after pictures of the office and the house that Luis had sent to her. He was a miracle worker.

She swiped too far and photos zoomed past, coming to a stop on a photo of her with Not-Erik. She thought she'd deleted them all, but she'd missed this one somehow. Not-Erik held up a bottle of tequila, his other arm draped across her shoulders and an inebriated grin on his face. Expanding the photo, she studied her own expression. She wore a smile but it was brittle, fake, and it didn't reach her eyes.

She tried to remember which of the endless round of parties this was from. It didn't matter really. What mattered was the look on her face. It served as a reminder that she'd been living a lie. Planning a wedding, pretending she was happy. Burying her true feelings just so she could have a husband and maybe a family. Settling for less-than because it was all she had.

And here she was heading down that road again. If Liam said he wanted to see Lily, would Georgia agree? Was she willing to let him walk in and out of their daughter's life whenever it pleased him? And by extension her life? How would she ever get over him if he popped in and out of her life? She and her daughter deserved more. She deserved happiness, even if that meant finding that happiness alone.

No. Not alone. She would have Lily. And her grandfather, and Alyssa and Dillon, Kristen and Tyler, Olivia and Zach, and Luis and Chase.

She had trust issues. Not the kind that made it difficult for her to trust, but the opposite. Despite the situation with Not-Erik, her default was trust. And she'd been trusting Liam to come around and at least be there for Lily, if not for her.

She glanced over at her tote bag hanging on a peg by the garage door. With reluctance, she pulled the manila envelope with the divorce papers and the wedding band out of the bag, and set it on the kitchen table. She'd give Liam one more chance to be a meaningful part of his daughter's life. If he refused, she'd present him with the long-overdue divorce papers.

WHEN LIAM ENTERED the kitchen wearing the same clothes he'd worn the night before, Georgia's heart sputtered. His hair was damp from his shower, and he smelled like her wildflower soap, which made her smile. She yearned for him to wrap his arms around her and kiss her, but instead, he stood apart from her, like he had the crowd last night.

He glanced over at the kitchen table where the envelope lay then back at her. He drew in a long breath then let it out. Is this where he planned to say goodbye?

"Georgia, I've been thinking."

Her sucker of a heart leapt. Had he changed his mind? Would he be a father to Lily? Would he stay?

"I'd like to see Lily after she is born. I'd like to be part of her life . . . somehow."

"You would?" The hope in her voice was audible. "Do

you mean you plan to stay? To be a father to her?" She laid her hands over her rounded stomach.

His gaze slid away, and she knew. "Uh, no. I have to leave. And I don't think I should take on the responsibility of parent to Lily. But maybe I could see our daughter every so often, in addition to supporting her financially."

Anger and disappointment shot through her. "You mean you'd like to see her whenever it suits you? What, once a year? Maybe whenever you decide to drop by?"

"It wouldn't be like that." He folded his arms over his chest.

"No? Then what, we'd agree on a visitation schedule? A regular one?"

He noticeably winced and looked down at the floor. "I'm not sure I could commit to a schedule."

"I see." This time she crossed her arms over her chest. "And when you visit, who shall I say you are?"

His head shot up at that. "Who? Her father, of course."

"You can't have it both ways. I won't have you waltzing in and out of her life. Either you're here for her as her father or you're not."

A muscle tensed in his jaw and, recalling the article, she decided on another tact. "Ben's death and Cole's addiction are not your fault," she said, so quiet she wasn't sure he'd heard her, but his gaze flew to hers. "You'd make a great father."

"Don't," he ground out, dropping his hands by his sides. "You don't know—"

"No, I don't know. Because you won't tell me!" She released a sigh. Yelling would get her nowhere. "But I can surmise. I don't know what happened in that apartment fire, but I can only guess that you blame yourself for Ben's death."

"No!" It was said with anguish and maybe fear. "No! I'm the reason Ben died. I was in charge, I was the oldest. I should have saved him." He jabbed a finger into his chest with each sentence. He lifted that hand to his forehead. "Or died trying. And Cole. Cole is a drug addict because of me. If I hadn't hacked ComEd and gone to prison, he wouldn't have gone into the foster system and been introduced to drugs. I can't. I can't be responsible for Lily's health and safety."

It broke her heart to see him torture himself this way. "Can't you see? You're a nurturer. You nurture the communities where you rebuild the mills. You nurture me, and by extension Lily. You've moved heaven and earth for Cole. And you anguish over Ben's death because you loved him."

"Godammit! No! I can't do it. I can't ruin another life."

His anger echoed in the room. She drew in a deep breath and blew it out through pursed lips. "Then I'm sorry. My daughter will have a full-time father or none at all." She cupped her belly. "Lily needs stability. And I plan to see that she gets it. Even if the judge has to make the decision. And if that means not taking your money, then so be it."

His head snapped up and his eyes blazed. "Do you really think I would withhold money in order to see my daughter? I'd never do that."

She pointed to the envelope on the table. "Then you can sign the divorce papers as is, or we tear them up and start over. The choice is yours." Blinking back tears, she left the room.

When Georgia came down later, the envelope was gone.

24

Liam entered his New York apartment, dropping his duffle bag on the floor by the door. He was exhausted. He'd spent the last week flying from city to city meeting with local officials, politicians, and community members to discuss his plans to revitalize manufacturing. He'd been met with suspicion by some, enthusiasm by others, and outright hostility by others. He got it. Who was he to come in and tell these communities he could improve their lives?

And then there was the insomnia. He hadn't slept a full night since he left Northridge. Every night, he relived his last conversation with Georgia, remembered every expression on her face, from hope to anger, to despair, and finally resignation. He got that too. He'd been angry, but how could he blame her for wanting to do what was best for her and Lily? He'd told her once that she shouldn't have to settle, that she deserved the best, and he'd meant it. Clearly, he wasn't the best for her.

He rubbed a hand over his chest where a constant ache had taken up residence. He missed Georgia. He missed her sunny smile and her bright laughter. He missed the way she bit her lip when she was nervous or thinking. He missed the tenderness she'd shown him. He missed laying his hand on her stomach to feel their daughter move.

Their daughter!

His breath hitched as a flicker of panic set in. He would never see her. She would never know him. He sank into a chair and doubled over, his face in his hands. What had he done? Drawing in gulps of air, he tried to relieve the tightness in his chest. Was he having a heart attack?

Calm down and breathe. In through the nose, out through the mouth. After a few minutes of breathing, the tightness eased, he leaned back against the chair, and he closed his eyes. He must have dozed because when he opened his eyes, the light in the apartment had dulled to the blue-gray of evening.

Enough. He slapped his hands on his thighs and rose in search of something to occupy his mind.

Taking his laptop out of his backpack, he set it on the dining room table. Then he saw the envelope—the one he'd been avoiding since he'd left Northridge. He hesitated before pulling it out. Opening the clasp, he removed the papers then realized there was something else in the envelope: the gold wedding band he'd given her. His chest tightened again at the sight of it. He set it and the papers aside.

He couldn't deal with this yet. He needed a cold beer and a hot shower first.

After his shower, Liam paced his apartment like a caged animal, realizing for the first time how cold and unwelcoming it was. There were no personal touches. No framed photos. No welcoming scents. No nursery with a crib and stuffed animals.

And the noise! How could he have forgotten the noise

from the streets twenty-five stories below—the constant car horns and sirens? He gazed down at the crowded sidewalks, the unfriendly faces, and longed for the relative quiet of Northridge—the open, friendly faces. One face in particular.

Anxious and restless, he grabbed another beer from the fridge and considered another adventure trip. Maybe to the Amazon or Antarctica. He could climb Mt. Vinson. Isn't that what he always did when life got too real? He ran?

Taking a long pull on his beer, he picked up the divorce papers. "Fuck it." He'd sign the damned papers, then he'd book a trip. In the paper-clipped packet, he found the divorce papers and the waiver of parental rights, helpfully marked with "sign here" tabs. There was no way he was signing the waiver of parental rights. He wanted to leave his options open. He ripped them up and set them aside. He knew he should send the papers to his attorneys, but he didn't really give a flying fuck about protecting his financial interests. The post-nup would have to be enough.

His phone buzzed and Cole's face appeared on the video app. A jolt of concern shot through him like a bolt from the blue. He didn't need another crisis. His hand hovered over the phone, then he accepted the video call and blurted, "What's wrong?"

Cole laughed and shook his head. "That's what I love about you, bro, your eternal optimism."

Gone were the dreads and the gaunt, hollow expression. Cole now sported close-cropped hair and a beaming smile. He looked good, Liam thought. Real good. In fact, he looked better than he had in years.

Liam scrubbed a hand over his face. "Right. Sorry about that."

"No worries, man. You have every reason to associate my calls with bad news."

Liam winced at the truth in that statement and took a different tack. "How are you?"

Cole glanced at something over his shoulder and laughed then turned back to Liam. "I'm good. Great actually."

For the first six weeks of rehab, Cole was not allowed communication outside the facility. And although Liam new Cole was likely the safest he'd ever been inside that facility, it hadn't alleviated Liam's worry over the lack of communication. Wondering if Cole was following the rules, going to therapy sessions, investing in his recovery. He wondered if it would work this time.

"I'm glad to hear it." Liam wanted to say more. Wanted to say he hoped this was finally it. That Cole would stay clean from here on out, that he would find his purpose, his happiness, but he was too much of a realist to think it, much less say it out loud.

"Hey, uh, thank your girlfriend for getting me into this place. It's been . . . life changing."

"She's not my girlfriend." She's my wife. My *pregnant* wife. But she wasn't his girlfriend. Not now. Not ever. And soon she wouldn't be his wife either.

"Uh-oh. Don't tell me you two broke up."

"No. It was never like that. We're just . . ." Married, soon-to-be-divorced, and soon-to-be parents, that's all.

"Riiight. And I'm not a drug addict. Whatever you did, bro, you need to make it right. Don't let her get away. And speaking of making things right," he continued before Liam could form a reply. "The phone isn't the best way to do this, but I need to speak what's in my heart, and I need to do it now."

Liam tensed at the serious expression on his brother's face. He knew intensive therapy was part of the drug treatment program, and as part of that therapy, addicts were encouraged to clear the air, get things off their chests, sometimes cut the cord on toxic relationships. Was theirs a toxic relationship?

He'd just lost Georgia and the daughter he'd never meet. Was today the day he'd lose his only surviving brother too?

"Listen, bro, I know you blame yourself for Ben's death, but it wasn't your fault. You were only fourteen at the time. Just a kid yourself. There was nothing you could have done. Nothing."

Though Liam's rational brain knew this, had always known this, it didn't alleviate the guilt.

"And before you disagree with me about it, I'm not done. I know you also blame yourself for my screwups. My time in foster care, my drug addiction," he laughed, "my whole fucked-up existence. Hell, I blamed you too."

Liam's chest tightened with feelings of inadequacy and self-loathing. "I—"

"I'm not finished." Cole held up a finger. "Don't do it. Don't blame yourself." Cole released a shudder. "I am the one who deserves the blame. I have to take responsibility for my own actions. My own bad decisions. There is no one to blame but me. I think I've known that all along. It was just easier to blame you. To pretend I was the innocent victim in all this." He shook his head. "It's all on me, brother. Not you. Never you."

Liam's eyes burned, and his throat tightened. He swallowed and tried to speak. "But—"

"I couldn't ask for a better big brother. You never gave up on me. Even when it would have been the easy thing to do. I'd be dead or living on the street if it weren't for you kicking my butt and carrying my burden. But that ends here—well, maybe the carrying my burden part, but I'll always need you kicking my butt."

Liam laughed out loud and felt as if a snarled, tangled rope inside his chest released, unfurling as it loosened. "I love you, my brother," Liam said past the tears clogging his throat.

"Ditto, my brother."

"Hey, how about coming to work for me again. I need someone I can trust to oversee the Georgia and Alabama operations." Especially since he'd be switching gears to the Northeast.

Cole tapped his heart with a closed fist. "Just hearing you say the words 'someone I can trust' fills me up, but nah, man. I need to stand on my own two feet."

"What will you do when you get out?"

"I got plans." He reached his free arm back and said something to someone behind him but out of view. A woman stepped into the frame, curly hair knotted on top of her head, a colorful bandana tied around her russet brown face. She pressed close to Cole and smiled. "This is Alesha."

Alesha waved at the camera. "Hi."

"Hi, Alesha," Liam responded.

"Alesha is a chef. CIA-trained."

"That's great." Where was this going? Was Cole saying he and Alesha were . . . dating? How'd they meet if he was in Shadow Mountain?

"Classes are part of the program here. Gardening, painting, sculpting, cooking, that sort of thing. Activities to refocus your mind. I took cooking classes, and Alesha was my instructor. One thing led to another and, well, she says I have a gift."

Liam blinked in surprise.

"Alesha has wanted to go out on her own for years, but she didn't have anyone who could help. Now she does. We're going to start small with a food truck, see how it goes. Then who knows, bro, maybe there's a Michelin-rated restaurant in our future." He hugged Alesha to him with his free arm and kissed her on the cheek. "You may not be the only successful businessman in the family."

Clearly Alesha was more than a potential business partner. The space that had held that tangled heap of rope filled with something else. Warmth, pride, and a heavy dose of brotherly love.

"If it's not too condescending for me to say so, I'm proud of you, Cole. So damn proud."

"I had to earn those word, man." He tapped his fist to his heart again. "Now, whatever you did to your girl, go make it right." Before he could say goodbye, Cole and Alesha had ended the call.

For the first time, Liam found himself on the receiving end of Cole's advice. He was right.

He'd lived a life of regret. Regret that he couldn't save his brother. Regret that he'd abandoned Cole. Regret that he couldn't save him from his addiction—but that was because Cole had to save himself. Did Liam want to regret giving up the best thing to ever happen to him?

He looked down at the phone still in his hand. Even with the brotherly pride and love that now filled his heart, there was still an empty space in his chest, and in his life, yet to be filled, and he knew the two perfect women to fill it.

25

Georgia should've been excited as Alyssa, Kristen, and Olivia put the finishing touches on the very girlie Christmas decorations for the baby shower. But while it was never going to be a couple's shower, she missed Liam desperately.

As she brushed on her favorite blush to add some color to her wan face, she thought some time away would make him realize he was wrong about himself. That he'd see how much he cared for the people in his life. Right down to his employees. But it had been two weeks and not a word. He hadn't even mailed the divorce papers back.

She paused, the blush brush poised between her cheek and the compact, and wondered if he was buried in plans to bring manufacturing back to the Rust Belt? And whether he thought about her? And Lily? She'd thought about texting him several times, even drafting a text asking how he was doing, only to delete it before she could send it.

Everyone had been kind and supportive. Alyssa invited her to lunches, and her grandfather often lamented he had too much food to eat and that she must come and eat dinner with him. And Luis had been especially helpful, handling some of the more tedious office duties without a word of complaint.

Her stomach undulated with what felt like an Olympic-style gymnastics routine as Lily adjusted her position. The baby had continued growing, seemingly oblivious to Georgia's broken heart, bringing Georgia closer and closer to her due date. Alyssa enthusiastically agreed to be in the delivery room with Georgia when the time came, and she appreciated that, but Georgia wanted the impossible. She wanted Liam. She wanted to share the most frightening, exhilarating, monumental day of her life with the man she loved.

But she'd presented him with an ultimatum, and he'd called her bluff.

"WHAT DO YOU WANT?" Alyssa asked, blocking the door, arms crossed over her chest. He could hear feminine laughter and the clink of glassware.

"Are you having a party?"

"It's a *baby shower*, asshole."

He guessed he deserved that.

Alyssa glowered at him. "Again, why are you here?" Her hands moved to her hips.

"To see Georgia."

"Why?" Her foot began tapping on the wood floor.

Liam's frustration threatened to boil over into anger, but in truth, he couldn't blame Alyssa's protectiveness. Hadn't he left Georgia? Hadn't he been a coward all along?

"I need to see her. I need to make this right?"

She tilted her head and narrowed her eyes. "Right how?"

He reached into his pocket and held up the plain gold

wedding band. Her lips parted in surprise, but before she could say anything, he heard Georgia's voice over the murmur of voices coming from inside the house.

"Who is it, Alyssa?"

She stepped back and extended her arm, allowing him to enter.

The last thing he wanted was to grovel in front of an audience. But grovel he would if that's what it would take. He stepped into the room and eight pairs of eyes turned in his direction, but he only cared about one.

Georgia's blue eyes widened—God, he hoped their daughter had her eyes—and his knees went weak.

"Liam!"

She sat on one of the sofas surrounded by boxes and bags in bright blues, silvers, and whites, colorful and beribboned in honor of Christmas, looking beautiful in a brilliant red cashmere sweater. If it was possible, she'd become more beautiful in the two weeks since he'd left. Now that he was here, he didn't know what to do next. All the words he'd practiced left him. The only words that came to him were "I'm sorry."

A chorus of *aw's* erupted, but Georgia appeared unaffected. She sat still as a statue, her face devoid of expression.

"I was wrong. So . . . wrong." *Smooth, real smooth.* He'd never been so unsure of himself as he was right now, when he needed confidence the most.

Finally, her lips parted and a frown knitted her brows. "What do you mean?"

He looked around at the bevy of women, some with fierce protective expressions on their faces, others with something akin to pity, but whether for Georgia or him, he didn't know. Approaching her like a bomb tech would an explosive device, he perched on the edge of the gift-crowded sofa. "I didn't think I was good enough. Trustworthy enough. Responsible enough. I thought Lily's life would be better without me."

"Oh, Liam." She set her hand on his cheek. "I told you, you aren't responsible for Ben's death or Cole's addiction."

"I realize that now. I also realize I don't want to spend the rest of my life without you or Lily. I love you." He knelt down on one knee, amid a chorus of gasps and sighs, and held out the plain gold wedding band he'd given Georgia at their Las Vegas wedding ceremony.

"Georgia Michelle MacKinnon-Dunbar, will you stay married to me and live with me as my wife and the mother of our child?"

There were gasps all around and someone blurted, "You're *married*?" but he ignored them.

"I promise to be a good husband to you," he laid his hand over her stomach, "and father to Lily and any other children we might have. I know I'll make my share of mistakes, but I will give you and Lily all that I have and all that I am now and for the rest of our lives." He held his breath, waiting, hoping, she would do something, say something, to put him out of his misery.

A tear sparkled on the edge of her lashes as she blinked rapidly.

"You *will* be the best husband. The best father. Because you're a good man, Liam Dunbar." She leaned forward and said, "I love you."

Lifting her left hand to him, she smiled behind her tears as he slid the wedding band back onto her finger where he hoped it would remain for the rest of their lives.

EPILOGUE

Atlanta, January 21st

Georgia's heart expanded with love at the sight of Liam holding his daughter. *Their* daughter. He gazed down at the tiny bundle with such raw emotion that tears pricked her own eyes.

Lillian Charlotte MacKinnon-Dunbar was born at six thirty-five a.m. weighing in at seven pounds, eight ounces. Liam had confirmed not long after that she had all ten fingers and all ten toes and declared that she was the most beautiful baby ever to be born.

Lily's great-grandfather and a bevy of unofficial aunts and uncles—including Alyssa and Dillon, Olivia and Zach, Kristen and Tyler, and Luis and Chase—had come to visit them. She certainly wouldn't lack for babysitters. Now, however, it was just the three of them in a hospital room filled with bouquets of pink and white flowers. Liam rocked a sleeping Lily, crooning to her, a sight Georgia never expected to see.

He still planned his new manufacturing venture, but his home base would now be Northridge instead of New York. With the Atlanta airport only an hour away, he'd purchased a private jet, so flying to the sites would be easy, and he would be home several times a week and on weekends.

Unsure whether he'd want to live in the small cottage she'd bought, she offered to sell it and buy something larger, but he wouldn't hear it. He'd put some of his own blood, sweat, and tears into it, he'd said. Why would he want to live anywhere else?

He rose from the rocking chair and approached the bed, Lily tucked into the crook of his arm. He leaned over to kiss Georgia, his dark eyes filled with emotion. "Thank you."

"For Lily?"

"For Lily. For loving me. For taking your honeymoon in Vegas. For our impulsive wedding. For making me see I do deserve love . . . your love. And Lily's." He gazed down at Lily again, smiling at her tiny yawn, then lifted his questioning gaze to Georgia. "When can we have another one?"

Georgia snorted and winced as she adjusted her position in the bed. "Now might not be the best time to ask that question."

He laughed, looking chagrinned. "Right." Easing into the bed beside her, he handed Lily to her.

As she cradled Lily, she could feel his eyes on her and she glanced up to see him smiling. "What are you thinking about?"

"I'm thinking I'm really glad that not everything that happens in Vegas stays in Vegas."

ABOUT THE AUTHOR

Rebecca Heflin is an award-winning, bestselling author who has dreamed of writing romantic fiction since she was fifteen and her older sister sneaked a copy of Kathleen Woodiwiss' Shanna to her and told her to read it.

Never quite sure what she wanted to be when she grew up, Rebecca didn't attend college until age 30, and earned her bachelor's in literature, before going on to complete her law degree.

Ever the late bloomer, Rebecca finally turned her attention to fulfilling her dream of writing, and published her first novel at age 48. When not passionately pursuing her dream, Rebecca is busy with her day-job at a major state university.

She and her husband are also co-founders of a non-profit organization, which raises money to help cancer patients and their families.

Rebecca's pen name is an abbreviated version of her great-great grandmother's name: Sarah Anne Rebecca Heflin Apple Smith. Whew! And you wonder why she shortened it.

Rebecca is a member of Romance Writers of America (RWA), RWA Aged to Perfection Seasoned Romance Writers, RWA Contemporary Romance Writers, and Florida Writers Association. Rebecca and her mountain-climbing husband live at sea level in sunny Florida.

Sign up for Rebecca's monthly newsletter, Rebecca's Readers, for all the latest news on upcoming releases, appearances, and contests.

facebook.com/RebeccaHeflinBooks

twitter.com/RebeccaHeflin

bookbub.com/authors/rebecca-heflin

ALSO BY REBECCA HEFLIN

THE PROMISE OF CHANGE

RESCUING LACEY

DREAMS COME TRUE SERIES

DREAMS OF PERFECTION, BOOK 1

SHIP OF DREAMS, BOOK 2

DREAMS OF HER OWN, BOOK 3

STERLING UNIVERSITY SERIES

ROMANCING DR. LOVE, BOOK 1

WINNING DR. WENTWORTH, BOOK 2

EDUCATING DR. MAYFIELD, BOOK 3

SEASONS OF NORTHRIDGE SERIES

A SEASON TO DANCE, BOOK 1

A SEASON TO LOVE, BOOK 2

9 781735 055169